W9-BES-707

"I can't stay..."

Sara answered Joe, a feeling of guilt settling heavily on her heart.

"Why the hell not?"

"Because it's too soon, Joe," Sara said in a resigned voice. "I'm supposed to be grieving."

"I don't see what that has to do with this," Joe stated calmly, biting back his hurt.

"You're getting in the way. You make me forget, and I don't want to forget. Joe, we were laughing on the phone. Laughing! Lala's only been gone seventeen days. I shouldn't be laughing." A tear rolled down her face. Joe caught it with his thumb.

"Take your coat off and come inside, Sara," Joe said tenderly. "I promise, I won't make you laugh."

ABOUT THE AUTHOR

Petra Holland still lives in the small town of her childhood, Holland, Michigan. She has always dreamed of writing and *Starlit Promise* is the culmination of perseverence, hard work and, as readers will discover, a unique talent for telling stories about real people and real emotions. The setting for her story is completely familiar to her. "I've always had wet feet and sand in my hair," she writes. "I've watched the lighthouse beacon flash when storms in my life rivaled those on the lake. I used this book as an excuse to spend many a wonderful hour on the shore of the big lake."

Starlit Promise

PETRA HOLLAND

Harlequin Books

TORONTO • NEW YORK • LONDON
AMSTERDAM • PARIS • SYDNEY • HAMBURG
STOCKHOLM • ATHENS • TOKYO • MILAN

Published August 1991

ISBN 0-373-70462-3

STARLIT PROMISE

Copyright © 1991 by Petra Walters. All rights reserved.
Except for use in any review, the reproduction or utilization
of this work in whole or in part in any form by any electronic,
mechanical or other means, now known or hereafter invented,
including xerography, photocopying and recording,
or in any information storage or retrieval system, is forbidden without
the permission of the publisher, Harlequin Enterprises Limited,
225 Duncan Mill Road, Don Mills, Ontario, Canada M3B 3K9.

All the characters in this book have no existence outside the
imagination of the author and have no relation whatsoever to
anyone bearing the same name or names. They are not even
distantly inspired by any individual known or unknown to the
author, and all incidents are pure invention.

® are Trademarks registered in the United States Patent and
Trademark Office and in other countries.

Printed in U.S.A.

CHAPTER ONE

"HEY, MISTER, do ya wanna help me fly my kite?"

Joe Fisher jumped slightly and spun around with a scowl, ready to snarl at whoever had dared to interrupt his solitude. Wasn't there any place he could be alone? No one in their right mind should be out here on a Lake Michigan beach in November. Okay, okay, it was early November and an almost-strong sun did warm the mild air so that only a thick sweater was necessary to ward off the chill of the coming winter. But still, he had hoped to be alone.

His interrupter was a young girl, tall and very skinny; the kite in question was bright red and yellow and seemed to be nearly as big as she was. She looked oddly young—too young for her height—and very pale under a light layer of freckles. Wisps of blond hair escaped from beneath her red ski cap. Her smile was wide and friendly, accented by terrific dimples that made her whole face seem to dance with happiness. Even her voice was striking.

She wasn't wheedling or whining for help; she was offering him the chance to help her. Her voice was matter-of-fact, as if she were offering to share a secret treasure with him. Hey, mister, do ya wanna have half my cookies? Hey, mister, do ya wanna have a million dollars? Hey, mister, do ya wanna help me fly my kite? It was an offer he could hardly refuse.

"Okay," he agreed, but his enthusiasm was less than complete. What he really wanted was to be left alone so that he could brood about Olivia's decision to move to California. One day a few weeks ago, on a cold, drizzly autumn day, she had decided to pack her bags and go somewhere where her suntan would never fade. She'd asked him to go along. She hadn't listened when he'd argued that a college professor couldn't leave in the middle of a semester. Which was beside the point, anyway, since he had absolutely no desire to move to California whether she went or not. So yesterday she'd left, alone. She was probably right: maybe he was a selfish bastard who never really cared for her. He certainly hadn't mistaken her for Ms. Right, Joe admitted with a sigh.

"Oh, good," the girl enthused, interrupting his thoughts. "You better hold this while I work the string." She handed him the kite, clearly doubting that he'd be much help. Joe suppressed a smile and helped her untangle the kite's thirty-foot-long tail of red-and-yellow bows.

"What's yer name?" the girl asked conversationally.

"Joe. What's yours?" he replied, wanting to reprimand her for trespassing on this private section of beach.

"Lala. Actually it's Michella, but everyone calls me Lala. Except my aunts. I'm ten." The girl blew on her fingers to warm them and then tackled a particularly difficult tangle. Joe stood by, wondering if he ought to do it for her.

"Why aren't you in school? Are you on vacation?" Joe asked, watching her and finally reaching out to take over.

"I'm sick," Lala announced and worked a bow through the loosened loop of string Joe held.

"Shouldn't you be in bed then?"

"Not sick like that. I'm gonna die. I got cancer of my blood. It's called leukemia," Lala stated calmly, adding the name of her disease in four equally stressed syllables as if she were a teacher instructing young children.

Joe stared down at the kite tail, wanting to step back, recoiling inside. He didn't want to hear about any little kid who was dying. Why was she telling him this? He immediately felt ashamed of his reaction. He had no right to recoil. Think about the poor kid, Fisher, think about her family. His hands were shaking slightly as he finished untangling the tail of bows and laid it in a straight line upon the sand.

Leukemia. Wasn't that one of the diseases that the doctors were finally beginning to cure? Joe was fairly sure he'd read someplace that only fifty percent of the children suffering from leukemia would die. Or maybe he had heard it on the radio during that telethon for Saint Jude's Children's Hospital. Lala probably wasn't going to die at all.

"How do you know you are going to die?" he asked without realizing that he was speaking aloud until it was too late. He felt a cold sweat start to form in his armpits and on the small of his back. Inside, his stomach and intestines seemed to be tying themselves up in a knot tighter than the one they had just untangled in the kite's tail.

"I heard my mom say it on the telephone when she was talking to Gramma Davidson. That's my daddy's mom. She said Dr. Smith said there was nothing more to do. That's why we came to the beach. I'm supposed to die before Christmas—I know 'cause I heard Aunt Melly say so. She was yelling at Mom. But anyway, I'm gonna wait 'cause I want to ask Santa Claus for something special first.''

Joe didn't know what to say in the face of Lala's calm acceptance of her own death and wasn't sure whether to correct her misconception about her ability to choose the time of her death or not. He was completely unprepared to deal with the subject and the discussion. All he had wanted to do was walk down by the water and feel sorry for himself, and instead he had to figure out how to deal with this situation.

''Do you eavesdrop a lot?'' he asked, changing the subject to one he felt more able to handle. ''There's an old saying that says you'll never hear anything good about yourself if you eavesdrop.'' Maybe he shouldn't have said that. Hearing you were going to die was more than not hearing anything good. Joe sighed heavily and picked up the kite.

''I don't eavesdrop!'' Lala protested vigorously. ''They sometimes think I'm asleep when I'm not and talk in front of me. It's not my fault.'' She glared at him with flashing blue eyes and dared him to contradict her.

''Okay,'' Joe said dismissing the whole conversation. ''Are we going to launch this kite or not?''

''Launch it, obviously,'' Lala replied, putting on the voice and mannerisms of someone much older. She shrugged one shoulder in an odd gesture that didn't fit her tall skinny body. It reminded Joe of Olivia in some way, maybe because it seemed so posed and artificial. ''You run and I'll hold the string, okay? Go that way,'' she directed, pointing so that he would run against the wind. "Hold it up over your head and go as fast as you can."

Joe obeyed, thinking that Lala reminded him of a boot camp sergeant. He looked over his shoulder to see if she was ready and then began to run, holding the bulky kite up so that the wind could catch it. The wind did pull on it, but it served as air resistance rather than loft. It was harder to hold the kite up in the wind than Joe had expected; he smothered a curse as his smooth-soled leather shoe slid sideways on the shifting sand and nearly deposited him on his backside.

"Wait a second," he called out in an expurgated version. While Lala pulled the string and rearranged the kite's tail in preparation for his next attempt, Joe levered off his slightly worn penny loafers and rolled up his jeans. He took off his elbow-patched tweed jacket and woolen scarf and set them aside before picking up the kite again.

"Ready?" he asked, looking back at Lala. She nodded at him; Joe grabbed the kite with both hands, held it over his head and ran until he could feel the wind grab it from him. Letting go, he ducked down out of the way and then watched as Lala expertly fed out the string, letting the kite soar higher and higher.

"Way to go! Let 'er rip!" Joe shouted gleefully as he pulled on his jacket and tucked the scarf back around his neck. The wind was quite chilly, and he wasn't dressed for the beach. He hadn't really planned to come. Ducking out through the back door instead of leaving by the front for his eleven o'clock class had been a last-minute decision. He wouldn't be surprised if the college was trying to call him right now; professors were expected to notify the school if they planned to miss a class. His students probably weren't too thrilled, either. And he couldn't blame them.

The kite rose nearly a hundred feet in the air, steadily moving up and away from them. "Watch this," Lala gloated, giving the string a yank and a sideways pull that Joe didn't quite see. The kite followed her cues and swooped and dipped. She continued to manipulate the string, making the kite dance in the sky for several moments. "I wanna get a two-string kite so I can really make it do tricks," she said wistfully.

Joe stopped himself from asking why she didn't, why she sounded so wistful. She was going to die soon. His stomach gave a jump and his head seemed to roar. It was hard to breathe past the sudden lump that caught in his throat. What the hell was he supposed to say now? He wished the girl's mother or father would come out here and rescue him. Didn't they know that a kid shouldn't be out alone talking to strangers? What if something happened? What would he do?

"Where do you live?" he asked. Lala was still letting out string, allowing the kite to go higher and higher until it was just a tiny dot in the sky. Joe could only see the tail by squinting and staring, and even then it might just be his imagination.

"At Arbor Manor. It's an apartment thing."

"Complex? An apartment complex?"

"Yeah. It's pretty cool. It's got a swimming pool— only it's empty now—and a playground with swings and a slide and monkey bars. Our apartment has a little balcony where we can make hamburgers and stuff in the summer. We used to live in a yellow house with a fireplace and a garden with a swing set, but we moved to our apartment after Daddy died. I was in second grade. It's called arbor 'cause there are lots of trees, but I don't know how come they called it a manor 'cause that means a big, big house and this is all little tiny apartments.''

Joe felt bewildered, not knowing how to respond to Lala's lengthy monologue. He could think of a hundred questions beginning and ending with what was she doing so far from her home? If he recalled correctly, the apartments she spoke of were on the other side of town—a rather bland complex sandwiched between two similar apartment complexes in what had once been a cornfield. He wanted to know more about her father's death but didn't dare ask. Where was her mother? In the end he said nothing, and Lala continued without any prompting.

"We're staying at my Great-Aunt Gert's house now. If my name was Gertrude I'd want people to call me Trudy, not Gert, wouldn't you?" Joe, who had never considered the issue before, nodded speechlessly. "Her house is really big and nice. It's got a fireplace in the living room and one in the bedroom. I wouldn't put a fireplace in the bedroom. I would put it in the kitchen so that you could always make toasted marshmallows. Don't you think that would be smarter?"

"Yeah, I guess so," Joe responded, hiding his amusement. He had a fireplace in his bedroom, and there was no way he was going to try to explain its appeal to a ten-year-old girl. "Is your Aunt Gert's house on the beach?"

"Yeah. It's the brown one. Can you see it? It's behind those trees a little bit. The one on the end. She's not my aunt, though, she's my mom's aunt so that makes her my great-aunt. Which is cool 'cause she's *really* great. I'm glad I'm not gonna have any kids 'cause my aunts wouldn't make very good great-aunts 'cause they're not great. Great-Uncle Corny's cool, too. He's really my great-uncle. His name is Cornelius. That's pretty neat 'cause he always tells really corny knock-knock jokes. People should have names that describe them, don't you think?''

Lala chatted on, not giving Joe a chance to get a word in edgewise, although she did note his considering nod. "Joe is okay, I guess. It's sorta ordinary. Are you ordinary? Mom says if people's names were like that, mine would have to be Lalalalalalalalalala. 'Cause I talk so much, get it?'' She grinned and this time paused so that he could reply or so that she could catch her breath.

"I get it," Joe said with a smile. He had recognized the home that Lala pointed out. It was next to his own, separated by a wooded lot. Cornelius and Gertrude Van Dyke usually stayed in it during the summer. They wintered in Florida, he thought, although it might have been Hawaii. One of the older couples in the neighborhood went to Hawaii each winter, but Joe couldn't recall just which one. "Are your great-aunt and great-uncle here now?''

"Yup. They just got back from the Seashells Islands in Africa. I like that name, too. Seashells. That's a good name for an island, don't you think?'' Lala tilted her head to the side and waited for his opinion, taking a break from the task of recalling the kite.

Joe assumed she meant Seychelles but didn't really feel like correcting her since her error was so charming. As an educator, even at the college level, he would normally be irritated by anyone who didn't bother to correct a child. "That is a good name for an island,'' he agreed.

"You wind for a while, okay?" Lala asked in a quiet voice. As soon as Joe took over the control of the kite, she sat down in the sand, stretching her legs out before her. Seeing how pale her face had suddenly become, Joe felt a momentary stab of panic. What the hell was he going to do now? "I'm okay," Lala assured him. "I just get tired sometimes."

"Are you sure?" Joe asked calmly, a sinking feeling in his stomach. Where was this little girl's mother or whoever was supposed to be taking care of her? You didn't just let a ten-year-old who was dying run around unsupervised. He had no idea what to do.

"Yeah, I'm sure. Are you gonna wind the kite in or not?" Lala demanded. Her cheeks seemed to regain a little of their color.

"I'm winding, I'm winding," Joe said heavily, not wanting Lala to sense the depth of his fear. He began to pull in the string and wind it on the bright plastic bobbin.

"Anyway—" Lala began to speak again, her voice not quite as strong as it had been "—I like that name, the Seashells Islands. I think there must be really a lot of seashells there. They only brought one home. I wished for them to bring me a starfish, 'cause I like this song about starfish, but they didn't."

"A song about starfish?" Joe asked, trying to recall any song about starfish he had learned as a child. He could vaguely recall a song about an inchworm and another about a giraffe who couldn't laugh, but no songs about starfish.

"It goes like this," Lala said and then began to sing in a voice that wobbled for a moment and then found the melody and grew stronger. When she was done, neither of them spoke for a moment and the only sounds were from the wind and the waves. Joe began to wind the kite string in again, stunned beyond words. He had heard the song before; it was a rock ballad that had been very popular back in the early seventies. That didn't diminish the horror he felt when Lala sang so sweetly about it being hard to die, about only being able to reach the starfish on the beach. A very big part of him just wanted to run. He hadn't skipped class and come out on the beach today looking for this. He didn't want to think about being unable to reach the stars.

"See, it's about starfish. I have an old record of it. I used to pretend it was my daddy singing, 'cause the song goes, 'Michelle, my little one.' And that's almost my name. Daddy died in the springtime. I remember 'cause it was just before school got out for summer vacation. I used to think the song meant that he wished he was still alive, you know, but now I think it means we'll be together again in heaven. Like that's what he wants so he'll be waiting for me. Don'tcha think?"

"Uh, yeah," Joe managed to squeeze out past the thickness in his throat. He didn't know what to say. How could such a young girl face her own death with so much calm, with such courage? If he were dying, Joe thought, he wouldn't be able to face it with such bravery and honesty. "Yeah, I guess you will be together in heaven."

He was in way over his head. What was he supposed to say? He tried to remember anything that might help—something he could have picked up from telethons or the TV shows that featured miracle cures in the last five minutes. Joe could only suppose there were no miracle cures left for Lala. So how did he deal with this disconcerting girl who was an odd mixture of childlike naiveté and uncommon maturity?

He felt confused—guilty because he didn't want to be involved in the discussion, and sad because in a short while Lala had managed to sneak into his heart. All he wanted, selfish bastard that he was, was to be left alone on the beach. He didn't want to know that Lala was dying. He wished he could believe that a miracle would still happen for her.

"Watch out! Watch out! You're gonna crash it," Lala's strident voice sliced through his gloom. Joe realized that his lack of concentration on the task at hand had brought the kite perilously close to the tree-tops on the wooded dunes by their houses. "Pull back on the string, Joe," Lala commanded. "Pull hard!"

Joe gave the string a yank and then, following Lala's instruction, a mighty yank. The kite rose for a moment and then made a graceful swooping dive into the top of a bare-branched maple tree. For a moment Joe stood in silence, wondering how the kite could one moment be almost alive in its graceful flight and then flutter like a lifeless scrap of fabric. He felt as if he had killed it.

He fought to hide his feelings. You didn't tell a dying kid that you just killed her kite. The last thing she needed was more death. Joe felt a shudder begin deep inside him and managed to suppress almost all of it before it rose to the surface of his skin as a faint ripple of dread. Finally he turned around and faced Lala.

She was staring at the kite caught in the distant tree. "Come on, kid, let's see if we can get that baby out of there." Joe forced his voice to sound cheerful. He held out his hand and hauled the almost-weightless girl to her feet. As they walked over to the tree, Joe kept her hand, bony and cold and very small, folded up in his. He felt big and protective. Trying to hide his concern, he casually supported her each time she began to slip in the loose sand. Lala was clearly more tired than she had let him know. He felt scared.

SARA DAVIDSON ROSE from the kitchen table where she'd been pretending to read and rubbed the back of her neck ruefully. Her muscles were tense and sore, a discomfort that had become constant even before she'd moved into her aunt and uncle's beach house with Lala. She heaved a sigh and slumped against the casement of the large bay window that looked out over the pale sand and deep blue water. Lala had insisted on flying her kite this morning even though Corny was in town running errands.

All she wanted to do, Sara thought for the thousandth time, was to grab Lala and somehow try to hold her safe, to protect her from the inevitable future and the inevitable pain. But she couldn't. No matter what she did, what she sacrificed, who she begged, there was no way to save Lala. She tried not to let Lala know her fear and pain, but maybe that was the reason her daughter had insisted on flying her kite without her mother this morning. "I'm not a baby, you know," she'd declared with the slight drawl of sophistication that she'd developed after watching afternoon soaps on TV in the hospital.

Lala, with her usual charm, had managed to find a friend, someone to help her fly her kite. Sara watched while the man tried to launch the kite and then paused to remove his coat before he tried again. It was impossible not to laugh as she watched the serious-looking man throw caution to the wind. When the kite rose sharply, soaring high, the man jabbed his fist into the air, clearly celebrating, probably yelling jubilantly. It was just like Lala to bring him joy. She brought everyone joy. If there was any justice in the world Lala would live to be a hundred.

But she wouldn't. Sara bit her lip savagely to hold back the tears that threatened to overwhelm her. She wouldn't cry until Lala was...until later. She focused on the brisk clipping of Aunt Gert's heels on the tile floor. If it wasn't for her aunt and uncle taking them in for Lala's last few weeks, Sara didn't know if she could have handled what was to come. The doctors weren't even holding out the hope of any more painful treatments. They'd given Lala a week. That was two and a half weeks ago, and now every additional day was another miracle.

"What's so funny?" Gert asked, coming to stand next to her niece. Sara smiled affectionately when Gert answered her own question, "Lala sure loves that kite! Hmm, that must be Joe Fisher with her. He teaches English at the college."

"He looks like it!" They giggled softly as they watched the pair on the beach. The wind was whipping up white-capped waves over the dark blue expanse of Lake Michigan. If she turned her head against the glass and peered sideways, Sara could see the end of the pier that stretched into the lake at the channel entrance. In the summer they had often walked down the sandy beach to the lighthouse and out onto the pier. Now it had become much too far for Lala to walk.

Almost as she thought it, Sara saw Lala hand the kite string to the man and collapse in the sand in a disjointed sprawl. She had been out in that cold for an awfully long time. Was she just tired or was something terribly wrong? Sara peered anxiously through the window, trying to discern the details of the distant figures. The man was bent down, ignoring the kite he was holding, obviously worried about Lala. Sara ran to the door, swearing under her breath as she struggled with the lock.

At the edge of the back patio a flight of shallow stairs led down a slight embankment to the sandy beach. Sara paused momentarily at the top of the steps. In that moment she noticed the man had resumed winding in the kite. Sara froze and watched the scene before her, wanting to run and join them but afraid to intrude. She had been guilty, so often, of cloistering Lala, of smothering her with love and protection.

Sara hugged herself and huddled into the side of the steps, trying to stay under cover while she watched. It was clear from the way Lala's head tipped and nodded, from the way her hands made graceful gestures, and from the way the man—Joe Fisher—bent toward Lala and then looked away, sometimes reeling the kite furiously and sometimes not at all, that they were engaged in a serious discussion.

Sara wished she could hear them. She had finally given up trying to teach Lala not to say everything that popped into her head. Luckily Lala was naturally generous so that she never intentionally insulted anyone. Sara had heard other people say this about Lala, particularly the nurses at the hospital. Everyone seemed to love her daughter.

Lala had always been that way, cheerful and happy and noisy, too. That was how she had gotten her nickname in the first place. Michael had thought up the name while their baby was standing up clutching the bars of her playpen and singing "lalala" at the top of her lungs, occasionally pausing to let loose wild peals of laughter. As a baby Lala had been a joy, laughing more than she cried; she had never changed, not even when her father died, not even in the face of this.

"You're going to catch pneumonia," Gert scolded, wrapping a coat around Sara's shoulders. Sara looked away from her daughter, silently thanking her aunt and begging for the reassurance that Gert couldn't give her. Gert shivered, and after squeezing Sara's shoulder helplessly, went back in the house; Sara focused on the scene before her again. Suddenly the man jerked the kite string so that the kite dived into the top of one of the bare maple trees. After a moment he reached down and helped Lala to her feet and they set off, hand in hand, toward the tree. Within a split second Sara was racing across the beach after them, unable to bear having Lala out of her sight for even a moment.

"WELL GOSH, LALA, that thing's really up there, isn't it?" Joe remarked as they found their way to the tree that clutched the kite in its upper branches. He casually sat Lala to the side on a moss-covered boulder and didn't mention her tiredness. He wasn't certain if that was the right thing to do, but it seemed far easier than asking her if she was okay. He wound the string that had trailed behind them as they walked.

"I'm going to give this thing a tug now, and we'll see if this old tree'll let go or if I've got to climb up there after it," Joe said, pulling sharply on the kite string. Lala was being far too quiet. He didn't like it at all. The kite remained firmly lodged.

Joe squatted next to Lala, looking at her wan face worriedly. She was staring sadly up at her kite. He didn't know whether to joke her out of the mood or read it as a sign of her exhaustion. What had happened to the babbling little girl who had been with him a few minutes ago? "Will you wait here while I go change my shoes?" he asked her quietly.

"Why?" Lala replied, brightening up just slightly, looking at him instead of at the kite.

"Why am I gonna change my shoes or why should you wait here?" Joe asked, and then answered without giving her time to reply. "I have to change my shoes cause I can't climb a tree in these ones." He held up the sole of his shoe for her to see its slippery surface. "Because I'd fall right out of that tree if I tried. And you should wait here so that I can find my way back."

"You can't climb this tree, anyway," Lala said sadly, "'cause you can't reach the bottom branches."

"You wait and see, girl, I'll be at the top of that tree before you can say boo!" Joe grinned at her and jogged off jauntily, carrying his shoes and socks. He hurried, not wanting to leave Lala alone for too long. It wasn't the danger in the woods that he feared, it was just that she seemed so vulnerable.

SARA SAW LALA ahead of her, sitting tiredly on a rock, her shoulders hunched within her ski jacket; even her bright red hat appeared to droop. Everything inside Sara seemed to move around and rearrange itself as she realized that Lala was dangerously tired now. She shouldn't have let her come outside today. It was too cold, too windy. She had been outside too long. Sara took one deep breath and held it for a moment before she released it in a long sigh.

"Hey, Lala, are you ready to come home for lunch?" Sara forced herself to sound bright and cheerful. Lala was paler now than when she had first come outside, and she looked so peaked that Sara just wanted to hold her. She was sure that her daughter was in pain, but she knew Lala wouldn't say anything until it became unbearable. That only made it worse when Lala did cry. Sara struggled to push her fear aside and to just be there for her daughter.

"Oh! Hi, Mom! I can't come home yet 'cause I'm waiting for Joe. He's gonna climb this tree and save our kite. He had to go change his shoes first. Then he says he's gonna be at the top of this tree before we can say boo. He got my kite stuck in it 'cause he pulled on the string too hard and then let it go all of a sudden. You know, like you always do," Lala's voice was thin but cheerful.

"I don't always do that," Sara defended herself, feebly since she knew her kite-flying ability was very low.

"That's true," Lala admitted graciously. "Sometimes you can't even get it to fly." She snickered merrily at her joke and squealed as Sara reached out to tweak her nose gently. "Hey, Mom, look at the doggy! Come 'ere, girl, c'm'ere," she coaxed the dog, which didn't hesitate before prancing up to Lala and licking her hands happily. "Look, Mom, she's kissing me."

"She's a he," a deep voice corrected her, and Sara and Lala both turned to see Joe striding up. He had changed his tweed jacket for a thick woolen sweater and put on a pair of heavily treaded black sports shoes. He had a rope looped over his shoulder. Lala just glanced at him once before turning her attention back to the dog, but Sara found herself staring at him in surprise. The man she had dismissed as serious-looking was in fact athletic and handsome.

"That's Roly Poly, but you can call him Roly if you want," Joe told Lala seriously, patting the dog that had trotted over in response to his name.

"Come over here. Come on, Roly," Lala crooned, and the frisky black-and-white spaniel danced back over to sit beside her, eager to be caressed.

"I'm Joseph Fisher, but you can call me Joe if you want," he said in a deep rich voice and stuck his hand out for Sara to shake. She felt disconcerted, unsure of her reaction. For a moment she forgot everything that was wrong and smiled at his little joke. His hand was warm and firm around her own. It made her feel safe for just one second, but she caught herself up shortly. She didn't have time for men or for silly feelings of safety. This Joseph Fisher wasn't going to save Lala.

"I'm Sara Davidson, Michella's mother," Sara introduced herself and then turned to check on Lala again. If her assessment of Lala's pinched look was correct, the little girl's joints were very sore again. It wouldn't do to have that bouncing dog bashing into her. But Roly was sitting still, leaning against Lala's side, almost as if he were propping her up. Only his eyes moved, closing with pleasure each time Lala began another long smooth stroke over his silky fur.

"Okeydoke, Lala, here I go. Are you ready for this?" Joe asked with a smile before turning to toss the coil of rope over the lowest branch of the tree. It sailed gracefully over the branch and unfurled as it descended, leaving Joe with a rope looped over the branch. After a nod and a grin from Lala, permission from the queen, he shinnied up the rope with an ease that bespoke of much practice.

Sara watched in awe. She could remember distant gym classes where she had to try to climb a rope dangling from the ceiling, and it had never been that easy. Joe climbed effortlessly; his thighs bunching muscularly, his shoulders moving smoothly. Lala, she noticed, had not stopped petting the dog but was watching Joe avidly at the same time. When he reached the branch, he wrapped first one hand and then the other around it, doubled himself over, looped one leg over it and then pulled himself up so that he was sitting on the branch. He made it look really simple.

"Did you see that, Mom? Wow! That is so cool. You like Joe, don't you? He lives in that house that's all made out of stones. He looks like he should live in a treehouse, huh?" Lala chortled merrily again, pleased with her own wit. "He's lucky he can climb trees better than he can fly a kite. I wish I could climb up there. I'll bet you can see forever. You can probably see all the way to the other side of the lake."

"Hey, Lala, you awake down there?" Joe called down in a cheerful voice. "I'm gonna loosen this kite and you pull on the string when I say to, okay?"

"Yeah," Lala called back.

"Okay, give her a pull," Joe called a moment later. Lala pulled on the string, but it was obvious that the effort was taxing her. Sara's insides all tightened, as did her stomach, her chest, her throat, and the skin and the muscles around her eyes. She ached so badly when her baby hurt.

"I'll pull it, Lala. Roly doesn't like it when you bump him," Sara offered, reaching for the string. Lala gave it to her without protest, a sure sign that she was not feeling well. Although she never seemed to rage against her illness, Lala stood up to everything she had to face and never accepted more limitations than were absolutely necessary.

Sara gave the string a sharp tug, and the kite came loose and slid down a dozen feet before it caught in another branch. She pulled on the string but the kite was caught. "Gosh, Mom, you got it caught again. You really can't fly a kite very good, can you? You must have a jinx or something. Like Charlie Brown. And don't try to blame it on the tree, either."

"Hold on," Joe called and scrambled down a level before going out on the limb where the kite was caught and releasing it again. "Okay, pull again," he called and watched while the kite sailed down to catch once more in the branches of the tree.

"Are you sure it's not the tree's fault, Lala? I'm doing my best here, and that old tree keeps grabbing it," Sara teased.

"Sure, blame it on an innocent tree, Mom. You should be ashamed of yourself. Look how hard you're making Joe work. He reminds me of a monkey the way he climbs from branch to branch. Except he doesn't have a tail. Wouldn't it be neat if we had tails? You could do all kinds of things. Like when you want to eat in front of the TV, you could carry your plate in one hand and your silverware in the other and use your tail to carry your glass of pop. That would be so awesome."

"Pull again," Joe called down from the tree. Sara did, and this time the kite came loose and tumbled to the ground. She began to disassemble it with practiced motions; this part of kite-flying she could handle. Joe climbed down from the tree and coiled his line while Lala sat and patted Roly very quietly.

"Where'd you learn to climb trees so well?" Sara asked, feeling uncomfortable with the silence that had fallen over them. She was used to Lala's ceaseless chatter. She would miss it so much when Lala was gone. The sadness welled up, and Sara had to force back the tears, swallowing fiercely at the lump in her throat. She made herself listen to Joe. There would be time enough to cry later.

"I don't know, I just learned. When I was a kid I always liked to climb trees, and I guess I still do. In the summer when I want to be alone I climb up a big tree with a book and no one can find me. It's like having a secret hideaway."

"What about Roly? Where does he go when you climb a tree?" Lala asked.

"He usually stays inside the house," Joe explained. He had never felt he was neglecting his dog before, but something in Lala's face made him feel that way now. "He likes to go in the basement and lie on the cement floor. I guess that must feel nice and cool against his fur." He paused for a moment, slinging the coil of rope over his shoulder. "Would you two like to come over for lunch? I made a big pot of minestrone yesterday."

Sara looked at Lala. She was petting the dog again and didn't grow enthusiastic at the prospect of lunch out. Not that Sara needed an excuse. She'd just met this man! Of course she wouldn't eat his soup. "Gert's making lunch for us right now."

Joe shrugged off the refusal. Lala needed to rest. He wondered if he ought to offer to carry her home. No, she probably wouldn't like that. She was an independent kid. He had a feeling her mother was that way, too. They were two of a kind: too skinny, too pale, too frail. He had a sudden urge to take care of them, to try to make everything better. He sighed quietly. He usually was attracted to strong, independent women. Whoever had said crime didn't pay had been right. He'd think twice before he skipped class again.

Sara had the kite wrapped up in a small bundle now, and Joe swooped down and gathered Lala in his arms. "I can walk," she promptly protested, just as he had expected she would.

"I know that," he said softly, cuddling her light body close to his chest, "but I always carry my girlfriends around. You're gonna be my new girlfriend, aren't you?"

"You probably already have a girlfriend," Lala challenged suspiciously. "I'll bet you've got ten of 'em."

"But none as pretty as you," Joe replied. "I had one girlfriend, but she moved away to California. So now you have to be my girlfriend."

"Okay," Lala agreed, "but I've already got me a boyfriend, you know. He gives me presents. Are you gonna give me presents, too? I'd let you be my boyfriend if you were really nice to me. If you let Roly come over every day and play with me. Especially in the summer when you're climbed up a tree. I wish I could climb trees like a monkey, too."

"I'll give you a starfish if you'll be my girl," Joe bargained as he came through the last trees and onto the open area of sand and beach grass around the rambling brown house where Lala was staying. Following Sara through the woods made him wish he had something to offer her, too, but he had nothing for a mother whose child was dying.

"Okay," Lala agreed. "You can put me down on the chaise longue on the patio," she instructed, and so Joe set her carefully onto the padded chair.

"G'bye," he said softly, starting to move away.

"You have to kiss me," Lala reminded him impatiently, clearly wondering how a grown man could be so ignorant about the proper treatment of a girlfriend.

Joe grinned and bent down to plant a loud kiss on her forehead. Lala wrapped a thin arm around his neck and kissed his cheek. "You're scratchy," she complained. Joe just grinned.

"Thanks," Sara whispered as he passed her on his way back into the woods.

"No problem," he said, shrugging off her thanks and smiling his goodbye to her. He wondered, as he walked home, if she had dimples as devastating as Lala's. She hadn't smiled that widely while they were together so he didn't know, yet. He reminded himself to make a note so that he would remember to go up in the attic and find that box of shells from a previous visit to Fort Lauderdale. He sure hoped there was a starfish in there. A starfish for Lala.

FOOL! WAS ONE of the milder epithets Joe used as he spent the better part of the next morning rummaging through the cartons and piles of junk in his attic searching for the little box of shells. He was worse than a materialist; he was a pack rat. A full three-quarters of the stuff in his attic served no purpose at all. And it was collecting dust. He would clear it out and have it hauled away—just as soon as he had some free time.

The elusive box, once found, held no starfish, only a sand dollar. On his way to see Lala, Joe called himself worse than a fool. Only an idiot made promises he couldn't keep. Made promises like *I'll give you a starfish* to a sick child. He hoped she would find the sand dollar, with its star-shaped pattern, a sufficient substitute for the starfish in her song.

Gertrude Van Dyke stood and blinked at him for a moment. "I thought you were the hospice nurse, but you're just Joe."

Joe offered a crooked smile. *Just Joe* summed up exactly how he felt today on his half-failed mission. He explained his errand to Gert, and she ushered him into the house with a shallow smile.

"Lala's not doing well today. She's still in bed. I suppose you can go on up. Lala will like the sand dollar. She was awfully disappointed when Corny and I didn't bring her a starfish from Africa. It's the first room at the top of the stairs. I'll come along in a minute with some coffee. Or would you rather have tea?"

"Nothing for me," Joe demurred. "I can only stay a few minutes."

"There's always time for a cup of coffee," Gert insisted, setting off to the kitchen with unseemly haste.

Joe frowned after her. Maybe she didn't approve of him bringing over the blasted sand dollar. She could probably tell he was more interested in seeing Sara again than in being nice to a little girl. Not that he didn't want to be nice to Lala. She was a sweet kid. Sure he wanted to do something to make her happy. But it's her mother you really want to see, his little voice insisted. Joe shrugged away its censure and trotted up the wide staircase, stopping in his tracks at the top, staring at the scene framed by the doorway.

Sara was curled in a chair beside the bed where Lala lay. Looking at the pale child, Joe realized that all the pretending in the world wasn't going to keep Lala alive. Of course he'd known Lala was ill, but he hadn't allowed himself to believe she was *dying*. Gertrude Van Dyke's stiff chatter made sense now; she wasn't getting a little senile, she was desperately trying to deny what was happening here. Lala looked awful, almost colorless and painfully skinny, her head quite bald. Sara didn't look much better. Her face was ashen and there were bruises under her eyes. Joe wanted to wrap his arms around her, around them both, to hold them close and stop this horrible thing, to fight off death as if it were merely an armed horseman.

"Mommy?" Lala's voice was raspy, little more than a whisper.

"What, pumpkin?"

"Will Daddy be able to find me, do you think? I'm afraid he won't recognize me 'cause I grew so much since he died. He'll be waiting for me, won't he?"

Sara drew in a shaky breath. "I'm sure he'll recognize you, Lala. He'll be waiting for you...." She turned her face away from Lala, and Joe watched as her shimmering eyes widened at the sight of him frozen in the doorway. "Oh, look, pumpkin. Joe came to see you. Remember how he helped you get your kite out of the tree?"

"My hat, Mom!" Lala insisted, bringing the shadow of a smile to Joe's face. Lala was caught in the awkward moment of transition, still a child, but almost a young woman. Sara eased a soft blue beret onto Lala's head with hands so gentle they etched the movement into Joe's memory. He felt sick with the knowledge that Lala would never realize the fullness of womanhood.

"Hi, Joe," Lala whispered. Joe could hardly hear her voice, and yet he could see the effort it took for her to speak. "Did you bring Roly with you?" Joe wished she wouldn't look so vulnerable, so exhausted, so sick. He wished she would start to chatter again, sit up in bed and wave her arms around like she had when she had talked to him on the beach. He wished he had brought the dog with him.

"Nope, not today," he admitted quietly. "I brought you something, though." He moved to kneel beside the bed. "I couldn't find a starfish for you, Lala, but I found you something else. It's a sand dollar." He handed her the flat white skeleton of the sea urchin. "See, it's got a star on it." He pointed it out for her and was rewarded with a faint smile.

"Thanks," she breathed. Joe looked away so Lala wouldn't see the wetness that darkened his eyes. Sara's hand touched his shoulder, giving him her strength. He couldn't meet her eyes because he feared the truth he might read there. With a smile for Lala, Joe turned to Sara, almost crashing into another man who was rushing into the room.

"Marcus!" Sara exclaimed thankfully and stood to bury herself in his embrace. Joe felt left out. For a split second he was filled with raging hatred for this man, an exceptionally tall golden blond god, who could do for Sara what he couldn't, what he wanted desperately to be able to do. His hatred shattered into shards of glass when Lala spoke.

"Daddy!" her voice was soft but decidedly happy. She sounded relieved.

Both Sara and Marcus froze. Joe watched as they moved simultaneously to the bed. "It's Uncle Marcus, Lala," Sara said in a thick voice.

"Daddy, I knew you'd wait for me." Lala's voice was faint but everyone heard her words. A small smile stole over her face. Her eyes closed and she was still. Marcus went down on his knees beside the bed and Sara stood beside him, his long arm wrapped around her shoulders. They were almost the same height that way, and they leaned against each other as if they were pooling their strength, as if they were partners.

Joe passed Gert as he left the room and descended the elegant flow of stairs. He felt anything but elegant. He felt small and ugly, tarnished by his helplessness in the face of death. He hadn't belonged there, but he wished he had. He wished he were part of Sara's family, wished he could have held her and helped her. Her tender movements and gentle voice hid a steely strength, but what would she do when Lala was gone and she didn't need to be strong for her anymore? How did a mother survive when a child as lovely as Lala died before she had a chance to live? Who would hold Sara when she finally cried? Joe asked himself as he trudged back through the woods to his empty house.

CHAPTER TWO

"MARCUS DAVIDSON is here to see you, darling. Should I tell him you're asleep?" Agnes Van Dyke came to the side of the bed and smoothed her daughter's hair. Then she turned away and began to straighten the knickknacks on the dresser, moving the wedding picture and the photos of Lala to the back and plumping the little stuffed lion, a souvenir mascot a dimly recalled boyfriend had given Sara in high school.

Sara looked around the room and sighed. Her mother hadn't changed a thing in here since she had left home. It was still a kid's room, an odd mixture of things she had left behind when she went to college. She had never even liked the pink ruffles. They were much too frilly for her taste. To her parents she had still been a little girl when they redecorated while she was in junior high. She'd graduated from college with honors, been married, had a baby, been widowed, and now had lost her daughter, too, and still she was their little girl.

"No, Mom, I'll get up and talk to Marcus. Will you please ask him to wait a minute for me?" Sara would have asked her mother to send him into the bedroom so that she could talk to him without getting up and getting dressed, but she knew her mother wouldn't allow that. When she and Michael had moved back to

Holland, they'd stayed with her parents while they looked for a place to live. Her mother had prepared two rooms, one for Michael and one for her and the baby. Sara had wanted to protest, but Michael had just turned the whole thing into a running joke, making elaborate plans for their good-night kisses.

"Are you sure, dear? Maybe you ought to take another one of those pills Dr. Miller left for you. You know he said there was no reason to push yourself now," Agnes said worriedly. She began to adjust the furniture slightly, and Sara realized that she was putting back the things that Sara had moved since she came home.

"I'm okay, Mom," Sara said as strongly as she could. "Please tell Marcus that I'm coming."

"Well..." Agnes drew the word out in a discouraging tone but finally turned and left the room with a disapproving sigh.

Sara pulled herself out of the twin bed and waited until the feeling of swirling weightlessness left her head. She was weak and knew she should be eating. If only everything didn't choke her when she tried to swallow. The week since Lala's death had passed in timeless periods of fog induced by tranquilizing drugs, and confusing moments of lucidity when she was forced to make decisions and take care of details. She felt numb, as if she were half asleep, watching a television show of her life.

Sara yanked on a pair of jeans and a big sweater and dragged a brush through her hair before she went into the living room to see Marcus. He was perched uncomfortably on the edge of a fragile chair, like an adult crunched into a child's playhouse. As soon as she entered the room he stood up with a look of relief on his face.

Marcus folded Sara into his long arms, and she felt secure for the first time since Lala died. When Marcus was there, it seemed as if Michael were still alive; she felt safe, felt loved. She clung to him while a wave of sadness washed over her. Pressing her face into the smooth, clean-smelling cotton of his shirt, Sara rested her forehead against his chest, just as she had when she hugged Michael.

Although eight years had separated Michael from his kid brother, Marcus looked enough like Michael that they might have passed for twins...if Michael were still alive. They had the same awesome height and athletic build, although Marcus lacked the innate grace that had served his brother so well on the basketball courts. Michael playing ball had been a dream to watch. Sara could close her eyes and still see the ball leaving his long fingers and rising in a graceful arc before dropping noiselessly through the hoop. After Michigan State, Michael had played for the Detroit Pistons for three years. Although he'd never been a star, Sara, staying home with the baby, couldn't resent the career that gave him such pleasure. His joy and enthusiasm had swept her along and had lived on in his daughter from the time she was born.

Of course Lala hadn't always been happy, nor had she been perfect. But her smile and her laughter and her incessant chatter had filled the days with the same sunniness that Michael always radiated. Michael hadn't even been depressed when he had to retire from basketball. He'd started selling real estate and found his happy nature made him a surprisingly effective salesman.

While Sara had enjoyed the money he made, she'd known it wasn't necessary for their happiness. With Michael she would've been happy in a breadline. But the extra money had been fun, and they'd been able to help others. When Marcus had started selling insurance, they'd been his first customers, taking out policies on their cars and their house and even their lives. Sara had already collected on the last of those policies, although the check still lay in her purse. She held Marcus tighter as she thought of it.

"Oh!" Agnes managed to make one syllable convey a massive amount of shocked disapproval. Sara felt suddenly guilty and irritated. The emotions lay heavy and thick, like a cloud of cigar smoke around her head. "Would either of you like a cup of tea?" Agnes inquired in a too-polite voice.

Sara looked up at Marcus, and he answered for both of them. "No, thank you, Mrs. Van Dyke. Sara and I are going for a drive. We'll be back in a little while." He gave Sara's arm a squeeze and spoke to her in a softer voice. "Go put on your shoes and a coat." Mindlessly she obeyed.

Once in the car she stared sightlessly through the side window at the trees and houses that flashed by. Marcus parked the car at the end of a road that looked out over Lake Macatawa. For a moment, she hardly realized that the car had stopped moving. It was such a relief to leave her parents' house. While they wanted to comfort and pamper her, they refused to allow her to really grieve in her own way for Lala. For years she had coped with her parents' protectiveness, but now she couldn't find the strength to fight their subtle oppression.

The lake was a flat expanse of dull blue-gray, like the heavy clouds above it. The color seemed to have been leached from everything. The banks were tan-gray stretches of dead grass and skeletons of trees. Sara sighed heavily. Without Lala the whole world was a dismal, colorless place. How was she going to survive?

"Sara, I know it's not my place to say anything, but are you sure you ought to be staying with your parents?" The silence following his question was deafening.

Sara felt something go cold and then hot inside her, and sudden sobs welled up uncontrollably from her chest. "I don't know," she tried to say, but her voice came out in a wail that turned into wrenching sobs. Although she'd shed a few tears at the funeral, this was the first time she had really let go, crying so hard she thought her body would break apart. She hated herself for being weak and helpless and out of control.

Marcus pulled her across the wide front seat of his huge sedan until she was gathered in his arms, and then he rocked her gently until the sobs lessened and she ran out of tears. Sara lay in his arms then, feeling drained and yet not relieved by her crying. Marcus gave her his handkerchief and she blew her nose, making a funny honking noise. She was embarrassed that she couldn't even cry right, but she had to smile as she recalled a joke that Michael and Lala had always made.

She moved back into her own seat and dried her eyes. "What are you thinking?" Marcus asked in a soft voice. That was one of the things that Sara liked about him. He showed concern but never demanded explanations or berated her for what she was feeling. When she smiled after sobbing her heart out in his arms, he only asked what she was thinking.

"Michael and Lala used to say, when you blew your nose noisily, that at least you weren't an elephant. I miss them so much, Marcus, I can't even tell you." Her voice broke and the tears prickled behind her eyes.

Marcus didn't say anything for a long time. When he finally spoke his voice was a little distant, as if he were far away. "Michael used to say that to me when we were kids. I don't know where he got it from, because neither Mom nor Dad ever used it. I can remember him saying it to me when I fell off my bike and broke my nose. I must have been eight or nine then, and I had been trying to ride without using my hands. I sailed right over the handlebars and landed on my nose on the sidewalk. Michael said that at least I wasn't an elephant. He said if I was, my nose would be like an accordion, like the coyote in those cartoons after the rock falls on him. He could always make me laugh."

Marcus chuckled quietly at the memory, and even Sara had to smile when she thought of Marcus as a little boy laughing and holding his broken nose. Michael could make anyone laugh no matter how bad things seemed. Lala had been the same way. Sara sniffled, but she didn't cry again. "Why'd you bring me out here, anyway?"

Marcus shrugged uncomfortably. "I probably shouldn't tell you. I'm rushing things a little."

"What?" Curiosity was drawing a frown between Sara's delicately arched eyebrows.

"I was downtown, waiting for a man I had to meet about a fire policy, and I stopped at the newsstand."

"And...?" Sara urged when Marcus paused again.

"And I got these magazines for you." He pulled out several gardening magazines and professional journals. Although he seemed to think she might be upset, Sara was merely surprised that he'd remembered. Once upon a time, before she'd married and had a baby, she'd participated in an innovative program that combined art and horticulture classes, preparing her for a career as a professional landscape designer.

"Thanks, Marcus." Sara leaned over and kissed his cheek, relishing the musky scent of his after-shave, exactly the same as Michael had always worn.

"Yeah, well, I was looking through them and I noticed that these two have job listings. I circled a couple of the ones that sounded right for you." Marcus flipped through the magazines and pointed out a couple of the ads he'd found. Sara stared at him and at the ads, and finally she read them.

"California? Texas? What do you landscape in Texas? Oil wells and cactus? I don't want to live in Texas." It didn't seem real.

"It's just a starting place," Marcus returned a touch defensively. "You don't really want to spend the rest of your life in your mother's house, do you?"

"No. I don't even want to go back there." She loved her parents, but her mother kept pushing those damned pills at her, turning her into a fuzz-brain. Marcus started the car and turned on the heater, warding off the chill that was seeping into the car. "I don't want to go back there, but I don't want to go to Texas, either. I want to go home. To my apartment." As she spoke, she realized she was making the right decision. It would be good to be alone, to have the time and space she needed, even if it meant hurting her mother. "Will you help me?"

Marcus looked at her sharply, as if he sensed her fear and was trying to understand it. "Of course I'll help," he said with a shrug. He quickly turned the discussion to the necessary details of what needed to be done. His questions seemed to cover everything, and Sara was grateful to have him take charge. To her, every little detail was still overwhelming.

"Is your car at your parents' house?"

"Yeah..." Sara replied, wondering how she was going to manage to concentrate enough to make the drive across town to her own apartment.

"Hmm, okay, you probably ought to let me drive you there. Then Dad and I will bring your car over tonight." Marcus made it easy.

But even he couldn't ease the situation with her parents. Sara's father, John, was just coming home from work when they returned to the house, and he was displeased that Sara had gone off with Marcus. Agnes fussed at their arrival. "I was so worried that you wouldn't be back in time for dinner. I wasn't sure whether to hold it or not. You shouldn't have just run off like that, darling."

"I guess I wasn't thinking," Sara apologized, rubbing her forehead. "I'm sorry, Mom. Can I do anything to help?"

"No, of course not! You ought to lie down and rest, dear. I can bring you a tray."

"I'm okay. Marcus is going to stay for dinner, all right?"

"Oh, my, I hope there's enough." Agnes bit her lip as she added an extra setting to the table. When she served the meal Sara could see there was enough in the pot to feed them for a week.

The meal was awful. Sara, torn apart by the tension in the air, could hardly force down a single spoonful of her mother's chili. And Agnes's horrified reaction to her news didn't help.

"But Sara, how can you want to go back to that empty apartment and stay all by yourself?" Agnes asked repeatedly. "Who's going to take care of you? It's not as if you've been up and about these last few days. Why would you go running back to that place when you can stay at home with us? You know we love you, darling. Couldn't you stay for just one more week, or maybe two, just until you've had time to get back on your feet again?"

How could Sara tell her mother and father that their love was suffocating her? She felt trapped in their need for her and knew she had to get away. If Marcus hadn't been there she might have capitulated, but she wanted to be strong in front of the man she had come to think of as her little brother.

After dinner she managed to pack her suitcase, tucking in the photos of Michael and Lala last of all. Agnes hovered in the background while she packed, draining her of energy and will she did not have to spare. As soon as Sara removed the pictures from the dresser, Agnes was there putting the remaining things in their rightful places. Sara had never before realized how strangely her parents had reacted to her growing up. This room, unchanged, seemed to be a shrine to the memory of her childhood. Sara was not sure why and was too tired to even try to figure it out.

The hugs and kisses and tearful pleas for her to stay, or at least call, would have been more appropriate if she had been moving to another continent. Her apartment was merely across town, less than five miles away. In Marcus's car she sagged immediately into the corner of the front seat and let the relief flow over her like the warmth pouring from the car's heater. She felt so tired that even breathing was an arduous task. Those pills seemed to have drained her of energy even while they were making her sleep. She wouldn't take any more of them no matter what her mother said.

Marcus carried her suitcase in one hand and supported Sara with the other arm. She walked into her apartment, feeling as if she had entered some strange place. It wasn't just that the air was cool and musty. Everything seemed to have changed, although it all looked the same as she remembered it. She felt as if she were a stranger in a foreign place where nothing made sense. Life was stripped of all its familiar meanings. For so long, her life had centered around Lala, and now everything had shifted. She didn't know who she was anymore, now that she was no longer Lala's mother.

Marcus called his parents from the apartment. Sara settled on the couch with a long sigh. She was so tired, and yet she couldn't relax. She was afraid to let go of her protective numbness, afraid to really let herself feel anything.

While they waited for the Davidsons to arrive, Marcus made a pot of coffee and brought Sara a cup. This was an immediate blessing, since her parents were steadfast advocates of tea. While Sara sat trying to find the courage to face the reminders of the past, Marcus bustled about, putting things into shape.

When she answered the door a short time later, Sara was enfolded by two sets of long arms. Vivian was the shortest Davidson at an even six feet, while Gregory, like his sons, was almost seven feet tall.

Sara was wrenched inside when they hugged her and offered to help her, their favorite daughter-in-law. They didn't even wait for her to ask, but jumped right in. While Greg ran to a nearby supermarket for milk and eggs, Vivian set about unpacking Sara's suitcase. She kept up a steady stream of conversation—their plans to move to Arizona after Greg's retirement, a description of the condominium they had bought there with enough room for Sara to come and visit. When Greg returned, he and Marcus busied themselves in the kitchen.

When everyone finally left, with repeated urgings for her to call for any reason, at any time of the day or night, Sara welcomed the silence and emptiness of her apartment. Finally she could sit back and let the tumult of emotions run through her. These feelings had been roiling and tumbling about inside her for a long time now, and the effort to keep them dammed up safely was becoming more than she could handle.

She crawled beneath the covers of her bed and waited, but she felt nothing. Then, slowly, irrevocably, the sadness came and the overwhelming feeling of wrenching loss. Losing Lala was like losing a part of herself, like having a part of her heart amputated. All the things she had wanted to think about were gone, and all she could do was miss Lala.

She curled into a ball, completely hidden under the covers on the bed, and cried until she was too numb to think or move. For a while she lay there in a state of suspension. She had the brief thought that this was good because when it passed she would be free from the pain. But when the numbness did pass, Sara was aware of a slowly increasing feeling of sadness and emptiness.

She began to cry again, wishing desperately she could fall asleep. But despite her exhaustion, sleep was something she could not find. She would drift into a doze only to jerk awake and realize, horribly, that it hadn't just been a nightmare, that Lala really was gone. Then she would cry herself back to sleep so that it could happen again.

The days that followed did not become any easier, and the nights remained long and restless. Sara's life seemed empty and borderless, a vague, unreasoned existence. During the days she drifted aimlessly, carried by the currents of whoever invaded the solitude of her apartment by calling or dropping by. There was a huge pile of cards and letters that needed to be answered and a barrage of phone calls.

Sara began to acknowledge the awful truth: at first she had deliberately embraced her sadness without knowing why. Then she admitted that she did know why. She felt horrible because a part of her was relieved that the long battle was finally over. Although she missed Lala desperately, a part of her was glad that she would never have to watch Lala suffer again, never see her crying and writhing in pain, never see her slowly wasting away into nothing when she should have been growing and blooming.

What kind of mother felt relief at the loss of her child? Sara was ridden with guilt over her relief and hardly dared to acknowledge that it existed. She didn't dare examine it. If only, she thought, there was someplace safe to hide, someone safe to talk to.

Instead, she sat in the apartment and forced herself to respond to the letters that had piled up. The notes expressing other people's sorrow and sympathy made her feel curiously ambivalent; her own grief seemed out of proportion. It was difficult to reply politely while everything seemed to be in motion and she had nothing solid to hang on to.

That wasn't quite true; she did have Marcus and her parents. Marcus came by quite often. Sara would lean back in her chair and squint her eyes and pretend that he was Michael. She would tell him stories about Lala, silly anecdotes and poignant observations, but they never mentioned Michael's death or Lala's illness.

Sara went into Lala's room again, and sat reading old papers from school and running her fingers over Lala's toys, trying to recapture her spirit, her life. She only felt alone. Alone with the terrible knowledge that Lala would never grow up. That she would never see her daughter graduate from high school or fall in love, that she would never welcome Lala's husband as her son or hold Lala's baby and look for Michael in his face.

Sara sank onto the edge of Lala's bed and hugged the battered teddy bear that nestled against the pillow. If only Michael were here to hold her, maybe letting Lala go would be easier. How had she ever survived losing him? In a way he had never really died, for he had lived on in their daughter, his namesake, Michella. Now his death was final and irrevocable. The despair that would have rushed into the hollow made by these thoughts was delayed by the jangle of the telephone.

Sara knew before she answered that her mother was calling again to see how she was or to ask her to come home. Agnes called ten or twelve times a day. Knowing she cared should have made it easier, Sara thought, but it didn't. Her father had only called once, to tell her how much she was hurting her mother by refusing to let her help. "Hello, Mother."

"Knock-knock."

Sara smiled. "Who's there?" she asked, knowing full well who it was. There was only one person in the world who would call and tell her a stupid joke, a man who was shy but who dispensed jokes to those he loved as others might dispense hugs.

"Say."

"Say who?"

"Say who do you do, it's your Uncle Cornoo!"

"Ugh! That's awful, Uncle Corny. It barely makes sense."

"Hmph! I wonder if I oughtn't call someone else and offer them a room in my condo on the lovely shore of the Gulf of Mexico. You don't seem to be properly appreciative," he snorted. Sara smiled even though she would miss Gert and Corny while they were in Florida. They were usually there by now, but they'd stayed late this year, waiting until Lala no longer needed them before heading south for the winter.

"Don't listen to him!" Gert insisted. In the background Sara could hear Corny complaining about rude women who snatched the phone away in the middle of a man's conversation. "There's always extra room," Gert assured her. "You come down any time you feel like it. And you call me if your mother upsets you too much and I'll have Corny talk to your father."

"Okay," Sara agreed, knowing she would never do it. She was pretty sure Gert knew as much.

"What Corny was supposed to be offering you was the key to the beach house. I thought you might like to come out sometimes. But I have to remind you to call Jan Heidema if you do. She's coming in once a week to clean and change which light gets left on, that sort of thing. But if she sees footprints in the snow, or finds something out of place... well, she's a little flighty. She'll probably call in the FBI."

"She'll call her husband first," Sara countered with the echo of a smile, recalling the woman from her recent stay at the beach house. A tiny bat had gotten into the house through a broken attic window and nearly given the poor woman a heart attack. Lala had laughed and laughed when Jan's husband, an elderly man with flopping white hair, had chased the bat through the house with a broom. He'd finally succeeded in evicting the bat despite his wife's shrieking and had calmly fixed the window while she continued to vent her horror.

Maybe going back to the house on the lake was exactly what Sara needed to do. It would be a place away from all the memories in the apartment, but not a place completely cut off from Lala's past. Sara knew the memories in the house would be both good and bad. There had been some moments of great joy between the trauma and pain. She was almost unable to trust the feeling of escape the house gave her.

"I don't know...." Sara hesitated. It sounded appealing. But she knew she couldn't escape her pain by escaping from her apartment, even though she longed for it to be that simple.

"Well, you don't need to decide this second," Gert assured her. "I'll have Corny drop the key off this afternoon. And I'll make him promise not to tell you any more bad jokes.''

"I like his jokes," Sara protested.

"Did he pay you to say that to me?" Gert countered.

Sara said goodbye to her aunt and wondered, sadly, how her aunt and uncle could make her feel so good when her own parents made her feel so bad. Then she thought about the peace she felt when she thought about moving back to the beach house. What was so special about it? Did she think Lala would be any less dead if she moved back there? And why did she keep thinking about Joseph Fisher, remembering how he had knelt beside the bed and offered Lala the sand dollar, tracing its star pattern with a gentle finger? Why had laying a comforting hand on his shoulder made her feel strong?

By the day before Thanksgiving Sara knew she couldn't stay in the apartment any longer. She couldn't handle the constant reminders of Lala or the construction paper cutouts of turkeys and pilgrims in the windows of the apartment opposite hers. She couldn't bear the holiday if she couldn't share it with Lala.

She called Marcus, who came to help her move to the beach house, but not without voicing concern. "Lala died there!" he exclaimed fervently. "How can you possibly think of it as a haven?"

Sara shrugged, unable to explain the feeling she had. "I just do," she insisted, but she was ready to change her plans if he fought her. She needed someone to like the idea. Her mother abhorred it.

"Okay, okay," Marcus conceded with a resigned sigh. "I'll clear out the fridge while you make sure you didn't forget to pack anything."

"I didn't." But she had. She hadn't taken anything of Lala's. Sara went into Lala's room, but choosing was an impossible task. Should she bring the drawing Lala had done of a man and a girl on a beach where the stars hung within reach? It was one of her favorites. Or should she take only the things that had been at the beach house before? Or no reminders of Lala at all?

Sara gazed around at all the things in Lala's room. Suddenly it seemed as if each item was the singularly most special thing to bring and at the same time wholly inadequate. Sara's head began to reel with the effort, and the tears rolled down her cheeks.

Marcus found her kneeling on the floor in a little ball and gathered her into his arms. "Sara, Sara, Sara," he said with a sigh. "If it hurts this much, it's not the right thing to do."

"Yes, it is." She wiped her eyes and sniffled. "I just need one minute." She packed her favorite drawings with the bedraggled teddy bear and the sand dollar from Joe before she announced, "I'm ready."

WHEN MARCUS LEFT after settling her into the Van Dykes' house, Sara was suddenly aware of the profound silence. Maybe she wasn't ready for this. She was alone in the huge quiet house, and she felt very solitary. A quiet little voice inside here was whispering that it would be easier to just shrivel up and let the wind turn her to dust and blow her away.

"No!" she said, and her voice seemed to be lost in the powerful silence of the house. "No!" she repeated much louder, shouting back at the demons who were pursuing her. She would not become a replica of her parents; she would not waste the rest of her life living in the past, living for things that could not be. She had to pick up the pieces and make a new life for herself.

For a little while she basked in the triumph of this moment of victory. She had found strength within herself that she had not known existed. But the sadness returned when she found Lala's kite leaning by the door, forgotten after the last morning she had spent on the beach. Sara picked it up and let the smooth nylon ripstop run under her fingers. The kite had been a present from Michael on their last Christmas as a family, before everything was destroyed. Lala had eventually learned to fly it and loved the excitement of sending it sailing into the sky. Cradling the hard bundle to her chest, Sara cried because Lala would never share her joy again.

When she finally stopped crying, heavy silence filled the house. She couldn't seem to catch her breath. The oppressive silence was crushing down upon her, forcing the air from her lungs; the pressure increasing. She grabbed her coat and tore the back door open with frantic fingers. Outside she could hear the rhythmic crashing of waves against the shore, and she took deep breaths as she yanked on her coat. Then she ran to the water's edge and listened to the lapping waves as they broke the silence that had threatened to overwhelm her.

CHAPTER THREE

THE ALARM ON THE CORNER of the desk buzzed like an irate wasp. Joe swore under his breath at the error that appeared in the line he was typing into the computer. He had gotten so involved in drawing together the threads of his argument for a grand conclusion that he had forgotten the time. It couldn't possibly be that late, and yet the clock insisted it was. He had to have the turkey in the oven within the hour, and he knew that if he started writing again, he would be at it for the rest of the night. He saved the unfinished article instead, storing it into the computer's memory without even risking the temptation of correcting that last mistake. Rising from his desk, he stretched and went to stand at the sliding doors that opened onto a small deck looking out over the beach below.

It was a cold, still night; a black sky glittered with diamond-bright stars above the crescent of moon that trailed ripples of pearly light onto the gently moving lake. Joe turned away from the view with a little shudder and then looked back. Was there someone down by the water? He flicked off the light so he could see into the darkness. Yes, someone was standing out there in the cold just staring down into the water.

He wondered if the person needed help. It was almost midnight and it was very cold out. Normally he wouldn't have looked twice at someone out for a walk along the edge of the lake, but for someone to just stand there and stare into the water seemed very odd. He decided it was a woman despite the shapeless silhouette of the person's winter parka.

Acting instinctively, Joe went out to the back entry and pulled on his boots and a thick woolen overcoat. He shoved his hands deep into his pockets and hurried down to the beach. His ears burned, making him wish he had thought to grab a hat. The idiot standing down there must be frozen solid!

She hadn't moved or looked up during his silent approach. Joe slowed to a stop while he was still a little distance from her. Either she was really frozen or she was so lost in thought that he was about to scare ten years off her life. He cleared his throat loudly. "Hello." He tried to make his voice gentle but firm enough to shatter the woman's trance. She squawked and spun to face him, her glimmering eyes filling her whole face in the dim light. The stillness that had enveloped her shattered with such speed that Joe felt himself jump in surprise.

It was that little girl Lala's mother. Sara. Joe couldn't think of anything to say. He thought of the house that had been dark and empty for several days. Of the ambulance he'd seen gliding silently past the end of his driveway a couple of weeks ago. Of the obituary he'd read in the paper and the way it seemed incomplete because it didn't mention Lala's gift of joy. Of the terrible pain Sara must be suffering after having her child torn from life too early. He was filled with a warm rush of rather melancholy tenderness and moved forward to wrap his arms around Sara and hold her tight.

He pulled himself up short. He'd probably scare her silly, suddenly grabbing her like that. "Are you okay?"

"Oh. Yeah, sure, I'm okay...I'm fine, thank you," Sara responded with a voice that was deliberately purged of emotion. Joe realized she was merely mouthing an appropriate response. He stared at her intently, trying to see how she really was and trying to figure what he ought to do next. He ignored the voice in his head telling him it was none of his business.

Sara felt like an insect on a pin, unable to hide what she was feeling or thinking. Now that her concentration on the mesmerizing ebbing and flowing of the waves against the shore was broken, she was suddenly aware of being very cold. The chill seemed to pierce the very marrow of her bones.

"Do you know who I am?" Joe demanded. A violent shiver shook Sara. "I'm sorry. That was rude," Joe said, sighing and shaking his head tiredly at his own unbelievable stupidity.

"You're Joe Fisher," Sara replied as if she hadn't heard his apology. She felt stupidly slow, as if the freezing temperature had made her brain sluggish, but his sudden smile took the edge off the chill.

"I saw you out here and I thought maybe you'd frozen solid. Couldn't you sleep?"

Sara shook her head. A crease appeared between her brows. What business was it of his?

"Good!"

Her frown deepened. Was this another one of those stupid coping theories?

"Really," Joe said with a chuckle, "it is good. I need someone to help me stuff my turkey, and you're just the person to do it. Come on. You can defrost while I make the stuffing." He clasped her hand and dragged her along the path and into his blissfully warm kitchen. Sara looked around the bright room, wondering what was happening to her.

Joe's house was built of rounded cobblestones in a very rough-and-ready style; several porches and decks looked out over the woods and beach. Warm oak paneling and a big black wood stove kept the kitchen in tune with the rustic atmosphere. Blue delft pottery accented the room, matching the tablecloth and chair cushions. It was cozy and cheerful. Sara looked around curiously.

"Let me take your coat," Joe insisted, standing close and waiting for her to shrug out of it. Sara complied, caught up in her inspection of the room. Delft pottery was a popular decorative accent in the area, which was home to the only factory in the United States using the technique. Somehow it seemed just right in this kitchen, not merely a touch of charm deemed appropriate by a decorator. To top it all off, a huge blue enamel teakettle gently steamed on top of the wood stove to add humidity to the winter-dry house.

"Sit here." Joe pulled a wooden chair away from the table and gestured Sara into the embrace of its high back and curving arms. She settled in its depths and watched Joe poke at the fire in the stove before adding a couple of thick logs from the wood bin. His hands weren't hardened by heavy labor, yet they handled the wood deftly. Heat began to pour into the room, and Sara welcomed it as it curled around her ankles like a cat. Fortunately it didn't dash away when the black-and-white spaniel clattered into the kitchen and sat down to study her curiously.

Sara waited for a reaction from the dog, or an explanation from Joe, something to explain how she had come to be settled snugly into his kitchen in the middle of the night. Roly Poly yawned suddenly and turned himself around three full times before he settled at her feet. Sara turned her gaze on Joe.

"Have some coffee," he exclaimed and strode across the kitchen to fetch her a cup which he laced with cream and sugar.

Their fingers touched as he handed her the cup, and Sara frowned at herself for noticing the casual contact. "I don't take sugar in my coffee."

"Sugar's quick energy. It'll warm you right up," Joe said, defending his action. Sara frowned harder, wondering why he seemed nervous. "Don't frown like that! Drink your coffee."

Sara sipped the coffee. At least it was hot and strong—if a little sweeter than she liked it. "What am I doing here?" she asked, feeling bewildered. Why should Joe Fisher care whether she froze to death on the beach or not?

"You're helping me stuff my Thanksgiving turkey. You know, neighborliness and all that," Joe explained. "Are you warm enough? You want me to get you an afghan to curl up in?"

"I'm okay."

"That's what you said on the beach," Joe muttered, but he went across the kitchen and started chopping onions into a deep skillet.

Sara stretched her feet toward the open door of the wood stove. The heat felt lovely. Although they lacked the steady rhythm of the lake, the dancing flames were as mesmerizing as the breaking waves had been. And both were almost as mesmerizing as the movements

Joe made as he worked by the stove. His hips swayed slightly as he stirred the browning onions, and his shoulder flexed rhythmically as he chopped celery.

He moved gracefully, sure of himself and of what he was doing. Michael had never even made coffee, joking that he couldn't boil water without help. What was she thinking? Sara's knuckles turned white on the handle of her coffee cup. She wasn't comparing them! She pressed her eyes closed until colored lights swirled behind her eyelids, and then stared once more into the flickering orange light of the fire.

This would be her third Thanksgiving without Michael. Her first without Lala. Aunt Gert and Uncle Corny were already in Florida. Her mother and father had invited her to dinner, just the three of them. The meal would be subdued and elegant, the tone set by the lengthy prayer her father would read from the church bulletin. Without Michael and Lala, it would be without laughter.

The first sob caught in her throat with a searing wrench. She swallowed the second but the next few escaped as strangled gasps. Sara ducked her head and bit her lip. She didn't want to cry again. She would be alone for Thanksgiving and for the first snowfall, for Christmas and for New Year's Eve. Every year Lala had tried to stay up until midnight, but she had never succeeded. Now she never would. Sara dropped her head into her hands and stifled the sobs into hiccups.

She heard Joe moving, and then he was standing beside her chair, setting a box of tissues in her lap. With one hand he stroked the blond curls on the top of her head, and Sara was surprised by how completely comforting his gesture was. "I'm sorry," she managed to gasp without losing control and crying out loud.

"It's okay to cry," Joe soothed. "Losing Lala has left a big hole in your life, Sara, and it's going to hurt until you find a way to fill that space." He frowned at his hand, watching it run through her soft curls, not saying how much he wanted to help fill some of the empty spaces in her life. "I can tell you this. It will never be the same again. It'll be good someday. It's going to stop hurting, but it will never be the same. And for now, it's okay to cry. You don't need to apologize."

His explanation seemed so natural. Slowly her tears dried up and her breathing became more regular. Joe's hand stopped moving and rested heavily atop her head. "Okay?"

Sara nodded, and Joe let his fingers trail through her hair as he pulled his hand back. She plucked a few tissues from the box, and he moved away. He turned the burner back on beneath his stuffing and finished sautéing the celery and onions. He glanced at her over his shoulder and sighed silently as he began to mix all the ingredients in a big bowl. It was almost too full, and some of the croutons kept edging over the sides and dropping to the counter. When it was finally stirred to his satisfaction, Joe stuck the spoon into the mixture and moved it aside.

He didn't know what more to say to her, but the silence was becoming uncomfortable. He grunted as he wrestled the turkey out of the refrigerator and awkwardly rinsed it in the sink. "You know, I had to special-order this bird," he announced. "It came unfrozen, but I figure I should cook it just the same as if it had been frozen and defrosted. I was worried when the butcher said it'd be fresh. I didn't want to have to pluck it! I wouldn't know where to begin. Will you come hold this for me?''

Sara moved to his side. Her jaw dropped at the size of his bird. "How did you decide how big a turkey to buy?"

"A pound per person, that's what Mom always says. This guy's a little small, but I think Mom will bring a second bird, so we'll be okay. It's the pies I worry about. There's never enough pumpkin to go around.''

"How many people are you having over? This thing's humongous!" Sara couldn't argue with his plan since she usually figured a pound and a quarter per person, double if the person was a Davidson giant.

"Mom and Dad is two," Joe muttered, "six kids, five in-laws, that's thirteen. Then the nieces and nephews. Three and four and three and two and three. There are two more on the way, but I didn't count them. So... twenty-eight altogether."

"In your family. Do you have any idea how lucky you are?" Sara demanded.

"Yeah, lucky me," Joe grumped. "I need you to hold the turkey while I fill it up. And you thought I was joking about needing your help. Where am I supposed to seat twenty-eight people, I ask you? I was going to rent a big table, but I decided against it. We'll just eat off our laps. I suppose we can put the kids in here at the table.

"You know," he added, "I forgot to count my grandparents. They're with us for Thanksgiving this year. That's two more. And that will mean a lot of my aunts and uncles and cousins will drop by. We'll have to stuff them, too. Mom better bring another bird.

We're going to need it. Maybe I ought to go out and get another one.'' Joe suddenly looked panicked, and Sara had to smile.

"Where would you cook it?"

"That's a good question...." Joe shrugged and had Sara hold a flap of skin in place while he trussed the bird with a wickedly huge needle and thick black thread. "Okay, Sara, I've got it sewn up tight now. You can wash your hands,'' Joe said as he set aside the needle and thread.

He rubbed the outside of the bird with herbs and salt and then heaved the huge thing into an extra-large pan. Slowly and deliberately, he tucked the heavy pan into the oven and then moved easily around the kitchen, cleaning up the mess and putting the dirty dishes in the dishwasher. Sara sank back into the comfortable chair and watched him work. She was very tired.

After Joe walked her home, Sara was surprised to find that she felt much better than she had earlier. Just watching him go about normal everyday things had helped her. It hadn't been like that at her mother's. Why was it different with Joe?

THE SILENCE that had haunted the house last night was welcome tonight, Sara thought as she leaned against the closed door and let her parka fall from her. If the excessive consumption of food at her mother's hadn't made her sleepy, the endless trips from the car would have. Agnes hadn't been inhibited by their limited number but had made a turkey dinner with all the trimmings, and she had sent nearly all the leftovers along with Sara. Hanging her coat up, Sara sighed; if only her mother didn't insist on fussing over her. But if she pointed out that the difference between mothering and smothering was one letter, Agnes would cry and her father would frown. No one was allowed to hurt his wife.

"Stop it!" Sara scolded out loud, disliking the edge of bitchiness that colored her thoughts. The dinner had been perfectly nice, and now she was back home—for the beach house did feel very much like home—with a counter full of delicious food. She tucked the food into the refrigerator and freezer, leaving the four pies—only the apple and one of the pumpkins had been touched—lined up on the counter. She'd have to call her mother and ask if you could freeze pie. But not quite yet.

Sara sat in one of the wing-backed chairs and stared into the dead ashes in the fireplace. A fire would be nice, but she could never make them burn. Maybe she'd give it a try in a few minutes. She didn't feel up to it right now. She didn't feel up to anything. The dinner hadn't been nice; it had been terrible. A travesty. She had never felt less thankful in her life. Her husband was dead. Her only child was dead. Joe had said there was a hole in her life that needed to be filled, but he was wrong. It wasn't a hole that could be filled; it was a giant vacuum, like a black hole in space, sucking everything good into it and leaving nothing but empty darkness.

It was easy for Joe to talk. He was sitting down to dinner with thirty of his relatives. The kids were probably playing games while the adults lingered over their plates. It would be like in the turkey commercials on TV: a grandmother with soft white curls, pretty young wives and handsome men, little girls in lace-edged pinafores, and little boys with their hair dampened to tame the curls. Joe's hair curled where it hit the edge of his shirt collar. Her mother had served dinner at one, but Joe had planned to serve at five. They were probably eating their pie right now. She hoped Joe didn't get a piece of pumpkin. It would serve him right for not counting the blessings he had.

No, that wasn't true. She hoped he got a big slice of pumpkin pie with fresh whipped cream. He deserved it for taking her in out of the cold last night. She was just being a grouch, wishing her misery on everyone else. But Joe had helped her feel less miserable for a few hours. She ought to bring him one of her mother's pumpkin pies.

Well, heck! She'd do just that! Crashing his family's holiday dinner couldn't be any worse than moping here in the gathering dusk. Or any worse than calling Agnes about the pies and being asked to come home and be her little girl again. Or than calling Marcus. He'd probably tell her to go landscape cactus and tumbleweed! The worst Joe could do would be to leave her standing on his front steps holding a pumpkin pie.

Sara took the time to brush her hair but didn't bother with makeup; she was still too pale and would only end up looking like a clown. She took both of the uncut pumpkin pies, balancing one in each hand as she took the long walk along the shoulder of the road to Joe's door. Mittens had been a mistake; they made the pies slip precariously whenever she tilted more than a fraction of an inch. She blew her curls up off her forehead and used her elbow to press the bell. If Joe didn't want these pies she was likely to toss one of them in his face. Maybe both!

"Hello, hello, come in, dear. Ooh, it's getting colder and colder out there. Now then, what have you got here? Pumpkin pie! Very good." The woman who answered the door was rather tall and stark, an ageless woman with steel-gray hair who could have been anywhere over fifty. Her smile was warm as she took the pies and waited while Sara added her coat to the already overburdened coat tree. "Come along now, we'll take these into the kitchen."

Sara shrugged and followed the woman, taking time to look over the chattering crowd as her leader struggled to get the pies into the kitchen before they were devoured. She spotted Joe and looked across the room at him, willing him to turn and see her. She needed to know she was welcome. Finally his head turned, his dark eyes looked her up and down, and then she was dismissed with the disdainful shrug of one pin-striped shoulder. But there was too much gray in this man's hair, and the lines of his face weren't those of laughter. It wasn't Joe. She didn't know who it was, some relative obviously, but she resented his sneer. She might not have an engraved invitation, but that wasn't stopping anyone from drooling over her pies. She tilted her chin up and followed the woman into the kitchen.

It was bustling with people. The pies, like the pied piper, seemed to be leading a crowd. The woman set the pies on the table and shoed away an eagerly proffered plate. "I ought to save a piece for Joey. He gave his first helping to little Kirk. That's how he is with babies and strays. He's got a soft spot as big as Texas. Now then, I can't seem to place you." The woman sliced boldly into the pie without bothering to determine if she would hit the exact center or not. "But I know everyone will be happy you came."

"I'll be happy if you put a piece of pie on this plate," a grinning man teased. He looked a little like Joe, but taller and skinnier, with light hazel eyes that crinkled with laughter.

"You're a pig, Timothy Fisher," the woman scolded, and Sara guessed that she was his mother.

"Ah, that I am, but not a male chauvinist pig!" he returned as he took a slice of the pie.

"There *is* more pumpkin pie!" Joe boomed as he came into the kitchen. Sara smiled at him, but he didn't seem to notice her. "That's your third piece," he accused Tim. "Mom!"

"I dispense pie, not justice," his mother replied, sliding a wide slice onto a plate and handing it to him.

"Who brought this, anyway?"

"Oh, hell! I still don't know her name. Over there." The knife pointed Sara out. She had slipped back through the crowd, letting herself get bumped back toward the windows. She blushed when people turned and looked at her curiously. Coming here had been a mistake. She wasn't ready for this many people. She had never even imagined that someone else besides Joe might answer the door.

"Sara!" Joe's voice seemed to boom out through the kitchen. "What are you doing here?" She was startled to find herself in his arms and held for a moment until her initial fear of his family seemed silly. "You brought these pies," he accused in a voice that made her glad she could nod.

"Are you going to introduce us, Joey?" the woman who let Sara in prompted in an exasperated tone as she ignored four people all competing for the last piece of the pumpkin pie.

"Yes, Mother," Joe said. "This is Sara. She's staying next door at the Van Dykes' place. Sara Davidson. Sara, this is my mom, Vera Fisher, and my aunt Lois, Betsy, my brother Timothy the Pig's wife, and over there is Drew, my oldest brother...."

"Don't forget about me, Uncle Joe," clamored a six-year-old boy intent on climbing up Joe's body as if it were a mountain to be scaled.

"I don't think I could forget you, Darryl," Joe said calmly, wincing as a bony knee dug into his kidney. "I guess you better meet them gradually, Sara, or you'll never keep their names straight," he confided with a warm grin.

"I didn't even have a piece yet," someone complained, and Joe sprang into action, sloughing off his nephew and grabbing Sara's hand. He ran her through the living room, ignoring someone calling his name. Sara was seeing his whole house in a ten-second tour. In the study, four kids were clustered around a computer, and in his bedroom a game of checkers was being battled out in the middle of the bed while a game of Monopoly took up the sheepskin rug in front of the fireplace.

"I'm winning, Uncle Joe, I'm winning," a redheaded boy about Lala's age announced proudly, setting off a tempest of protest that Joe disregarded as he led her away. There was a large spa in the next room with a hot tub containing six or seven giggling teen-aged girls who tried to look alluring for their bachelor uncle or cousin.

They were back in the hallway, and Joe was starting to look frustrated when a preschool-aged boy came out of the bathroom. "There ain't no TP in there," he warned, and Joe led Sara into the bathroom and locked the door. He set his pie on the spattered counter and replaced the supplies, including hanging up a dry set of towels by the sink.

"There are disadvantages to having a large family," he announced factually as he closed the lid and sat down to eat his slice of pumpkin pie. After a bite he closed his eyes and smiled in satisfaction. "Perfect. This is the best pie I ever tasted. Kirk stole my first piece. He said he hadn't had one yet," Joe said with a pout.

Sara didn't understand why they were hiding in the bathroom. She felt wobbly-kneed and sat down on the rim of the bathtub. She had not expected the chaos and noise that accompanied the high good humor filling the whole house. It was really quite draining. A sigh of tiredness and relief escaped from her as she relaxed. Maybe it *was* a good idea to hide here. Where else would Joe get to eat his pie in peace, without anyone claiming they deserved it more?

"I'm surprised you're here. Not that you're not welcome. The more the merrier is the only way to survive with my family, but I didn't expect you." Joe waggled his fork in the air.

"My mother cooked for an army, but there were only the three of us to eat what she made," Sara explained. "She gave me most of the leftovers, and I thought you might need the pies. Did you have enough turkey?" She didn't want to talk about feeling lonely now that she was with Joe.

"Mmm, yeah," Joe said as he finished another bite of pie. "Mom brought one that was almost as big, and Aunt Wendy brought a good-sized ham. There might be enough left for a sandwich, if you hurry, but I wouldn't bet money on it." Joe shook his head in disbelief. He put the last bite of pie in his mouth and chewed it slowly with his eyes closed. "That's the best pie...."

Loud pounding on the door interrupted him and shook the little room. "Hurry up in there," a voice whined petulantly through the door panel. "I can't wait all day, you know."

"Just as I was going to say the quiet was nice," Joe muttered disgustedly. "Who is that?" he called back through the closed door.

"It's Robbie. Hurry up."

"Can't you use the bathroom by the kitchen?" Joe asked.

"Grandpa's in there. Again. I got to go now. Hur-r-r-y."

"Maybe we better get out of here," Sara suggested, almost keeping a straight face.

"I suppose I've had my solitude fix," Joe agreed and opened the door. "Okay, Rob, we hurried." The door slammed almost before they were through it. Joe just shook his head and looked amused. "You can make yourself at home, Sara. Hardly anyone bites. I'm going to the kitchen. I'll bet you anything they've drained another pot of coffee."

"I...um...I'll come with you," Sara decided.

"I can't believe you're here," Joe murmured, and his smile was so warm that Sara felt its electricity race through her body. For a second they were alone together in one of those special places only lovers go. Sara frowned and shook her head: what a silly thing to think! At least Joe couldn't read her mind; he just led her to the kitchen, introducing her to an aunt, a brother and three nieces along the way. He pulled a chair into the small arc around the wood stove and sat

Sara down. She wasn't sure she wanted to be shoved into the family circle, but he didn't give her a chance to protest before he was making coffee and restacking the dishwasher.

A woman introduced herself. "I'm Deanna." A head of short black hair bobbed as she spoke. "Matt's wife. Mother of Samantha, Victoria, Byron and Geoffrey. They're thirteen, eleven, nine and eight."

"Joey introduced us, but I'll bet you don't know my name," a glowing golden woman challenged with a twinkle in her eyes. "Betsy."

"Timothy the Pig's wife," Joe's mother clarified, and the women all laughed. Sara smiled. Timothy must be one of those bony men who ate and ate and never gained weight. "So, Sara, tell us about yourself."

Sara was saved from having to answer immediately when a toddling little girl trotted to her side and leaned on her leg, rubbing her eyes with grubby fists. Sara took advantage of the business of picking up the tired child and settling her on her lap to think of something to say. She didn't know how to define herself; she wasn't Michael's wife anymore, she wasn't Lala's mother anymore.

"Do you have any kids of your own?" Betsy asked. Then, without waiting for a reply, she continued warmly, "You'd make someone a wonderful mother. That darling little girl is Grouchy Grace, James and Marie's youngest. She's usually such a scaredy-cat, but I guess she likes you." She leaned over and tapped the tip of Grace's nose; the little face crinkled up and then hid against the softness of Sara's breast.

Sara turned her head to the side and stared at the edge of the table where the tablecloth hung in a fold at the corner. The cloth was exactly the same shade of blue as Lala's eyes had been. The line of shadow in the fold blurred and began to waver as Sara's eyes filled with tears. She bit down on her lip, trying to use the pain to distract her. She had made someone a wonderful mother, hadn't she? She'd done her damnedest. So why had her baby been taken away from her? She missed Lala so much. Two tears overflowed and Sara sniffed and tried to keep the others back.

"What's wrong, dear?" Betsy's voice was calm yet compassionate, the practiced voice of a mother used to dealing with problems.

"What did you say to her?" Joe demanded suddenly. He wrapped an arm around her shoulders and leaned over to smooth Grace's hair and twitch her nose, diverting her before she copied Sara's tears. Grace grabbed his hand and pulled it to her mouth. Sara watched him through her tears and saw her own hand stroking through Grace's hair.

"Betsy said she'd make a great mother," Deanna informed Joe in a puzzled voice.

"Oh." Joe smoothed Sara's hair back and perched on the arm of her chair, his hip pressing against her arm. His arm tightened around her as he explained, "Sara lost her child recently. Lala was ten."

"What happened?"

"Leukemia," Sara sad, raising her head and wiping her eyes. "I'm sorry. I don't mean to be a crybaby and spoil everyone's holiday."

"It's okay," Joe asserted before anyone else could speak. He massaged the back of her neck with his free hand. The tension in her muscles seemed to melt away magically.

"You don't need to apologize," Vera declared. "I lost a child once. There is no way to describe the pain." Joe seemed to stiffen, but he didn't stop massaging the back of Sara's neck.

"Do you have other children?" Deanna asked.

"No."

"Oh. Well, at least you're young. You and your husband will probably have others."

Sara almost choked on hysterical laughter. She wasn't young; she felt even older than she was. Of course she and Michael would never have any more children. And even if Michael wasn't dead and it was possible for the two of them to have another baby, did anyone really believe it would make Lala's death any easier? Sara was damned sick of hearing people say stupid things like that. She didn't know whether to laugh or cry or simply scream in frustration.

"Sara's a widow," Joe informed them calmly. He extracted his fingers from Grace's damp grip and wiped them on the bib that was tied around her neck. Sara caught the corner of it and held it steady for him. What was she supposed to say in response to all the apologies and expressions of sympathy? She never knew the right words to use. She felt as if she really was one of Joe's strays, a poor pitiful thing. "Are you okay now?" he asked her quietly. She nodded. "I have to go wash my hand." Her smile felt strange, like it was cracking the mask left by her tears.

"I feel so awful." Deanna's apologies and self-derision continued to gush forth after the general hubbub faded. "I can't believe I said that. You poor thing. I'm so sorry. I can't begin to tell you what a fool I feel."

"It's all right," Sara assured her quietly. "You had no way of knowing."

"Oh, but I'm such an airhead. My kids say I'm a space cadet, and I guess they're right. Open mouth and insert foot—that's me! I'm just so sorry...."

"Yes, dear, we understand," Betsy said decisively, patting the other woman on her arm. "Perhaps we ought to change the subject." Sara smiled gratefully, and Vera nodded in approval. Enacting the plan without knowing it, people stormed into the kitchen, gathering dishes, rounding up and then bundling up kids, saying good-bye to all and sundry. The confusion nearly rocked the solid stone house off its foundations. Joe brought Sara a cup of coffee and stood behind her chair as if to protect her, but was soon caught up in helping Aunt Wendy find her ham platter and wrestling with a slightly recalcitrant zipper on a size four winter coat. And then he had to figure out which mitten went on which hand. Sara rocked Grace gently until she had to relinquish the sleeping child to her mother.

The kitchen got noisier and noisier. All the kids who had been upstairs were milling around, the younger ones petulant and cranky, the older ones reluctant to depart. Sara wanted to help Joe somehow, but she found the confusion overwhelming. Everyone was talking at once. She finished her coffee and went into the living room. She spotted an armchair tucked back in a corner near the fireplace and curled up there, out of everyone's way. After a few minutes a very old man came up to her. "Who are you?" he demanded querulously.

Sara wasn't sure if she had ever talked to someone so old before. The man was tall but very skinny, and his skin was saggy and wrinkled and liberally sprinkled with liver spots. She stood and shook his hand, afraid that she might break the fragile bones that showed through his papery skin. "I'm Sara, a friend of Joe's," she said loudly since the man had a hearing aid on the frame of his glasses and had spoken loudly himself. He peered at her closely and then broke into a wide smile that lit up his whole face.

"Dora, Dora, come here," he called imperiously to the room in general. He was soon joined by an equally elderly lady who Sara guessed was his wife. These must be Joe's grandparents, she decided, and wondered exactly how old they were. "This is Lois's daughter, Karen," the man introduced her to his wife.

"No, I'm Sara, a friend of Joseph's," Sara corrected him loudly.

"Lois's? Lois married that Irishman, you know that, Charles. She's your daughter. You'd think you'd remember that she married an Irishman. Her daughters all have red hair. You're a mixed-up old coot. Why don't you get a new battery for that hearing aid?" Sara thought that Dora hadn't really seen her, but then the old woman turned to her and confided, "Ignore him, he's old."

Sara smiled wordlessly. She didn't know if Dora knew who she was, and she knew that Charles still didn't. "Hi, Sara," Joe said at her elbow, and Sara jumped slightly, not having heard him coming up behind her. He caught and squeezed her elbow slightly, supporting her. "Are you introducing yourself to my grandparents? They're Dad's parents. Charles is ninety-six and Dora is ninety-three."

"Speak up, boy. Didn't anyone ever tell you not to mumble?" Charles demanded, reverting to his irritated tone.

Joe just grinned and spoke again in a loud, slow voice. "Sorry, Grandpa. Did you meet Sara? She's a friend of mine. Sara Davidson."

"He thought she was Lois's daughter," Dora confided.

"She said she was," Charles countered.

"No, she's not," Joe said. "She does have the same blue eyes, though. Is Dad going to drive you two home?"

"Who are you?" Charles demanded of Joe then.

Sara was appalled that Joe's own grandfather didn't recognize him, but Joe just laughed. "I'm Joseph, Robert's youngest son."

"Humph," Charles grunted while he frowned at Joseph suspiciously.

"Yes, Joey, Robbie's going to take us back to the home in a few minutes. I don't think your mother is ready to leave yet," Dora remarked, ignoring her husband's rudeness.

"Have you seen your mother around this zoo recently?" a gray-haired man asked as he joined the group. Joe's father had the same serious, almost-professorial look as his son. His glasses and pipe added to the image.

"Mom was in the kitchen a few minutes ago, helping Suse with the kids," Joe answered his father's query. "Dad, I'd like you to meet Sara Davidson, a friend and neighbor. Sara, this is my father, Robert Fisher." Sara shook hands with Robert and felt as if her hand had been crushed to a pulp.

"Davidson. Michael Davidson, the basketball player, right?" Robert demanded.

"Huh?" Joe turned a puzzled frown on his father.

"Yes," Sara answered Robert's question a bit shortly. Men! She had worried about squeezing Charles's hand too hard, and now her own was being crushed in a vise. "Michael was my husband. How did you know that?"

"I heard Joe say you had just lost your daughter, and it was on the sports page that Mike's little girl just died. I'm really sorry. I saw your husband play once."

"Play what?" Dora asked her son.

"Basketball, of course!"

"He went on to play for the Pistons, right?"

"So you saw him at State?" Sara clarified.

"Of course," Robert declared. "Professional basketball's a joke. I only watch college sports. The rest of it's nonsense. Now, your Michael Davidson was a pretty fair player. Good at free throws, but he didn't handle the pressure well. That's an indication that his ability to judge the angle of an arc from sight wasn't quite fast enough. I'll bet you didn't know that basketball is a game of geometry. Most people don't. That's why they can't understand the game."

"Bah!" Charles harrumphed. "They can't understand it because it makes no sense. Baseball is the sport for true fans. An American game. Skill, strategy, luck. A splendid game. It actually can be used as a perfect example of Taoist principles."

"Now we'll be here until midnight," Dora complained. "Mention baseball at a thousand yards and Charles can hear you just fine, but tell him something important at three feet, and he's deaf as a doorknob."

"Are we leaving now?" Joe's mother asked as she came up carrying an armload of dishes.

"We'll be here until midnight," Dora predicted gloomily, gesturing at her husband and son.

"Dad and Gramps are discussing the relative merits of basketball and baseball," Joe explained. His mother rolled her eyes expressively.

"Robert," she interrupted, "please carry these dishes to the car for me while I find Charles and Dora's coats." To Sara's amazement, the outspoken Robert obeyed his wife without protest. Charles followed him still arguing.

Soon after Joe's grandparents and parents left, Sara was the only guest remaining. The house seemed huge and quiet now that it was empty. Joe collapsed onto one of the sofas in front of the fireplace and sighed loudly. "Thanksgiving's the only holiday that makes sense. They give you the long weekend after it instead of before. Heaven knows I need time to recover!"

"I better go so you can get started."

"Whoa! Give me a second to catch my breath. I should check the house and make sure no one got left behind, and then I'll walk you home."

"I live next door, Joe. I can find my own way home."

"It's dark out."

"I'm not afraid of the dark," Sara insisted, but she remained curled up in the chair by the fire.

"This neighborhood may seem safe, Sara, but only a fool takes unnecessary chances. And don't tell me that the world ought to be safe for women. It's not. Too bad, but true. I'll walk you home."

"Okay, okay," Sara agreed with a half smile.

"Okay, okay," Joe parroted. "Let's go look for leftovers. Last year James and Marie left Grace behind. She was sleeping on the bed, and they just forgot her in all the confusion. I've never seen a more mortified mother! Of course, little Grace slept through her entire abandonment."

He dragged himself to his feet and then held out his hands and pulled Sara to hers. He kept hold of her hand as they walked through the rooms. "You're going to have to clean everything," she observed. There were piles of damp towels in the spa, and the Monopoly game players had left more than one playing piece on the bedroom floor. In the upstairs guest rooms where the older boys had been watching football, there was a large collection of soda cans, and stray kernels of popcorn were strewn everywhere.

After he had assured himself that there was no one left behind, Joe walked Sara home, accompanied by an exuberant Roly, who had spent the day in the basement, safe from the children's attention. "So what did you think of the Fisher mob?" he asked as they crunched along on the gravel shoulder.

Sara smiled. "I'm still not sure I have them all straight. What order did you come in?"

"Drew, he's married to Dria. Then Matt and Deanna, James and Marie, and Tim and Betsy. And finally, a girl! That's Susan. She's married and has three kids. That's where they were going to stop, but seven years later I snuck along, colicky and crying, messing up their retirement plans."

"Oh, sure," Sara laughed, "I believe that. I don't think your mother will ever retire."

"You don't know how right you are," Joe laughed. "Mom and Dad are supposed to be retired, and they're still running off to give lectures and attend conferences all the time.''

"Just what do they do, anyway?''

"You've never heard of Robert and Vera Fisher?'' Joe asked incredulously.

Sara paused and felt embarrassed as she tried to recall them. She couldn't think of where she ought to have heard of them, except as Joe's parents. "No,'' she finally admitted to Joe's delight. He threw back his head and let delighted laughter rumble into the night while Sara glared at him.

Finally he relented and explained. "At one time my parents were considered the best team of geometers in the world.''

"Geometry! How am I supposed to know them from that? Geometry was the only class I ever flunked. I could never figure out what to do with all those stupid triangles and hippopotamuses.''

Joe almost started to explain that they were hypotenuses but caught himself in time. His eyes glittered with suppressed laughter as he caught Sara's hands and turned toward her. Only after he pulled away did Sara realize he'd been about to kiss her. She frowned and barely listened as he chattered on about how his brothers and sister had all followed, more or less, in their parents' footsteps, while he had become the black sheep by studying literature.

"You're not much of a black sheep,'' she protested, recovering her wits. "You're a lot like your brothers.''

"Am I being insulted here?''

"Of course not. I think it would be wonderful to have a family like yours. I always wanted a brother or a sister.''

"Spoken like an only child!"

"Admit it, they make a nice crowd. I had Thanksgiving dinner with Mom and Dad. Three people don't make a very good holiday crowd." She didn't add that Lala's absence made the holiday with her parents unbearable.

"I'll bet your grandfather remembers your name," Joe challenged.

"Actually you'd lose that bet," Sara stated with a frown.

Joe paused at the bottom of the steps and whistled for Roly. "Well, if you'd asked me when I was ten, I'd have given you all of my brothers and my sister, too!"

"Joe!"

"I don't think you would have enjoyed them much. They like to talk about triangles and hippopotamuses." Sara stood on the bottom step and smiled at him. The wind was gusting strongly around the house, swirling around them, but she didn't feel cold. "You better get inside before you catch cold," Joe ordered protectively. "I'm glad you came tonight, and I'm glad you brought those pies. You single-handedly saved my Thanksgiving. I suppose you know I'm your slave for life now."

"I'll keep that in mind," Sara told him dryly before she went inside and closed the door. She stood still, listening to him walk back toward his house, whistling for Roly as he went. If anything, Joe had single-handedly rescued her Thanksgiving, not the other way around. Trust a man to get it all backward.

CHAPTER FOUR

"I thought you were coming to the game with me, Lala. Don't you want to see your old man hit a grand slam against the dreaded Bill's Bowling Alleycats?" Michael sneered the name as if it were far less silly to be known as a Goldbricker for the real estate office's team.

"I wanna help Mom make the cookies for my class. I specially asked to let her make the cookies so I could help. I almost had to make punch, and that's no fun at all." Lala leaned over and snitched a glob of the chocolaty dough. Michael imitated his daughter and earned a slap on the wrist.

"Dad!"

"Okay, I won't snitch any of your batter, but you have to promise to save me a cookie. How about one for every hit I make?"

"Every run," Lala bargained, knowing Michael often got stranded on base when his teammates failed to match his success.

Michael threw her a pleading look, but Sara just smiled and left Lala in charge of striking the bargain. "You're a mean girl, Lala. I think I'll have to tickle you."

"I won't save you any cookies if you do."

"Meanie."

"Okay, every hit, but only if you win the game."

Michael threw back his head and laughed. He tousled Lala's hair and planted a hurried kiss on Sara's cheek before dashing out the back door, leaving his rich laughter echoing in the kitchen. Sara heard his car door thud closed. Her blood turned to ice. "No!" she screamed. "Michael, come back, come back. Michael!"

SARA'S FACE WAS WET when she woke up. It always was—every time she had this awful nightmare. If only she had called Michael back. But she hadn't; she'd laughed and let him go. On the way home after the game, Michael was killed by a drunk driver who didn't bother to stop for a red light.

Sara sighed and wiped her face on the edge of the sheet. It was silly to wake up sobbing; all she did was give herself a headache and worry Lala. In fact, she ought to get up and make sure Lala was still sleeping. It wasn't fair to let Lala worry about her mother. Lala had her own grieving to do. It had probably been unfair for her to move her daughter to this apartment. It eased her own pain, but Lala didn't quite understand why they had lost the house as well as Daddy.

Sara climbed out of bed and shrugged into her robe as she took the three steps across the room to the light switch by the door. Only there was nothing there. She took another step and another, and a vertiginous fear enveloped her; it felt as if she were going to walk forever reaching out to touch the wall and finding nothing. Then she stepped into the edge of the old-fashioned maple wardrobe and hurt her toes.

"Dammit all!" Unlike her hysterical sobs, the whispered curse did not echo in the room. Sara bent down and curled her fingers protectively around her sore toes, using the physical pain to hide from the overwhelming emotional one, for she now knew where she was. At Aunt Gert and Uncle Corny's, hiding from the pain of Lala's death. Sara bit back her sobs and rocked herself for a moment before she stood back up off the floor. She walked through the dark house to the bedroom that had been Lala's, and only then did she turn on a light.

The room was empty. The bed neatly made up again by the cleaning woman. The few things of Lala's that Sara had brought back were set on the dresser. The flat white sea urchin. It was dead; without so much as an echo of the sea. The room was dead, too. It captured nothing of Lala. Even the teddy bear was starting to look unloved, simply a bedraggled leftover that no one really wanted anymore. There was nothing of Lala here anymore. The room was completely empty. Sara moved the few things to the room she was using, but it only took a minute, and it didn't make her feel any better.

The night was dark and cold, and the wind had grown fierce and now whipped across the lake and buffeted the land. It shrieked through the trees and around the house, howling under the eaves, rattling and whistling in the storm windows. Sara moved through the dark rooms feeling as if the house were surrounded by demons.

She suddenly went to the stereo and put on Beethoven's Fifth Symphony loud enough to obliterate the sound of the wind. When the music diminished, Sara ran through the rooms turning on every light. Then she built a roaring fire in the fireplace, using lighter fluid from the barbecue supplies in the garage to make it burn. She wrapped herself up in a blanket and curled up into a ball on the floor in front of the fireplace, shivering and edging closer to the warmth of the fire.

The flames crackled, throwing sparks into the air. The music pounded dramatically as it swelled to grandiose proportions. Sara didn't feel safe or secure, but the haunting loneliness was held at bay. Like a camper sleeping within a circle of fire to ward off starving wolves until dawn, Sara was momentarily safe. The music stayed loud, the fire kept roaring, and the lights burned in every room until the windows turned pale gray with the dawn light. Only then did Sara allow the stereo to remain silent while she slowly grew drowsy, savoring the lethargic warmth of her blanket cocoon.

When she woke up the house was filled with a dismal gray light. The November day was without sunshine as heavy banks of clouds roiled toward the shore, driven by the wind. Sara felt disoriented as she gazed around the living room and into the cold embers of the dead fire. She could barely remember why she had wandered through the house in such desperation. The strength of those midnight emotions seemed foreign in the light of day.

When she stood, every muscle in her body protested. Stretching and a hot shower removed only some of the stiffness. Sara moved slowly through the house as she turned off lights and straightened up the already neat rooms. At midafternoon she scrambled an egg and made toast and coffee, but she wasn't hungry. She was bored. She had nothing to do now that she was no longer a wife and no longer a mother. She was nothing; how could she have anything to do?

Sara sat at the kitchen table with her cup of coffee and the magazines Marcus had given her. The pictures were nice, but they didn't make her feel like digging in the yard and planting anything. And who would go out and garden in this windstorm, anyway? The positions-available ads he had circled were ridiculous. She hadn't enough experience for one, and too much training for another. She didn't want the one in Texas, and she didn't like the sound of the one in California. Still, she might as well get a job; she'd nothing better to do. It seemed rather dreary; no job would ever substitute for what she had lost. Nevertheless, she wrote a letter to the man who had been her adviser, although she doubted that he was still at the school. It didn't really matter anyway.

There was a mailbox at the hotel that nestled against the channel from Lake Macatawa into Lake Michigan. It would be a good walk, and good to hear the waves breaking against the pier by the lighthouse. Big Red, as the squat red lighthouse was affectionately known, would be standing up to the waves as sturdy as could be. It was somehow satisfying to see it in a storm. If buildings could be considered brave, the red lighthouse certainly was. She'd walk down to the mailbox and mail her letter to Professor Black and watch the lighthouse weather the storm. Maybe it would help her weather her own emotional seas; they were running high.

AFTER HE FINISHED dusting the last shelves and running the carpet sweeper through the living room, Joe heaved a tremendous sigh of relief: the house was finally clean. He had been working all day and now it was done. Thanksgiving was over. He put away the rags and set the papers he had to correct on his desk so that he would remember to do them before he tried to finish his article.

Before he did anything else though, he was going to soak in the hot tub until he turned to a prune. It looked most inviting after he had scrubbed it and re-filled it with fresh water. He deserved to indulge him-self. He took a brief shower so the tub would stay clean and then settled into the relaxing water and let it lap against the bottom of his contented smile.

Two minutes after he had closed his eyes, relaxed his muscles and emptied his mind, the phone rang. Couldn't Ma Bell have come up with a phone that didn't make you jump when it rang? He ignored it, knowing it was another member of the Fisher clan trying to find out exactly who Sara was and what their relationship was. At thirty-four, he was a disgrace-fully old bachelor; everyone in the family wanted to help him find the right woman so he could settle down and raise another five or six Fishers.

He had learned to distrust their judgment; they had no idea what he wanted in a woman. His older brothers picked intellectual women who wanted a Fisher who took after the mathematical parents. And Susan sent him every blonde who crossed her path. Of course, Olivia had been his own selection, and she hadn't been a good choice. Now that she was in Cali-fornia he felt bad that he didn't miss her, just the con-venience of her presence in his bed and on his arm. Without her, the barrage of blind dates would start again.

Maybe he was better off without a woman. He'd never been swept off his feet by passion. Maybe he was incapable of feeling that kind of emotion. Maybe it was just a fairy tale, a joke everyone else was in on.

Even in his large family he sometimes felt like an out-
sider. He loved them and they loved him, but he didn't
quite fit in.

Leaning back against the hot tub's molded seat, Joe
suddenly lurched forward and ducked his head beneath the churning surface of the water. Pulling his
head back up, he shook the water from his hair much
like Roly did after he went swimming. Spatters flew
everywhere. The mood of melodramatic introspec-
tion broke. To make sure it stayed broken, Joe
climbed from the hot tub and wrapped up in a heavy
terry robe. A glass of crisp white wine would keep him
on track for the rest of his soak.

He had the bottle uncorked and a glass pulled down
from the cupboard when he glanced out at the windy
beach and saw Sara Davidson. He nearly dropped the
bottle of wine in his rush to dash out onto the porch
and call her. The bitter wind whipped his voice away
and sent a debilitating draft billowing up under his
bathrobe. The damned thing was too short, a skimpy
present from his mother. Was it supposed to make him
attractive to women? Didn't his mother have enough
grandchildren without him contributing more? Joe
glared, angry that his mother found him inadequate,
angry that the wind was so cold, angry that Sara was
ignoring him.

Finally, when he was about to abandon the effort,
she noticed him. He gestured for her to come up, and
she lifted an arm in reply and walked on. Joe gestured angrily as he stormed back inside. He wasn't
going to literally freeze his butt off over a damned
woman! If she wanted to ignore him, that was just
fine. And if his stupid dog wanted to desert him to run
in circles around her ankles that was fine, too. He

didn't care. All he wanted was to return her damned pie plates.

He went into the spa and wrestled the insulated cover onto the hot tub and then jerked on a pair of old jeans and a sweatshirt with a torn collar. He didn't care. He stomped to the telephone and punched in her number.

"Hello," Sara answered breathlessly, still wearing her parka, dropping her hat and mittens onto the counter. The phone *would* ring just as she'd dashed in to grab the rest of the pumpkin pie before she went back to Joe's. She knew he'd love it. Why had he wanted to talk to her, anyway? Maybe something was wrong. He was wearing his bathrobe. If he was sick, he was stupid to have gone out in that wind. She'd had on her winter parka and was frozen; he'd have caught his death of a chill.

"Why didn't you come when I waved to you?"

"Joe?"

"Yes! I wanted to talk to you. Why the hell did you ignore me?"

See if she was going to share her pie with him! He had no right to yell at her! "I didn't ignore you. I waved back," she informed him icily.

"I know you waved back. I saw you wave back. I was standing out there freezing my tail off, trying to get you to come on up to the house."

"Why are you yelling at me?"

The silence stretched and stretched until finally Joe sighed audibly. "I don't know. Can I blame it on the cold?"

"Hey, I walked all the way down to the channel and back. I'm colder than you are, and I didn't yell at you . . . at least not until after you yelled at me. I was just coming back here to pick up some pumpkin pie. I thought you might like a piece.''

"And I blew it?''

"Well...''

"If I apologized real nice?''

"Well...''

"If I said I was more sorry than words can say? That I lost my head in the heat, ah, chill of the moment? That it hurt to be rejected by a woman of your devastating beauty?''

"With my nose as red as Rudolph's? I think I need a pair of hip boots!''

"Well?'' Joe prompted.

"Well...'' Sara teased. "Okay. I doubt your sincerity, but I'll bring it over if you'll make some coffee.''

"Great!''

Sara was smiling as she hung up the phone and covered the pie securely. Before she left she went into the bathroom and brushed her hair. It had been crushed by her hat. Silly idiot, she thought; she was going to put her cap right back on. Her cheeks glowed from the cold, and she thought she looked a little better, a little less pale. If only her nose wasn't bright red! If only she didn't have a sappy grin plastered on her face. It was just a cup of coffee with a neighbor. He was probably sick and wanted someone to make him chicken soup.

She walked back to his house along the road. Roly came scampering out of the woods to join her again, bobbing around her exuberantly. Lala had wanted a puppy or a kitten, but Michael was allergic to pet hair, and then the lease in the apartment forbade them. Sara sighed. She'd done it all wrong. The feeling of guilt settled heavily on her heart. Her daughter had just died; what was she doing dashing off to have coffee with a man, making jokes and blushing at the thought of his skimpy bathrobe?

Joe had been pacing between the doors, but he stood and waited when he spotted Sara and his fickle dog coming up the driveway. She didn't look very happy. She was probably tired from her walk. That was a damned cold wind that was blowing. But the coffee would do the trick. When she reached the steps he threw the door open and ushered her into the house. Roly bounced in with her but Joe ignored him.

"Hello, Sara." Suddenly he couldn't think what to say. A minute ago his thoughts had been racing in circles, his head dizzy with all the things he wanted to tell her. "Come in. Let me take that for you while you get your coat."

"I can't stay."

"What?"

"I can't stay. What did you want?"

"Is something wrong? Did something happen since we talked on the phone? You didn't go home to get this pie just to hand it to me. You were going to have a piece, too. I made the coffee."

"I said I can't stay."

"Why the hell not?"

"Because Lala's dead, that's why!" Sara's eyes glittered with tears and her voice was strained, fierce but rough with emotion. "My daughter's dead, dammit!"

Joe stared at her. He didn't understand at all. He felt betrayed and hurt, like he'd been sucker-punched. He knew Lala was dead. He wanted to help. "She's dead, Joe," Sara repeated in a resigned voice. "I'm suppose to be grieving."

"I don't see what that has to do with this," Joe stated calmly, biting back his hurt.

"You're getting in the way."

"What?" Joe interrupted with a squawk.

"You're getting in the way. You make me forget. I don't want to forget. Dammit, Joe, we were laughing on the telephone. Laughing. Lala's only been gone for seventeen days. I shouldn't be laughing." A large tear rolled down her face, and Joe reached out and caught it with his thumb.

He sighed silently. "Take your coat off and come inside, Sara. We'll have a cup of coffee and a piece of pie, and I promise I won't make you laugh."

"Joe," Sara protested, and he immediately regretted the callous remark.

"Please."

Sara left her coat and mittens on the couch and followed Joe into the kitchen, where he was already pouring the coffee and slicing the pie. He pulled out a chair for her and set a plate in front of her, but he didn't sit down with his plate and cup. Instead, he rummaged through the stack of dishes on the counter and pulled out two pie plates. "These are yours, right?" He held them up for her inspection and Sara nodded. "I'll put them by your coat so you don't forget them." Sara stared after him. He didn't sound angry but the friendliness had left his voice. She didn't quite know what to do. Eating pie as if nothing had happened wasn't appealing.

"I wanted to talk to you," Joe said as he slid into the chair next to hers and picked up his fork. "I wanted to apologize for Betsy and Deanna and my

mother. And also for my father and grandfather. I'm
afraid my family's more outspoken than tactful. But
they didn't mean to make it harder for you."

"I don't think you need to apologize for them,
Joe." Sara took a tiny bite of the pumpkin pie.
"They're adults, responsible for their own actions.
Besides, I've heard a lot worse. My sister-in-law thinks
I killed Lala by taking her out of the hospital at the
end. And Melanie, my other sister-in-law, thinks I was
utterly cruel to let them use experimental drugs on
Lala. She says she doesn't know what kind of mother
would let a sick child be used as a guinea pig for sci-.
entists. At least Betsy was complimenting me, even if
she was wrong."

"She said you'd make a wonderful mother. What's
wrong about that? I watched you with Lala and you
were a wonderful mother. You don't believe that crap
about using her as a guinea pig, do you? I'm quite
certain you did what you had to do in the best way you
knew how. Come on, Sara, don't be dumb!"

"What do you know about being a mother? You
think you can tell in five minutes if someone's a good
mother or not? Sincerity isn't what counts. Sure, I
tried, but did I succeed? No. I ignored Lala's complaints when she started to feel under the weather. I
dismissed it all as a stress reaction because she'd just
lost her father. I didn't take her to the doctor until it
was too late. You know the earlier they catch the cancer, the better chance they have for curing it. I wasn't
a good mother."

"Sara."

"You can't argue with the facts, Joe. If I had been
a better mother, Lala might be alive now." Sara had
been poking at her slice of pie with her fork and now

she gave it a last vicious stab and shoved it away from her. Joe picked up her plate and his empty one and set them in the sink. He leaned back against the counter and crossed his arms.

"Wrong. You're absolutely wrong." He topped off his coffee cup and replaced the one sip Sara had taken from hers. He took the cream from the refrigerator and stirred some into his coffee before he continued. "You just wish that were true."

"You're crazy."

"Think about it. If Lala's death is your fault, you are implicitly saying that you can control death. Okay, you admit you didn't, but since you're capable of doing so, you can prevent this from happening again. The truth of the matter is that you can't control death. You didn't have the power to save Lala. It means you're vulnerable and you could get hurt again."

"I won't."

"How can you prevent it?"

"I'll never have another child. It hurts too much."

"Give yourself some time. I'll bet you change your mind."

"What makes you think you know so much about it? It's easy for you to sit there and lecture me. You never lost a wife, did you? You never lost a child. Hell, your parents are still alive. Even your grandparents are still alive. What do you know about losing someone you love?"

"You make it sound like a competition," Joe said bitterly, stabbing the handle of the spoon he had used to stir his coffee into the tablecloth, making tiny dents in the pad beneath it. "If I haven't hurt as much as you, I'm not allowed to hurt at all, is that it? You can't lose what you never had, and there's a different kind of hurt that goes along with that. And I have lost someone I love." His voice dropped. "I lost Jeremiah."

Sara felt duly chastised. She put her hand over his white-knuckled grip on the spoon and squeezed gently. "I'm sorry. You're right, I'm being a jerk." Joe dropped the spoon and turned his hand over, meshing his fingers with Sara's. She looked at their clasped hands; they looked right together. She held his hand a little tighter. "Why don't you tell me who Jeremiah was?" she invited.

"You'll think I'm a melodramatic fool," Joe warned, "but I'll try to explain because it just might help." Sara wondered if he meant help himself or help her, but she didn't ask. "Jeremiah was my twin brother, but he died right after we were born. I always missed him. It's like a piece of me is missing. How can I miss someone I never knew? It's not like anyone ever blamed me. My mom won't even talk about it. Except maybe I blame myself. I was the big one, you know, the dominant twin. I was ready to be born and he wasn't. He was just too small to live. Sometimes I feel like I killed him."

Sara stared at Joe in amazement. He couldn't possibly be serious. But his hand was tight around hers, and he was staring out at the wind-whipped lake with glittering eyes. "Joe," she protested, "you can't possibly hold yourself responsible for something that happened before you were born. You weren't in control of what was happening. It's just…just life, that's all. It's nobody's fault. I don't know where you got such an idea." But she heard the echoes and understood, a little better, what he had tried to tell her before. Maybe Lala's illness had been out of her control.

Maybe, but that didn't ease the hurt any. "Oh, Joe," she said, and sighed sadly.

He turned and looked into her eyes, and something electric stretched between them. They were caught in a timeless place where their souls seemed to meet and touch. It was magical. Something strange happened to Sara's blood, making it tingle. Joe could feel his stomach knot and his throat tighten. He'd never felt anything like this before in his life. It was more than desire. He didn't want Sara's body, or rather, he did, but he knew it would never be enough. He didn't know what to say or do. This feeling was so strange, exhilarating and positively frightening. He was vulnerable now in a way he did not like.

Sara thought he might kiss her. There was something fiery in his eyes. But before she could decide if she liked the idea of Joe wanting her or not, her stomach growled loudly. She stared down at it in disbelief. For the past month food had been the last thing she wanted. Why was her stomach picking this moment to make itself heard?

"You're hungry! You should have eaten your pie." Joe was on his feet and rummaging in the refrigerator in a second. "Let me make you something to eat. Here's some leftover clam chowder. How's that sound?"

"It sounds good, but I have to get on home." Joe's pleased expression faded, and he put the bowl back in the refrigerator. "Marcus said he thought he'd come over tonight. He's my brother-in-law. You saw him when you brought Lala that sand dollar. You have no idea how happy you made her. She really liked that."

"Well, that's good, anyway. I didn't realize it was so late. It's already getting dark. I'll walk you home."

"Okay."

They didn't seem to have anything to say to each other as they walked along the edge of the road. Joe waited on the bottom step while Sara fumbled with the lock. She opened the door and turned to whisper good night. And he smiled briefly and walked away, wishing he, instead of Marcus, could be the one to comfort her. Instead, he had made things worse—attacking her feelings when they were quite normal, comparing his old hurt to her new, much worse one. He walked home quickly, feeling cold and empty.

Sara waited for Marcus, but he didn't come by after all. She ate a cold turkey sandwich and wished it was steaming clam chowder. She thought about what Joe had said. It did make sense. She had wanted to be in control. Who didn't? Feeling like a fragile leaf tossed on the stormy sea of life was no fun at all. She wished she could make herself invulnerable, but she didn't know how. Except to never give her heart away again. Although the only effect of her campaign so far had been that she had become unspeakably rude, thinking only of herself, putting her own pain above everyone else's.

CHAPTER FIVE

"CHRISTMAS IS COMING, the goose is getting fat...."

"Shut up," Sara growled under her breath, glaring at the ceiling of the mall where the music seemed to be coming from.

"Did you say something, dear?" Agnes asked without taking her eyes off the display of pipes in the window of the tobacconist's shop. "I think you ought to get your father that nice black one on the left."

Sara knew her mother wouldn't understand if she tried to explain that she didn't want to celebrate Christmas. She wanted to hide from the world, filled as it was with holiday cheer and exhortations to be happy. All the Christmas specials on television had poignantly happy endings, and miracles were promised on every street corner and during every commercial break. But where had the miracles been when she needed one?

She'd thought she could avoid the holiday, but it was proving to be omnipresent. Jan Heidema had decided that Christmas decorations were part of her job as caretaker for the beach house. Sara knew the woman meant it as a kindness, but it was exactly what she didn't want. The pine boughs on the mantle, the red-ribboned wreath on the front door, the red candles surrounded with holly and ivy in the kitchen table centerpiece: small decorations that were pathetic in the huge house. Sara wanted to smash them. She wanted to see the pine boughs burn with showers of hot spitting sparks. She wanted to watch the candles melt into lumpy pools of useless wax. She wanted Christmas to vanish.

"Mom, I really have to get back. Marcus is coming by at seven." She had stopped by her parents' house late in the afternoon in order to pick up some old photos. Only a mother would keep a record of the gardens her daughter had designed for friends over the years, photos which would now make up a portfolio. Marcus wanted to help, and she had promised to get the pictures. But Agnes had insisted that Sara go out for dinner with her because she hated to eat alone and John had to stay late at work. And now they were in the mall looking at Christmas displays. Sara wanted to scream.

"I thought you said he was coming by after his business dinner."

"Well, yes, but it should be around seven. Marcus was going to meet someone at five-thirty. I figure an hour and a half is plenty of time for dinner and talk. It will only take him a few minutes to drive over from Zeeland."

"Oh, look, there's Santa Claus! I can remember how excited you always were to sit on his lap and ask for your special Christmas wish." Agnes pointed at the red-flanneled man sitting on a gilt throne surrounded by white cotton snow and a long line of children. Some of them bounced impatiently while others slumped against their parents or the velvet ropes that herded them into a single-file line. Lala had never believed in Santa Claus, but she had loved the ritual of sitting on his lap and had taken great joy in visiting as many Santas as she could.

Sara turned her head away. "Well, I don't have time to sit in his lap tonight," she muttered. Sarcasm seemed the best defense against the painful memories that assaulted her.

"You know, Sara, Marcus Davidson isn't really your brother-in-law anymore. You don't need to see him. I wouldn't come to depend upon him. He must want something from you, though I can't think what. Aren't the children lovely? Look at the sweet little girl in her red dress. Wouldn't you like to pick up that pipe for your father now? It will be one less worry for later on. It's getting close to the big day. I'm so excited. I think this will be the best Christmas ever!"

The best Christmas ever? Sara had to struggle to make her lungs work; the band of pain tightening around her ribs almost prevented her from breathing. "I'll get the pipe later," she said thinly. "I have to go, Mom, if I'm going to pick up those pictures and get back home in time." The best Christmas ever? How could her mother even think that?

An angry mother dragged a bawling child across their path hissing threats at him. Sara felt sick; she wanted to grab the mother in a grip as fierce as the one on the child's arm and shake her. Didn't she know how lucky she was? How fragile that child's life was? How easily it could be snatched away? This was the time for her to be patient and loving, even when the child insisted on acting like a child. What was Christmas all about, anyway?

"Home? I thought you were meeting him at Aunt Gert's house." Agnes turned back to look at the pipe again.

"That's what I meant," Sara said through clenched teeth.

Finally Agnes seemed to sense Sara's urgency, and she allowed herself to be led from the mall, pausing only once in front of the card shop. "I bought the most lovely silver paper to wrap your father's presents. But I'm not sure yet which color bows to buy. I was going to get all red ones, but then I thought maybe some red and some green. What do you think? Shall we go in and I'll show you the paper?"

"No, Mom, let's just go. Please!"

It was nearly eight o'clock before Sara pulled up in front of the beach house. Marcus was already there, waiting in his car. He jumped out to open her car door when she arrived. "Well, thank goodness you got here! I was turning into an icicle! Let's go in and make a fire. Here, let me carry those for you." He swept the photo albums out of her hands and loped up the stairs to the door. Sara didn't believe for a minute that her mother was right; Marcus didn't want anything from her. He was just lonely—his brother was dead, his only niece was dead and his parents were in Arizona. He had two older sisters, but they were married and wrapped up in their own lives with little time for a gangly younger brother.

Once they were inside, Sara made coffee while Marcus lit the fire. She was secretly relieved that he was as unenthusiastic about Christmas as she was. He wouldn't ask her to play Christmas carols or suggest they make eggnog. They would just look through the pictures and pretend it was an ordinary time of the year.

Looking through the pictures wasn't so easy. Memories of Michael and Lala came rushing back, although actual photographs of them were very scarce. Marcus helped, quietly listening to her reminiscences. They sat cross-legged on the floor in front of the fire and paged through the albums. Sara was surprised at the number of pictures they found. She'd forgotten half the gardens she'd designed. She'd have to sort the pictures and choose the best for her portfolio.

"You've done a lot of work," Marcus confirmed. "You'll have no trouble getting a job. I think it'll be good for you. It's just a shame you've never had a chance to work before."

"Well, Michael said every mother was a working wife and that I didn't need the aggravation of a second job," Sara explained. Michael had proposed at Christmas during their last year at college, and they'd been married that June. Lala had come before she had properly settled into being a basketball player's wife, and then, when Lala was a little older, Michael had retired. With the move and his career change, her career had been put off again, and then she'd been busy with Lala starting school. It just had never been the right moment. Michael's death had opened a door, but Lala's illness had slammed it shut. Now she wondered whether Marcus was right, whether working would fulfill her.

He didn't like her explanation if his grunt was anything to go by, but he didn't elaborate. He plucked a couple more photos from the album and added them to the growing pile between them. "There," he said with satisfaction, "that's the last of these. Are you almost finished?"

"Almost."

"I'll take our coffee cups to the kitchen." A moment later he called to her from the other room.

"Sara, come look!" She turned the last page in the album and closed the cover on a picture of her in the dress she had bought to celebrate her fifth wedding anniversary. Michael had bought a new suit, but there was no picture of him in it. Marcus called again, and Sara found him standing by the kitchen window. "Look! It's snowing!"

Sara leaned against the frame of the window. Small white flakes twirled through the cone of light cast by the floodlight on the back of the garage. "Lala always loved the first snowfall. So did Michael. They used to go outside when there was only an inch and make snowmen. These tiny, muddy, lopsided snowmen. And they would call me to come out and look because they were so proud. Then we'd have a snowball fight." Those fights had been messy, with more giggles than snowballs. She felt a fragile smile touch her mouth, but she knew she might be hit by pain at any moment.

Marcus took Sara by the hand and led her back to the fire, lying down and cuddling her against his body. Closing her eyes almost all the way, Sara squinted into the fire. The bright orange flames turned into diamonds of liquid color. The fire burned warmly. Michael used to build fires like this in their fireplace. They would put Lala to bed and then cuddle in front of the flames. Sometimes they would lie for hours without speaking, just enveloped within a cloud of tender togetherness. She had loved those nights.

Marcus's long body stretched beside her felt just like Michael's. Sara rolled over so that she could bury her face against the smooth folds of his shirt—cool crisp cotton that smelled of him. His familiar musk aftershave was like Michael's, different than the woodsy spice scent of Joe's cologne. Sara inhaled deeply. She slowly unbuttoned his shirt and experimentally kissed his smooth chest, tracing the outlines of his bones with her mouth. His long sternum and ribs were smooth and flat and warm, like satin, like marble. He was just like Michael.

His hands eased beneath her sweater, and she could feel his long, smooth fingers tracing up her spine, spanning her ribs with his thumbs against her sides. His hand was large enough to capture both her breasts at once. He cupped a mound of flesh in each hand and used his thumbs and forefingers to tug the rosy tips into peaks. Sara tilted her head back and his mouth found hers.

He pulled away a moment later, sitting up abruptly. "I can't. I'm sorry, Sara, but I just can't think of you as anything but my sister."

"I know," Sara agreed in a mournful voice. She'd wanted to feel something when she touched him, when he touched her. He was the embodiment of her perfect man—almost an exact replica of Michael—and she felt nothing more than a certain pleasantness when he touched her. She didn't expect sirens and bells and exploding skyrockets; Michael had made love to her for ten years, and she'd never experienced that. But she should have felt something if they were going to risk making love. "I guess this won't work."

"I guess not," Marcus sighed. He buttoned his shirt and leaned back to look at her. "Are you okay? I could try if you wanted me to."

"No, Marcus, it wouldn't work. You might look like Michael, but you're not him." Sara pulled her sweater down a little tighter and rubbed her nose with the back of her hand. "Do you want something to drink or something?"

Marcus chuckled at her solution. "No, I think I'll just head home before the snow makes the roads too slick. You want to come over on Christmas Eve and decorate the tree? Mary and Melanie planned this progressive dinner for Christmas. We're supposed to have wine and cheese at my place, dinner at Mary's, and then dessert and presents at Melanie's. It sounds dumb to me, but I didn't have much to say about it. I guess you'll spend the day with your mom and dad, huh?"

Sara nodded. She felt horrible about trying to make love to Marcus. She didn't want to make love to him; she wanted Michael. It had been unfair to put him in the position of feeling he had to try for her sake. She got Marcus his coat and let him out the door into the night. "I'm sorry," he said again, and she told him to drive carefully on the way home.

It wasn't easy to fall asleep that night. What was it about her grief that had made her so awful? She was always striking out, like a wounded animal backed into a corner. Sara wasn't happy with that image of herself, but she found a certain wry justice in having to admit it. She felt as if she no longer knew who she'd been or who she had become. Had she been a good mother? Joe had almost convinced her at Thanksgiving, but she still felt guilty about not taking Lala to the doctor earlier. And what was she going to do with her life now? She had no definition except what she wasn't anymore. It was just as well Marcus was pushing her to get a job. At least then she'd be something.

By CHRISTMAS EVE there was nearly a foot of snow on the ground, making it a very white Christmas and giving kids the excitement of looking for reindeer tracks in the morning. Sara had abandoned her effort to resist Christmas and spent part of the day helping Marcus decorate his tree. Unlike his sisters—Melanie favored matching satin balls and lights on her tree, while Mary would use only silver and gold stars—Marcus used one-of-a-kind ornaments. The special ornaments brought back memories, but Sara found she wasn't sad when she looked at the tiny imprint of Lala's kindergarten hand pressed in clay and painted red. Instead she remembered how happy Lala had been when she gave it to her Uncle Marcus.

Even so, it was a relief to have Marcus drive her home. He'd grown increasingly morose through the afternoon, not even smiling when it came time for him to stretch on tiptoe and crown his tree with a battered star of filigreed silver. She had smiled as a feeling of peace came over her, but Marcus had sighed gustily yet insisted nothing was wrong. He sighed again, loud and long, as he slowed down to approach the entrance of Gert and Corny's driveway. The plows had come past and piled heavy chunks of snow across the entrance.

"Maybe you better just drop me off here. You might end up stuck in that," she warned. Marcus grunted and turned into the driveway, gunning the engine and spinning the wheels as he slid through the barrier of snow. Fishtailing just once, he drove up and stopped in front of the door, letting the car idle while Sara climbed out. "Have fun tomorrow. Don't forget to give your sisters my presents and tell them I said Merry Christmas, okay?"

"Yeah, okay. Mom and Dad sent a present for you. It's in the trunk. Let me get it out, and then I've got to go."

"Don't you want to come in and having something warm before you head back to Grand Rapids? You could watch me open it."

"No," Marcus declined shortly. "It looks like it might snow some more," he added when she frowned at him, bewildered by his curtness. "The roads might get bad." He shoved a big box at her and then climbed back into his car. "Bye, Sara," he said and slammed the door.

She watched him drive off, trailing a thin vapor of white exhaust, spinning his wheels through the snow, not looking back. "Merry Christmas, Marcus," she said softly. He must still be upset at their attempted lovemaking. Any romantic relationship between them was doomed to failure. Marcus might feel like Michael when he hugged her, but however much she might long to recapture the past, the reality was that Marcus was *not* Michael.

She went inside and opened her package alone. It wouldn't do to save it until tomorrow morning when she opened presents with her parents; they wouldn't want to be reminded that there was another set of parents who had a claim on their daughter. Vivian Davidson had made her an afghan of brightly colored granny squares bordered in white. It was soft, cheerful and warm, like one of Vivian's affectionate hugs. Sara smiled as she wrapped it around her shoulders. But her smile soon faded.

It was no fun to open presents alone. She stood at the kitchen windows, watching the stars begin to pop out of the darkening sky, sparkling over the even darker lake. She no longer wondered if she would survive without Lala, but she knew merely surviving was not enough. She needed to fill her life again. Obviously Marcus would never fill it. And neither would a job. So what would? Sara asked herself. And shook her head when Joe popped into it. The man kept sneaking into her thoughts at the weirdest moments. She shook her head again and bundled up for a walk along the edge of the lake.

In a few hours it would be Christmas—her first Christmas without Lala. She wished there was some way to go back in time and watch more carefully how her daughter had enjoyed the special day. She had let those Christmas mornings slip past without paying attention to enough of the details. Some years she had even missed the expression on Lala's face when she first saw her stocking. Why had she let herself be tucked away in the kitchen making coffee when Lala first came down the stairs?

She walked along the edge of the lake where the damp sand had frozen into a surface as hard as concrete. The waves slushed against the shore, thick with little pieces of ice. If it stayed cold for the rest of the night, by morning huge chunks of ice would form. Already the snow had piled up against the trees and in the woods away from the windswept shore.

It was a white Christmas this year. Did that matter when she was all alone? She gazed up at the huge black sky and the perfect shining stars, and it seemed as if her memories of Michael and Lala were as perfect and shiny as the distant stars. How had Lala's song gone? Something about the only stars within reach were starfish on the beach.

At least she had those starfish, Sara realized. She had walked as far as the channel and now stood on the pier gazing back at the solid bulk of the land and the lighthouse with its red blinking light. As she walked back toward the house, Sara envisioned a whole treasure chest full of glittering starlike memories of Michael and Lala. She had known their special joy and magic. It would be wrong to forget it now.

The night didn't seem so cold and dark anymore, and the stars seemed to have dipped lower in the sky, coming almost within reach. She would never be really alone, Sara realized, for she would always have the memories, like stars, to keep her company.

As she walked past the stone house where Joe Fisher lived, Sara looked at the softly lit windows and the silvery smoke drifting from the chimney and wondered what his Christmas would be like. In his huge family the holiday must be filled with laughter. She imagined the house full of happy children playing with their new toys while the adults shared in the merriment. Tonight his house was quiet, and she imagined him in front of the fireplace wrapping the last of his presents. She almost went up to tell him about how peaceful she felt seeing the stars tonight, but something held her back. She wasn't sure he wanted her crashing into his life with her every little problem and victory. She didn't want to be one of his strays. She wanted to be his lover. The thought sent Sara scurrying home in confusion.

THE FLAMES FLICKERED lower and lower in the fireplace until there was nothing left of the blaze but glowing coals, and still Joe did not add more logs. He stared at the orange embers. He felt lonely, and he knew it was stupid. He could have gone to any one of the four parties he'd been invited to this evening. Or he could have gone over to his parents' house as they had asked. But no, he had decided it would be nice to spend the evening alone—quiet and peaceful before tomorrow's rush of confusion and noise. So why had he chosen to be alone if he was going to wallow in the misery of his self-inflicted loneliness?

Hell! he thought, it wasn't even a question. He knew why. Sara Davidson was just an ordinary woman. She wasn't breathtakingly beautiful, nor did she possess any superhuman virtues or capabilities. She was attractive and strong, but that wasn't enough to make a man mad, was it? He'd spent so much time walking back and forth on the beach hoping she'd join him that Roly was beginning to roll his eyes whenever Joe suggested a walk. Twice since Thanksgiving he'd seen her walking and raced out to accidentally bump into her. Once they had walked to the mailbox at the hotel together and once he had talked her into joining him for a bowl of soup. It was hardly a grand seduction scene.

But he didn't want to seduce her. He wanted to love her and be loved by her. He wanted to protect her from more pain, to wrap her in his arms and keep her safe. He wanted to come home to her at night instead of to the empty stone house with only a silly dog to keep him company. He knew she would understand the secret part of him no one else ever had. But he feared he couldn't give her everything she needed. How could he ease the pain of Lala's death? He wasn't full of free-spirited joy like Lala, like her husband had been. If he were still sane, he'd give up all hope, but he wasn't; he was mad about her. If he weren't crazy he'd hate her for making him feel so vulnerable and inadequate, so utterly foolish.

A log in the fireplace suddenly split, and the two parts shifted onto the bed of coals with a shower of sparks. Joe stared at the fire. In the morning the logs would be cold and gray and lifeless. He gave them a few vicious pokes with the wrought iron poker that hung at the side of the fireplace. Then he closed the fire screen and went into the kitchen.

From the window he could see the lake and the starry sky, but neither held any appeal for him. The stars were so beautiful and so perfect, but so far away that they could never be reached. A vague and heavy feeling that he would be alone and incomplete forever settled over him. He knew Sara wouldn't be out walking now, but he put on his coat and followed Roly down to the beach, anyway.

Roly jangled as he dashed through the snow, and the noise grated on Joe's nerves. Tim and Betsy had stopped by earlier in the day, and their kids had strung sleigh bells around the dog's neck with red ribbons. Joe was about to yell at poor Roly for making so much noise when he realized the spaniel was following Sara's tracks through the snow toward her house. She must have been out on the beach recently. He took it as a sign that they were supposed to be together and whistled piercingly for Roly as he hurried home.

He stomped a few times at the door in a rushed attempt to clear some of the snow from his boots and jeans. But he didn't care about keeping his floors dry nearly as much as he cared about hurrying over to Sara's with her present. He slowed down only once, as he passed a mirror and wondered about a shave. He certainly needed one, but he didn't want to look as if he'd primped for the visit. Sara might be uncomfortable with a late-night visitor. She'd always be beautiful to him, but women could be strange that way. His sister Susan wouldn't have a flat tire without first combing her hair and freshening her lipstick. But he was sure Sara wouldn't be like that.

With a shopping bag over his arm, Joe walked through the woods to Sara's door with Roly jingling merrily beside him. Now that he was going to see Sara, albeit uninvited in the middle of the night, Joe smiled at the happy sound. He no longer felt lonely. The snow had drifted up from the beach and lay in ridges between the trees, sometimes coming halfway up his thighs as he tramped a path through the woods, but he didn't mind at all.

His knock sent Sara flying from her chair, her heart beating wildly. Who in the world would be pounding on her door in the middle of the night? When she opened it and found Joe standing on the steps with a crooked grin on his face, she didn't know whether to yell at him for scaring her or welcome him into the house. Roly didn't bother to wait but snuck across the threshold, jingling like some oddball reindeer. "Can I come in?" he asked, and she found herself stepping aside and letting him in the house. His pants were white from the thighs down from plowing through the snowdrifts. He must have come through the woods. Just like a little boy. Men! they had no sense whatsoever!

"Hang up your coat, Joe. I'll dry the dog." Sara kept a towel by the door for brushing the snow off her legs when she returned from the beach, and she knelt down, setting aside her new afghan, to dry Roly. He stood patiently and raised each foot in turn. Sara grinned up at Joe, amused by the spaniel's tolerant air, but he was busy brushing off his jeans with the tips of his mittens. Sara used the towel to brush the back of his legs, just as if he were a child coming in from playing in the snow.

Joe froze under her touch as the blood rushed to the surface of his skin. The towel brushed against his legs without passion, he knew, but part of him only knew that the woman he loved was caressing him. She was almost irresistible in a high-necked granny gown made of white satin. The contrast between the old-fashioned style and the sensuous fabric was driving him wild. But he knew that if he made one false move, all would be lost. Sara wasn't ready for anything more than friendship. Yet.

He was ready for more than friendship. He longed to respond to Sara's touch, to turn around and touch her soft blond curls, to trace the shell-like contours of her ears, to run his hands across her satin-clad shoulders and pull her to her feet and press her against his body. He wanted to find her silky skin behind that high-buttoned collar. Damn! If he didn't stop his thoughts he wouldn't be able to stop himself until he was buried within her warm silkiness. Stop it, Fisher, he ordered himself. But he didn't.

It wasn't until Sara grabbed the loose fabric at the back of his thigh to hold the material steady while she brushed the towel down the whole length of his leg that Joe forced himself to stop her. One more minute and his heart was going to pound right through the wall of his chest. He bent over and swiped at his legs once more with the mittens. "Good enough," he croaked.

Sara pulled back as if she'd been burned. One minute she was brushing the snow off his legs like he was Lala. All he did was bend over, and she was set afire. The muscles at the top of his thigh had flexed beneath her hand; the fabric she held pulled his jeans tight across the contours of his hips. Joe wasn't a boy; he was a man. She wrapped herself in the afghan, too embarrassed to look at him.

"You wouldn't happen to have any coffee, would you?" Joe asked, relieved that his voice didn't crack.

"I'll go get you a cup. I just brewed it fresh a few minutes ago. I couldn't sleep so I figured, why not?" Why not indeed! She should have gone to bed and put the lights out, then she wouldn't be making a fool of herself now. Could he tell that she had contemplated taking him as a lover? There'd never been anyone else before or after Michael. It was time, wasn't it? She was a normal woman, but that didn't mean Joe wanted her. "Are you any good at starting fires?" Oh Lord, he didn't think she meant *that,* did he? "I mean, I was trying to start a fire, in the fireplace, and I couldn't get it to burn. I never can. I think it's that thing on the chimney, the flue. I don't know what to do with it."

Joe smiled, and the fire in her blood flared. "I like fresh cream, but skip it if there's only that powdered stuff. I'll get us burning in no time."

What a stupid thing to say, he berated himself as he knelt on the hearth. He was not going to get them burning. He might want that; hell, he was already burning. But Sara wasn't ready for his love scenes yet. He had to give her time. He had to slow down. He rearranged the logs Sara had stacked in the fireplace so there was room for the air to move between them. He added a few sticks of the kindling wood and a wad of newspaper. A moment later he leaned back with a smile.

"I think I hate you," Sara announced as she set their coffee on the table and settled into one of the wing-backed chairs that flanked the fireplace.

Joe spun around, a frown crumpling the skin between his eyebrows. "Why?"

"I saw you. That only took one match. One. I always need to go get the lighter fluid from the garage," she admitted.

"It's how you stack the wood. See, you need to put the logs like this, so the air can move around them. A fire needs oxygen to burn." Joe was demonstrating his technique with a couple of logs from the woodpile on the hearth. "Just add a couple of sticks of kindling, a wad of loosely crumpled newspaper, and voilà! There you go." He thumped the logs back onto the pile and moved to sit in the other chair, calling Roly back from exploring the dining room. The dog flopped on the hearth with a final jingle and stretched out as if he belonged there.

Joe sipped his coffee and stretched his feet toward the fire, resting his toes against Roly's back. There was a moment of silence while the fire hissed and snapped with a profound loudness. "You don't have a Christmas tree," he observed.

"I didn't feel like it this year," Sara explained. "I helped Marcus decorate his earlier today, and tomorrow I'll go to my Mom and Dad's house. They'll put the tree up tonight, just as if I were a six-year-old who's going to come running down the steps in the morning and not know how it got there."

"I've got a big one again this year," Joe said. "Every year I promise myself that I won't do it again next year because I hate taking down the decorations afterward, but I still put one up every year. If I didn't decorate, my family would do it for me. In fact," he said, jingling Roly's bells with his toes, "they decorate even if I've already done it. This is the handiwork of Liza and Darryl, Tim's kids."

Sara liked the way Joe's feet looked in his socks. They were compact rather than long and skinny like Michael's had been. She wished she could be part of his family for tomorrow's celebration instead of going to her parents' house. "I wish Christmas were over," she sighed.

"I can understand that. It must be different now, without Lala. I think kids are the thing that really makes Christmas fun. I love to shop for my nieces and nephews and watch them open their presents. That's the fun stuff. I guess we never really outgrow toys."

"You know," Sara mused, "I miss having a kid. I mean, different than missing Lala. There are places you can't go and things you can't do without a kid." She sighed. "I miss McDonald's Happy Meals," she admitted sheepishly. "They were so funny."

"I know, and you can't really do it by yourself, either," Joe agreed. "I wish I had kids—well, I've always wanted to have children, someday, you know what I mean—but I wish I had kids. I feel silly watching the cartoon specials by myself, especially when I cry about Rudolph or poor old Charlie Brown. Have you ever noticed that if a man is swimming with a kid and he stands on his hands, he's a neat guy, and if he's with a girl he's a show-off. But if he's by himself he's loony-tunes? Alone, it's a well-executed overhand crawl or nothing. And it's like that with everything. Boring!"

Sara had to laugh at Joe's complaints. Joe stared at her for a moment and then let his own laughter break free. Not because he thought it was so funny, but because he couldn't quite contain the joy that ran through him when he knew he had made Sara happy enough to laugh.

After their shared laughter, there was a silence while the fire crackled merrily. "So," Sara said finally, "did you come here in the middle of the night just to tell me you cry when you watch Christmas specials and like to stand on your hands in the water? If you want to go out there now and stand on your hands in the lake, I promise I won't laugh at you," she said solemnly.

"Not tonight, darling, I have a headache," Joe quipped back, lightning fast. "I'd need to be more than loony-tunes to swim off an iceberg," he added while Sara still struggled to deal with the easy intimacy of his first joke.

When Sara didn't respond, Joe knelt on the hearth and fed another log to the fire. Still kneeling on the small rug spread over the wall-to-wall carpeting, he scratched Roly's soft ears with a distracted hand and gazed into the flames. The log spluttered and steamed before small flames began to lick up its side. Joe gave it a couple of pokes that didn't do much but gave him time to tell himself to slow down.

Sara watched the play of the muscles under his soft sweater. He wasn't tall and sleek like Michael, but there was something enormously attractive about the way he was put together. He had a touch of the same athletic grace. And his dark brown hair curled at the back of his neck where it lay against the collar of his dark green sweater. She wanted to lean forward and run her fingers through it. She shook her head to clear away the thought.

"Actually," Joe admitted as he settled back into his chair, "I came to bring you your present." Sara felt a wash of dismay flow over her. She hadn't bought him anything. She'd gone back to the mall and bought a few presents: the pipe for her dad, a cashmere sweater and a delicate necklace for her mom. She had hurried through the stores, concentrating so fiercely she gave herself a headache. She'd never considered adding Joe to her list.

"I didn't get you anything," she confessed in a soft voice.

"It doesn't matter."

"Yes, it does."

"No, Sara, it doesn't. Christmas is supposed to be about giving, not about exchanging things of similar value. Do you know how much of a headache it is to find presents of equal value for fifteen nieces and nephews who have completely different needs and wants and wishes? I have twelve sets of aunts and uncles and a slew of cousins that no one can count anymore. If I tried to keep everything even, I wouldn't have any fun at all. I have to argue enough with relatives who figure Christmas is a giant score-keeping game to see who's loved the most. Don't make me fight with you, too."

Sara was taken aback by Joe's vehemence. For a moment she just looked at him, and then she said in a very small voice, "I still wish I had gotten you something. I didn't do much shopping though. I was tired and it wasn't any fun."

"It's okay, Sara," he said in a much gentler voice. "It's not your fault the Fishers never heard the theory of zero population growth. Here. I just brew this up to give everyone I owe a present: colleagues, and the secretaries who type for me, and all those sorts of people. It's orange-lemon-grapefruit marmalade.''

Sara stared at the jar of marmalade Joe had handed her. It was a beautiful light golden color, studded with delicate fragments of citrus peel, like sunshine poured into a bottle. It was strange that her throat had tightened with disappointment at the thought of being just one of the people Joe felt he owed a present. She wanted to be special to him. Wasn't that silly when she hadn't even thought to buy him anything!

It was still a beautiful gift. She smiled as she thought of her singular attempt at jam-making. It had been an unmitigated disaster.

"You actually made this yourself? It's funny. I guess I assumed that bachelors were helpless in the kitchen, and motherhood was a guarantee of culinary skill. Do you know, when I saw your Thanksgiving turkey, I thought you were one of those macho cooks who figured the bigger the better? And the one time I tried to make jam it turned out awful. It was supposed to be peach jam, and it came out like brown soup." She shuddered at the memory. "It looked so terrible, Lala didn't even want to taste it."

"Well, you ought to taste this before you go overboard with your praise," Joe warned, "because I didn't. I guess that means I'm either confident or stupid."

"Let's make some toast," Sara suggested, hungry for the first time in weeks. She grabbed Joe's hand and pulled him protesting behind her into the kitchen.

Within moments, they were seated at the kitchen table, each with a helping of warm toast. Joe watched while Sara carefully spooned marmalade onto her piece and spread it neatly to the very edges of the bread. She closed her eyes as she took the first bite, and they popped back open in surprise. He couldn't contain his grin. "There's something else in here," she accused, taking another bite and chewing it slowly.

"Grand Marnier liqueur and a little dash of cinnamon," Joe explained. After a moment he spread a tiny spoonful of the confection on his slice of toast and ate along with her. Mostly he watched her, enjoying the fact that she was eating. She was too fragile. She needed some more meat on her bones.

After Joe explained just how he had made the jam, Sara started to tease him. "You could get rich selling this stuff. It's like liquid gold."

"Isn't that what they call crude oil?"

"No, I meant . . . never mind. We'll call it Joseph Fisher's World Famous Orange-Lemon-Grapefruit Marmalade."

"We will?"

"What's your middle name? We can use that, too. Long names sound gourmet, you know."

"I don't have one."

Sara was about to go on when she caught the guilty look on Joe's face and knew he was lying. "Everyone has a middle name. I'll tell you mine, if you'll tell me yours," she bargained.

"No."

"Alfred? Horatio? Percival? At least give me a hint," Sara wheedled.

"Okay, I was named after a mathematician."

"Gee, that helps a lot."

"A Greek geometer."

"Aristotle?"

"Generally considered a philosopher."

"Euripides?"

"You're getting colder. He wrote plays."

"My middle name is Jane."

"That's not so bad," Joe argued.

"Plain old Jane," Sara complained. "Please tell me."

"Euclid," Joe muttered into his coffee cup.

"What?"

"Euclid."

"I never heard of him."

"My mother did."

"It's not so bad, not really. It could be worse, I guess. I think I need another piece of toast. Lying makes me hungry."

Joe groaned and hid his face against the table so Sara wouldn't see his goofy smile. She was laughing, teasing him! Her dimples were like Lala's; combined with her twinkling blue eyes they were enough to make the hardest man fall in love. And he didn't even have that much resistance. She ate a second piece of toast and Joe just watched. No one had ever made him feel bigger and stronger and more capable...more masculine. He'd made her feel better. He'd made her laugh!

They went back into the living room, and Sara collapsed into her chair in front of the fire feeling happy and contentedly tired. It had been a long day, but it was good to sit up late and eat toast and laugh with Joe instead of pacing the rooms alone feeling haunted by her guilt and grief. She was still smiling when Joe handed her a box wrapped in gray paper with feathery sprigs of dark green pine. She wanted to repeat that he shouldn't have or that she wished she had something for him, but she knew he would argue.

Joe stood awkwardly while she opened the box and pulled out a hand-knit sweater with a windmill pattern in a deep, rich delft-blue. Sara didn't know what to say. It was beautiful. She jumped up and wrapped Joe in a hug that tried to tell him what she felt.

Joe put his arms around Sara's fragile body with great care. He was afraid that if he moved too fast the whole embrace would turn out to be a figment of his imagination. It was too perfect. A bubble of excitement and happiness was swelling in his chest. He knew Sara was hugging him to say thank-you, but he felt so much more than that.

"It's too much," she whispered, pulling away from him and returning to her chair, wrapping herself back up in the afghan. Joe could still feel her too-thin body against his. He could feel the satin folds of her nightgown beneath his hands, and he could feel her hands against his back. Sara spread the sweater in her lap and looked down at it. "It's so beautiful."

"It's exactly the color of your eyes," Joe explained. "That's what made me choose it for you." He didn't say that it had been outrageously expensive, more than he could afford to spend, but too perfect for her to be resisted. He was afraid Sara would protest again and maybe refuse the gift, but she didn't. After a while she told him how she had walked on the beach and thought of Lala's song and decided to treasure the moments that came her way.

"Moments of memory, moments like stars," she had called them, and her words had reverberated within Joe as he watched her fall asleep in her chair. He knew he should wake her up and tell her to go to bed, but this was his moment of memory, watching her sleep and thinking of her smiles and her laughter and her hug. She'd given him a present tonight that was more precious than anything she could have wrapped up in a box. And someday she was going to give him her heart.

CHAPTER SIX

SOMETHING DISTURBED her sleep, and Sara moved uncomfortably, scowling at the stiffness in her muscles. Another rotten night's sleep. The telephone was ringing. Her feet were freezing. The phone rang again, imperiously demanding that she open her eyes. Sara did.

There was a man sprawled in her aunt's wing-backed chair!

Sara scrambled for the phone, dropping the blue-and-white sweater, tripping over the tails of the afghan that was tangled around her. "Hullo," she muttered thickly into the receiver. Joe sat up slowly and looked across the room at her, blinking groggily. He rubbed his eyes as if he wasn't sure he could trust them. His hair was standing up in spikes, and there was a red crease on one cheek above the shadow of his beard.

"Merry Christmas, Sara!" Agnes Van Dyke sang happily into her ear. Sara yawned.

"Hi, Mom." Joe reminded her of a little boy, Sara thought, a half smile quirking one corner of her mouth.

"Are you just waking up now, Sara? We're waiting for you before we open the presents, and you know how impatient your father gets, just like a little boy." Agnes's voice was warm with indulgence. "You are coming, aren't you?'' Sara winced at the sudden fear in her mother's voice. Had she been avoiding them that much?

"Of course I'm coming, Mom,'' she said in her most reassuring voice. "I just overslept a bit without Michael and Lala to drag me out of bed before the sun rose.'' She was sleepily amused at the similarity between her rush of tenderness for Joe and her mother's similar reaction to Sara's father. If only she could share that with her mother instead of being trapped in this mother-child relationship. If they could just be friends.

Roly shook himself heartily on the hearth, making his Christmas collar jangle noisily. He trotted to the front door and yapped to have it opened. "What was that sound?'' Agnes demanded.

"Oh . . . that was just the neighbor's dog.'' Joe was stretching. His muscles were taut under his jeans, and his stomach was flat and hard where his sweater had ridden up. He gave her a searching look and then walked across the room and let the black-and-white spaniel out into the cold. He djdn't meet her eyes as he walked past her to disappear into the kitchen. Sara bit her lip.

"The neighbor's dog? It sounds like he's sitting at your feet. I knew you shouldn't move out to that empty house all by yourself. It's no wonder you can't wake up in the morning with a dog barking like that all night long. You ought to call the police and complain.''

"Mom,'' Sara complained. Her mother had righteous indignation perfected to an art form. "I let him in the house. I can hardly complain if he barks to get back out.''

"You let him in the house?" Sara grimaced at her mother's aghast tone. If she'd been awake she wouldn't have made that tactical error. "Whatever made you do such a foolish thing, Sara Jane? You know better than to let a stray dog into the house. What if it had attacked you in the middle of the night? You insist on staying out there all alone in the middle of the woods. The least you can do is be careful. What if that dog has rabies?"

"Mom, it's a neighbor's dog, not a stray. It doesn't have rabies and it doesn't bite. His name is Roly Poly, for goodness' sakes!" Sara caught herself before her irritation flared; it was Christmas Day and she wasn't going to argue with her mother.

"You know your aunt and uncle showed a great deal of trust by generously allowing you to use that house. That dog could have messed the carpets. You mustn't forget your responsibility to your aunt and uncle."

"Mom, Roly Poly is very well-trained. He barked when he needed to go outside." Sara was tempted to say that his very masculine master had been right beside her all night long and would have taken care of any problems his dog caused. That would send her mother into a real conniption! And ruin her Christmas.

"I still don't think you should've let him in the house. You never know what's going to happen. Jane Hoffmeyer lived next to these people who had one of those German fighter dogs, and one day that dog got loose and bit Jane on the leg. She needed fifty-three stitches and..." Agnes's voice trailed away, and Sara could hear the rumble of her father's voice in the background as he said something to her mother.

"Sara?"

"Yes, Daddy, Merry Christmas," Sara said, relieved that she wouldn't have to hear the story of Mrs. Hoffmeyer's bitten leg again.

"Are you going to come over today, Sara? Your mother is looking forward to seeing you, and it would spoil her Christmas if you weren't here with us." John's voice held a deep note of warning.

I'm not a child! Sara didn't say the words to her father. She concentrated on the tantalizing aroma of brewing coffee and decided that with this kind of service she'd be a fool not to keep Joe. That thought made her shrug the afghan tight around her shoulders. She could barely think to say, "Yes, Dad, I'm coming over. I have to get off the phone in order to get ready, though."

"Sara," her father said urgently in a dramatically lowered voice, "did you have time to get your mother something for Christmas? If you didn't, I have an extra present that you could give her. She would be very hurt if you—oh, I'm sure the roads will be fine, Sara. There was no new snow overnight, and the salt trucks were out yesterday. You shouldn't have any trouble getting here."

Sara guessed her mother had returned to the room. "Sure, Dad, I'll see you in a little while. I did get something for Mom, and for you, too, so don't worry. Bye, now." She quickly hung up the phone before he could say anything else. She frowned at it for a minute and then went into the kitchen. Joe was just emerging from the bathroom. His hair was slicked back with water, but the heavy shadow of his beard remained to give him a rakish look. Sara wasn't quite sure what to say to him; she felt awkward and rumpled.

"I didn't mean to fall asleep on you," Joe said. "I'm sorry."

He sounded so solemn. Sara couldn't read anything on his face. Her eyes skidded away and landed on the coffee maker. "I'm glad you did this," she said, pouring two cups and handing one to him.

"It's the least I could do, given the circumstances. I didn't want to interrupt your phone call to say goodbye." He sipped his coffee briefly and set it aside.

"Joe," Sara protested as he started to leave the kitchen.

"Yes?"

Yes, Sara noted, not yeah; my, but we were formal in the morning, weren't we? She shrugged uncomfortably, not remembering how she had handled this sort of awkward moment when she was dating Michael. There hadn't been any that she could recall; they lived in the dorms until they were married. Besides, this was different. Joe had kept his clothes on and slept in an armchair; he wasn't her lover. "Thanks for the presents. The sweater's wonderful."

"You're welcome." He finally smiled and his eyes thawed again.

"Why don't you let me make you some breakfast? Please. I could make waffles. My waffles are really good, not like my peach jam."

"What about your mother? Isn't she expecting you?"

"Well, how about eggs and toast, then? It'll take two minutes. Please."

The second please did it. How could he refuse when staying was all he wanted to do? Well, not all he wanted to do. There was kissing Sara, and making love with her until they were both too weak to get out of bed. "Okay," he agreed mildly, "eggs and toast. Do you want me to help?"

"Nope. Sit down. This will be your Christmas present from me. Not as nice as the sweater, I admit, but the best I can do on the spur of the moment." Joe pulled a chair from the table and watched as Sara hurriedly took eggs and milk from the refrigerator. She cooked their meal quickly, setting steaming plates on the table long before he was ready to stop watching her move around the kitchen. She could have cooked an eight-course dinner and he wouldn't have tired of watching her. "There you go. Merry Christmas, Joe."

Joe picked up his fork. "Merry Christmas, Sara." Their eyes met, and he forgot about eating. Someday, he promised himself, someday she'd make him breakfast and he wouldn't have a stiff neck from sleeping in a chair. "I'm sorry if I made things awkward with your mother."

Sara frowned. "You didn't. Roly did. Mother was worried that he might be rabid. Or mess the floor."

"Two dire possibilities to be sure. You should have told her I was here to protect you."

Sara almost missed the laughter in Joe's eyes. "Thanks, Fisher. I wouldn't rush home. I'm pretty sure Santa left you coal in your stocking." Joe gave her such a mournful hound dog look that Sara had to laugh. He grinned. Electricity ran up and down her spine.

"I'm really glad you're here this morning," she admitted. Joe looked at her for a second and then slid his fried egg onto his toast to make a hot sandwich. Sara watched the way the tendons in his hands and wrists moved. It was beautiful. His skin was tan, dusted with dark hair on his forearms. "I'm really glad," she insisted.

"I didn't want to admit it last night, but I was scared. Even after I went down to the beach. I was afraid that peaceful feeling was too fragile to survive waking up on Christmas morning without Lala. I was afraid to go to sleep. I was just sitting here, and I didn't know what to do, and then you came with your silly, jingling dog." She smiled at him. "You're good for me, Joseph Euclid Fisher."

Joe felt like he'd been electrocuted. If Sara knew the way he was feeling right now, she'd be scared all over again. But at the same time he felt a deep calm. He could wait. Sara thought he was good for her. He'd helped her. He could wait. "I was hoping you would forget that." She just grinned at him, not even realizing his heart was about to burst with love for her.

Sara knew her mother was going to call again at any moment to find out what the delay was, so she didn't try to stop Joe when he rose to leave. She held his mittens and scarf while he put on his boots and coat. He held out his hand to take them, and Sara slid his mitten over his hand as if she were dressing a child. Joe grinned and held out his other hand. She looped the scarf around his neck and then hugged him. He felt warm and solid. She wished she could make the moment last forever. His mitten came up to ruffle her hair as his arm tightened around her, pulling her close.

"Sara." His voice felt like it was clogging his throat. Slow down, his mind screeched the warning, but he paid it no mind when Sara tipped her head back. Her blue eyes darkened, her lips parted slightly, and Joe leaned over and touched them with his own. By sheer force of will he managed to hold back and keep the kiss easy, gentle. He didn't take advantage of the softness of her mouth parted beneath his. He was glad of the thick coat that protected her from the knowledge of what she was doing to his body. He pulled back long before he was ready.

Sara looked at him with a curious, confused, dazed expression. Joe smiled slightly. "If I don't leave, your mother is going to come looking for you and I'm going to be late for church. And then my mother and father and brothers and sister will all want to know why. And we aren't even under the mistletoe." He stepped back away from her and opened the door. Roly came jingling across the lawn to leap against his legs. Joe smiled at Sara and walked away. She watched until he disappeared into the woods, one hand unconsciously touching her lips.

"AMEN."

They spoke the word together, solemnly. For a moment Sara felt as if she were a child again, slightly awed by the deep note of conviction in her father's voice, always surprised by the confidence in her mother's. She watched as her father straightened up and surveyed the table. Agnes smiled into his eyes and placed her napkin on her lap. "Isn't this a marvelous Christmas?" she asked.

A smile slowly deepened on John's face. "It will be, once I carve this ham," he agreed. Sara watched him as he used a polished silver knife and meat fork to cut and serve slices of ham. He dished new potatoes and *snijboontjes*, the traditional Dutch fermented green beans, onto thin china plates edged with holly. Deep green napkins and candles decorated the table. Her father passed her a plate laden with more food than she wanted.

"Thank you." It was useless to protest. This was her mother's party; she wasn't going to spoil it. If it had been hers the plates would have been paper—no dishes to wash!—and decorated with Santa Claus or a grinning snowman. But it wasn't her party. Sara bit back a sigh and smiled at her mother. Her face felt stiff, as if she'd forced the smile once too often. "Everything looks wonderful, Mom."

"Did you like your present?"

"Yes, Mom," Sara replied for the third time. "It's beautiful. I'll wear it for good luck when I go on job interviews." The floral motif of the silk scarf was elegant and understated; the rich claret and pink would add the perfect touch to her favorite pink dress.

"Job interviews? Are you going to work?"

"I'm thinking about it," Sara answered honestly, for she hadn't enthusiastically embraced the idea yet.

"Do you need money, Sara? I could help you out. You ought to bring your papers by and I'll look them over for you. We can work out a budget for you, and I'll take care of your tax forms, too. Your mother can tell you when would be a good night for me. Sometime after the New Year, I think."

"Marcus already promised to do my taxes, Dad. He worked on them when we decided how to invest Lala's insurance money."

"I told you that man is up to no good." Agnes frowned worriedly and sipped her wine. "He's after your money. I wouldn't be one bit surprised if he tried to marry you. I knew he was up to something when he came and dragged you out of the house that day. He couldn't wait to talk to you about that insurance money.''

John patted his wife's hand. Sara protested, ''He's Michael's brother, Mom, and besides, it's his job. Michael and I bought the insurance policies from him. And anyway, I'm not getting a job because I need the money. I just need something to do.'' She concluded sadly, ''My life is so empty now that Michael and Lala are gone.''

''You could join the church choir again. I never did understand why you couldn't once you came back from Detroit. We can always use another good voice.''

Sara swallowed a lump of ham that caught in her throat and landed heavily in her stomach. She hadn't joined the choir because she had a young child and a husband to take care of, no time for two practices and three services every week. Why couldn't her parents stop pretending that she was still their little girl?

''Your mother's right, Sara. The choir meets every Tuesday and Thursday at seven. The Reverend De-Vries would be glad to have you. Your voice is as lovely as your mother's.''

Agnes rewarded John's remark with a smile. ''Yes, and there's the Women's Charity Circle. We meet on Wednesday mornings. Right now we're working on a project to send bibles to a missionary in South America.'' She chattered on about the need for their work and how Sara could help, although Sara couldn't see that she'd be doing much more than occupying a chair at endless meetings. She almost missed Agnes's next idea.

''What?''

John gave her a rather quelling look, as if to remind her not to indulge in outbursts at the dinner table. "I said," Agnes repeated patiently, "come spring, we could join the garden club."

"But, Mom, you don't do any gardening," Sara protested. It was her mother's black thumb that had gotten her started in gardening in the first place. Someone had to keep the yard from looking like a plant cemetery.

"No, I don't, but the garden club would be a nice way to get started, and we could go together."

Sara shook her head slightly. The garden club wasn't at all what she wanted. Mostly the women met for tea and practiced growing and arranging nice specimens for the plant shows. She designed landscapes. And Agnes needed lessons, not a club.

"I think that's a splendid idea," her father agreed.

"We never do anything together anymore," her mother mourned. "I know these last few weeks have been stressful for you, but I want to help. You shut me out of your life. Don't you want to spend time with me? I won't force you. All you have to do is tell me."

The look John sent Sara brooked no hesitation on her part. "Mom, I don't try to shut you out of my life. You're my mother, for goodness' sake. Of course I like to spend time with you," she argued, before she realized she was being sent on a guilt trip. By then it was too late to get off the boat, but she quickly tried to change the destination. The last thing she wanted was to join the garden club with her mother; neither of them really wanted to belong to the organization. "I want to get a job. You sent me to school to learn how to design gardens, and that's how I'd like to spend my time.

"But that doesn't mean we can't do things together, Mom," she added quickly. "In fact, you could help me choose the photos for my portfolio. You could come over for lunch some day next week. We haven't done enough things together. I didn't have any time while Lala was sick. She needed me."

"We know that, Sara," her father stated calmly. "But your mother needs you, too, and you don't understand how hard it was for her to see her only grandchild suffering. Now, how about some more ham? This is supposed to be a Christmas celebration."

"I think I'm full, Dad." Sara said. She wouldn't argue. She wouldn't spoil their holiday. She might not understand how her normally sensitive parents could be so blind about how they hurt her, but she wasn't going to act like a spoiled child and ruin their Christmas. They'd never accepted Michael or his daughter, and it was far too late to change that. Sara pasted a false smile on her face. "Maybe just a tiny little piece," she said, and handed her plate to her father.

"Wasn't the church lovely?" her mother asked. "I thought the white poinsettias were a beautiful touch."

HAPPY NEW YEAR, Sara growled to herself. The snow on the front steps was piled into a drift as high as the top of her pink cap. She attacked it with a fury, heaving it onto a rapidly growing pile, working off the frustration of having been snowbound with her parents for three days. A blizzard to start the New Year might have met with the approval of the kids who had an extended Christmas break, but it didn't meet with hers. Three days of being treated like a child. Three days of drinking tea and playing cards. She'd buried herself in putting together her portfolio and perfecting a résumé, but they were done in far too little time.

Sara dug her shovel into the snow with a muttered complaint. Three whole days cooped up in the house with her mom and dad. She loved them, but it had been about two-and-a-half days too many. She never should have given in to her mother's tears and pleas; she would have survived here just as well, maybe better.

"Three days," she grumbled and swung another full shovel at the top of the pile. The snow was getting heavier and heavier. The pile taller and taller. The snow landed near the top and rolled back down to land at Sara's feet. She scooped it up and threw it again. It rolled back to her feet. "Three whole days," she grunted as she sent the snow up once more. Even more tumbled down. "Three entire days and nights," she seethed through gritted teeth, filling her shovel with snow.

"Interesting technique," a deep voice observed.

Sara spun around and flung the whole shovelful of snow at the grin on Joseph Fisher's face. It missed. He laughed. The second scoop caught him on the chest. He yelped and stumbled back, still laughing. Sara stared. The white snow was clinging to his dark wool coat. She could feel a blush start to climb up her neck. She couldn't believe she'd just done that.

Too late, she realized Joe's intent. She was caught in the vise of his arms, the shovel dropping into the snowbank with a soundless ploop. She tried to wiggle free, but Joe was too strong. "Hi, Sara," he greeted her, his casual words a little breathless from their continuing struggle. She didn't reply except to try to slip down against his body and thus duck out from under his arms. It had worked better with Michael, who was so much taller than she. "Feeling a little hot under the collar, are you?'' The words puffed out in white clouds of frost.

"No!" Sara redoubled her efforts. Joe managed to get a mittenful of snow past her scarf, but the effort had loosened his grip and Sara escaped. Joe lunged after her and sent them both falling into the snow, their laughter mingling in one white cloud. Their eyes met and the laughter died.

"Sara?" Did she know, Joe wondered, that her eyes turned dark blue and sparkled when she laughed? Would they darken like that when he made love to her? Her cheeks were pink from the cold. He bent toward her lips, still parted with laughter.

"Ack!" Sara squawked, while Joe made a sound more like an oomph. Roly yipped excitedly and grabbed Sara's hat, clearly enjoying this human game that gave him such an advantage. His only problem had been choosing which hat to take.

"Damn dog!" Joe complained, brushing snow from his face with a damp mitten.

Sara took immediate advantage of the moment, cramming snow into his collar. "Who's hot under the collar now?" she taunted, slipping free and laughing down at him.

Joe leaped to his feet, trying to get the snow off his bare skin and to lunge after Sara simultaneously. She skittered away, dancing down the smooth surface of the plowed driveway, laughing at him. Joe was filled with delighted disbelief and a kernel of fear that this happiness might be fragile. The delight beat out the fear and he gave chase. Roly growled past the hat in his mouth and dashed in circles around Joe's ankles, hampering his attempt to catch Sara. She laughed and stayed just beyond his fingertips until they were near the end of the driveway.

"Joe?" she asked breathlessly.

He paused. "Yeah?"

"Catch!" She grabbed the tip of a snow-covered pine bough and pulled it back so that it sprang free and showered Joe with snow. Sara laughed at the stunned look on Joe's face. His cheeks and nose were red with the cold. He looked nothing like a serious-minded professor just now. Joe was grinning with devilish intent. Sara decided flight was prudent and scrambled up the bank of snow the plow had piled along the edge of the driveway.

With Joe following, Sara raced along the clods of snow, stumbling and slipping on the awkward surface. Joe's fingers closed on her scarf, but she slipped away. This wasn't going to work. She jumped down the back of the pile and tried to hurry across the smooth surface of the snow-covered front lawn. She sank to her waist. Running was impossible. Sara pushed on anyway, her arms making struggling swimming motions at the snow. Joe would sink even deeper, she thought, and turned to see.

He grabbed her and tumbled them both into the snow. "Uncle," Sara laughed breathlessly, squirming as white flakes crept under her collar and around her unprotected ears.

Joe just laughed triumphantly. "It's too late now," he chortled. Sara squeezed her eyes shut and waited for him to scrub her face with snow. Instead, she felt a warm puff of air on her face and opened her eyes to glimpse Joe's dark eyes as he bent and touched her mouth with his own. His lips scraped back and forth across her mouth before his tongue flicked out to run a heated path across her lower lip. His head pulled back. Sara blinked up at him.

A clump of snow fell from the lopsided brim of his cap and splattered on her forehead. Sara was suddenly cold. She shivered, and Joe pulled them both to their feet and led her back along their trail through the deep snow to scramble over the bank onto the flat driveway. "Look at the mess you made," she scolded. "The whole driveway needs to be reshoveled."

"The whole driveway?" Joe asked skeptically, sounding very much like an English professor, although Sara thought he bore a distinct resemblance to a snowman at the moment.

"Yes."

"And it's all my fault?"

"Yes. But I think it's very chivalrous of you to volunteer to shovel it for me."

"Haven't you heard," Joe asked as they walked back to the house, "that chivalry is dead?"

"Well, it's a good thing I have such nice neighbors then, isn't it?"

Joe had to look away from the glee in Sara's bright eyes. She was covered with snow. He wanted to kiss her again. Instead, he picked up the shovel from where it had fallen in the snowbank, forgotten in the ensuing skirmish, and called Roly to bring back Sara's hat. The black-and-white spaniel looked like a moving snowball. The hat was a blob of frozen snow. Joe handed it to Sara without comment and quickly shoveled the rest of the snow from the steps, tossing it onto the pile with apparent ease.

Sara stared at her hat and then at Joe as he worked. Even bundled in a coat he was sexy as he moved, strong and graceful. Another shudder of cold ran through her, and she turned away to get her suitcase from the car, now that the steps were cleared enough that she could get into the house. Joe paused when she returned. "I figured you'd gone somewhere to hole up for the storm," he accused with a smile.

"Mom and Dad insisted that I stay with them. I went over before the storm even got here," Sara explained. "How'd you know I was gone?"

"When the power went off I walked over to see if you were okay, or if you wanted to come over and sit around the wood stove with me. Anyway, when you didn't answer the door I checked the garage. With the car gone I figured you'd gone someplace for the duration."

"Oh." The thought of spending three days trapped with Joe in the midst of the blizzard was breathtaking. She pictured his warm, cozy kitchen; Roly on the rug in front of the wood stove, and a hot pot of soup simmering gently. His arms around her to keep her warm. "I was with Mom and Dad," she repeated, trying to banish the wayward thoughts from her head. "It was...I got my portfolio finished and a résumé typed up. Why don't you come in and tell me what you think? That way I'll know if they're really good or if I was just suffering from cabin fever."

"I've got a better idea," Joe said when Sara shivered again. "I'll finish this shoveling while you run inside and get a swimsuit, and we'll soak in the hot tub for a while. It's the perfect thing to do after a snowball fight."

"It sounds perfect, but I don't have a suit out here. I only brought winter clothes."

Joe refused to say what he was thinking, and suggested, "Wear a T-shirt."

Sara hesitated, but the thought of immersing her whole body in a lovely tub of warm, bubbling water was irresistible. She'd always liked bubble baths, and this sounded even better. "Hurry up and finish then, I'm freezing."

"Still freezing?" Joe asked a short while later. He wasn't. He was warm all over. Sara was already in the hot tub. He didn't look at her as he handed her a drink and slipped into the water across from her. He wasn't going to lose control. He wasn't going to rush her. He was going to make sensible conversation just as if he wasn't burning up.

Sara almost laughed. Freezing? After watching Joe's muscular body slip into the swirls of foamy water? He wasn't long and sleek and blond like Michael. He was compact, tan, dusky with dark hair. She wanted to touch him. She took a sip of the drink, only to have the hot buttered rum heat up her insides even more. "What are you doing, trying to drown me?"

"What?" Joe sounded bewildered, but Sara didn't look over at him.

"A girl could fall asleep with a drink like this. I feel like I'm in heaven. This is wonderful."

"Good." Joe sipped his own toddy and wished he could think of something interesting to say. "So, you spent the blizzard with your parents. That sounds nice." The edge of wistfulness in Joe's voice was faint. He wasn't about to admit that his normal self-reliant independence had vanished. Three days of isolation should have been a satisfactory ending to the busy holiday season. Instead, he'd spent his time pacing from window to window wondering where Sara was and how long it would be until he saw her again.

"Well," Sara hedged, some protective instinct making her hesitate to say anything bad about her family. "Maybe it was better than being snowed in all alone, but I was sure glad when they opened the roads today. My parents tend to treat me like I was still a kid."

"I suppose that's fairly typical," Joe observed.

"Maybe," Sara agreed reluctantly. "But it does get tiresome. My mother wants us to spend more time together, but I don't see how I'll stand it. If she would just be my friend instead of my mother! I need somebody to talk to, but with her I can never mention Michael or Lala."

"Why not?" Joe asked, his curiosity piqued. "Didn't they approve of the marriage?"

"It wasn't Michael. They didn't approve of any marriage. I don't think they wanted to share me with anyone else. And it proved that I was grown up and didn't need them anymore. I used to think it was just empty-nest syndrome, but lately I wonder. You know, they wouldn't come to the hospital to see Lala when she was sick? They would invite me to dinner."

"Maybe they thought you needed a little time to be away from the strain."

"You have to be the most generous man on the face of this earth," Sara said with a laugh. "How about this? In their photo albums they have hundreds of pictures of me and only three with Michael, and that's including the one where his head is cut off. And there are maybe ten of Lala. She was their only grandchild." Sara's voice became strained. "How can you explain that?"

"You're more photogenic?" Joe teased, only to feel like the world's biggest heel when Sara's face crumpled. He surged across the hot tub and caught Sara in his arms. "Please don't cry, honey, I'm sorry. I shouldn't make fun. I can't explain it. My parents were more than ready to treat me like an adult, to have an empty nest. Of course by the time I left home there were already a bunch of grandchildren. Maybe that made it easier for them. They moved to a little house and said, whoa, we've already played the parenting game. You want to have kids, great, but don't expect us to baby-sit. Which is only fair."

Sara had pulled out of his embrace and moved to sit beside him. The difference between their families intrigued her. "My parents really did have it different."

Joe moved back to his own seat and sipped his drink, trying to hide his dismay at her rejection. He frowned. "It doesn't make sense. If they didn't want an empty nest, why didn't they welcome Lala? She was obviously a wonderful kid. Hell, for all my parents' talk, you can hardly walk through their house it's so cluttered up with pictures of the grandkids. They're going to have to move back to a big house just to hang up all the pictures!"

"That's what I'm saying! It doesn't make sense."

"Unless..." Joe frowned into his drink and idly took a sip as he thought it through. "Okay, let's say your parents want to keep you as a child. Now what would that accomplish? Are they afraid of getting old?" he asked, poised for triumph.

"No."

"No?" Sara shook her head. "Well then, why? I can't think of any other reason why they would want to keep you dependent but wouldn't welcome Lala. What other reason is there for a time warp?"

When had she thought about time warps recently? Sara frowned. When she had tried to make love with poor Marcus in order to recapture the past. "To keep everything the same, safe and happy. The future can be awfully scary sometimes."

The distant note in Sara's voice made Joe look at her intently. "So you think your parents are scared of the future and trying to hide in the happiness of the past? Was the past really that great or is the future really that frightening?"

"Maybe the past was nice for them. They eloped, you know, when they found out I was coming. My mother's parents disowned her. I only saw my grandparents twice in my life, and both times it was when they were forced to acknowledge our presence in some social situation. The first years were rough on Mom and Dad. Instead of college, Mom had me and Dad got a job. It turned out okay, though. Dad bought into the car dealership, and he's a partner now. But I don't see how the past was any better than the present."

"So they had to get married, huh? It'd be more usual if they'd been eager to get rid of you so they could get a divorce. The old staying together for the children's sake trip."

A light flared in Sara's eyes. "What if Mom thinks Dad married her only because he had to? Then if there wasn't a reason to stay married, me, she'd lose him. She's the one who wants me to be a little girl. Dad just wants her happy. He's very protective of her." The light in her eyes faded. "But how could she doubt that he really loves her? If she asked for the moon, he'd give her the moon and stars."

"Her parents stopped loving her," Joe observed. "That's got to change a person. You kind of take your parents' love for granted. They have to love you because you're their child. If they can stop, just about anybody can.''

Sara slumped back in her seat and stared at him. ''You're brilliant,'' she observed. ''Absolutely brilliant. I've tried to figure out my parents for ten years, and you do it in ten minutes.''

''We've been in here longer than that, and what's more, you figured it out. I was just sitting here asking dumb questions.'' But Joe was grinning. It felt damn good to have Sara think he was brilliant. ''I'm glad we worked that all out, but it was hardly the relaxing soak I thought it'd be. Why don't we get out of here now and take a look at that portfolio of yours?''

''Okay.'' Sara stood up in the center well of the hot tub and found herself two inches from total contact with Joe. She swayed forward. He was as firm and solid as she imagined.

''Careful,'' he said, catching her elbow and holding her steady, two inches away from him. ''It can be slippery in here. Just step up on the seat to get out.''

Sara felt like a fool as she turned and climbed out of the hot tub. She grabbed the big towel Joe had laid out for her and wrapped it around herself protectively. ''I'll change in the bathroom,'' she said and scurried away to hide.

Joe watched her go with mixed pleasure and regret. She had great legs. Short women weren't supposed to have great legs, but Sara sure as hell did. And he doubted she had any idea just how sexy she looked in a soaking wet teal-blue T-shirt. It clung to every curve and dip on her perfect body. Lord, he'd almost exploded into a fireball when she leaned up against him in the tub. He'd wanted to strip off the wet shirt and make love to her right then. But he could wait. He hoped.

CHAPTER SEVEN

HE COULD WAIT, Joe repeated to himself as he covered the hot tub and pulled on a pair of faded jeans and a ragged sweatshirt with the collar slashed three inches down the chest. He didn't need to dress up, he was waiting, going slow, not trying to impress Sara, not attempting to seduce her. He was waiting. Patiently.

Which would be a hell of a lot easier if she didn't look so damned good, he thought as Sara stepped from the bathroom. Her blond curls were frizzy from the humidity of the hot tub; he wanted to feel their silkiness around his fingers as he caressed them smooth. Her cheeks were flushed pink, and her eyes were big and dark, as blue as the lake. Her lower lip was caught between her teeth. She was probably still embarrassed because she fell against him, which only proved how necessary it was that he wait until she was ready. So he'd wait. Patiently.

"Are you hungry? I should've asked before we got in the hot tub."

Sara smiled, a little relieved that Joe couldn't read the thoughts that had swarmed in her head while she got dressed. She was hungry, but not for food; this appetite hadn't been tempted in the three years since Michael's death. "Mom made me eat lunch before I left. I practically had to tie Dad up to keep him from coming along to shovel." Sara shook her head in affectionate exasperation. She did love her parents in spite of everything.

"How about another drink?"

"No, thanks. One was enough."

"Do you want anything?"

"To show you my portfolio."

Joe rumpled her curls, unable to keep his hands to himself. "You're an impudent little thing, aren't you?"

"Impudence implies that I owe you respect...." Sara started to challenge him, but her voice trailed off when he slung his arm across her shoulder and steered her toward one of the leather couches in the living room. How could she talk when his hip was rubbing against her own, nudging her with every step he took? Joe didn't seem to notice that she left the sentence unfinished. He guided her to the couch and sat beside her, so close their legs touched. Sara looked into his dark eyes, but he was staring at her mouth. She thought he was going to kiss her, but he suddenly seemed to jerk away.

"So, let's take a look at your portfolio," he urged with false heartiness.

Sara couldn't decide if Joe was attracted to her or if it was her imagination. He'd initiated the kiss outside, but he seemed to be pulling away now, although he was sitting so close. Was he or wasn't he interested? Did the college offer any continuing education classes in the fine art of flirting? She desperately needed one. She suddenly realized she was staring at Joe and jumped up to get her portfolio. She desperately needed something!

She settled for distracting chatter and a chasm of leather between her and Joe's taut thigh. "I'm not real sure about the order of these pictures yet. I'm not going in a strictly chronological order. I was afraid that if I started with the best I would lose the impact by going steadily downhill, but..."

"But if you start too low, no one will ever get to the end," Joe concluded, thinking it was a balancing act, just like loving Sara.

"Exactly," Sara agreed, passing him the portfolio. She watched the expressions on his face as he paged through the pictures, biting her lip when he examined the pictures with a little frown making a crease between her eyebrows. "Well?" she demanded when he was finally done.

"I had no idea you were so talented. These pictures are beautiful. The gardens are beautiful." Joe closed the portfolio and read over her résumé. He looked over at her with one of his crooked smiles. "It's a lucky thing for me that you can't see what passes for my garden. You'd never speak to me again."

"I could help you pick out some new plants," Sara offered.

"I don't know. I think the yard's too shady and the soil's too sandy. It's pretty hopeless."

"There are all kinds of beautiful plants that grow out here. Look at what's in the woods and around other people's houses. We could put in some trilliums for the spring, or daffodils, and a couple of dog-woods, maybe, down by the creek...."

Were they a we? She probably didn't mean it like he wished she did. "I don't own the creek, your aunt and uncle do. I have a narrow little lot squeezed in here. How did you think I could afford to live on the lake?

I'm only an associate professor, not president of the college."

Sara bit back a sigh. "If you ever want any expert advice..."

"I'll know who to call. You're good, damned good." Joe flipped through the portfolio again, stopping at the photograph of a large weeping cherry tree standing alone in a landscape of weathered gray rock and lush greenery. Almost hidden beneath the cascades of pink blossoms was a boulder, sized so that a woman could lean against it while a man kissed her. At least that was the image that popped into Joe's head. He could see Sara leaning against the boulder, the cherry tree weeping delicate pink petals as he leaned forward and pressed against her softness, parted her pink lips and kissed her deeply.

Hell! That's exactly what he was putting himself through by being too stupid to control his own body. Joe set Sara's portfolio on the leather seat and slid down to sit on the floor, leaning back against the couch. Waiting would be easier if he wasn't drowning in Sara's eyes. It was purely accidental that he ended up with his head resting on her knee. Purely accidental.

Roly saw his opportunity and came padding across the room to lie with his head in Joe's lap, available for caressing. Joe obliged by rumpling the dog's soft ears with a distracted hand. He'd had no idea Sara was so talented. How could he feel both irritation because her late husband hadn't encouraged her to use her skills more fully, and distress that she was talented? Or was it fear that her talent wouldn't leave enough room in her life for him? He'd never hesitated to date highly intelligent, capable, talented women. And it never mattered that they weren't always available, that they didn't have room in their lives for him. But Sara was different. With her he wanted everything. Marriage, babies, everything.

He froze when he felt her fingers stroke through his hair. He had to force himself to relax again, to lean casually against her leg just as if every nerve in his body hadn't leapt to attention, demanding equal time. Face it, he might want everything, but he'd take whatever he could get. That it wasn't everything did matter, but he could wait. He didn't want Sara as an appendage, merely a body in his bed. He wanted her whole: her intelligence, her spirit, her skill, and yes, her body, too.

Joe was doing it to her again, Sara thought—moving away and then leaning against her, giving signals that she couldn't read. Sara consoled herself by touching his hair, smoothing it with her palm, combing it with her fingers, letting it caress her hand like she wished he would caress her body. His hair was pure brown, without red or gold highlights, a deep rich color; it slipped silkily through her fingers. She didn't notice that her breath had become shallow until Joe cranked his shoulders around and caught her eyes. Suddenly her lungs were empty; electricity was stretching between them again. Joe's eyes were dark, deep, melting, capturing her own.

She sucked in a deep breath as he turned, displacing Roly, and knelt before her, resting his forearms on her knees, looking into her eyes. She leaned forward. He leaned against her, used his hands to part her thighs and knelt between them, pressing against the edge of the couch. The heated flow of her blood started where his hands touched her legs, pounded in her ears, tingled in her lips and breasts, and centered deep in her abdomen. After a million years he leaned forward and rubbed his lips across hers, breathlessly gentle, then again with a little more pressure. And again, and again.

Sara moaned and struggled to move forward on the couch, to press her body tightly against the lean muscular hardness of Joe. His hands ran up her thighs, tripping sparks and flames along the way, up her hips, to span her waist and slide up her slender ribs and stop with his thumbs pressed into the soft undersides of her breasts. He eased her forward until the tense points of her breasts skimmed his chest. She hated the thickness of her sweater, the padding of his sweatshirt. Her hands rested on his shoulders, her thumbs sliding together where his collar was slit to rub in the crisp hair on his chest.

Joe's hands caught her cheeks and cupped under her jaw to hold her while he kissed her again, his tongue parting her lips and delving deeply into her mouth. He moaned and tilted his head, moving to gain greater access to her mouth. Sara kissed him back, responding to the movements of his tongue. Her thighs quivered where Joe pressed against the tender inner flesh. Her breasts thrust forward against him. Her whole body hummed with passionate energy. She wanted him. She wanted his kisses, his hands on her breasts, his skin against hers, his mouth on her tight nipples, his body inside her own, moving against her, moving with her.

He pulled back and drew in a shuddering breath. His hands moved to cup her breasts through her sweater, his eyes glittering as he watched her hard nipples peak the clinging fabric. Sara felt her breath catch at his excitement. She placed her hand against his cheek. Joe turned his head and kissed her palm, his eyes watching as his hands moved to slide up under her sweater, pushing it up, baring her breasts. His tongue slid up her finger and then he sucked it into his mouth. His mouth moved on to the next finger while his eyes devoured her breasts. His fingers started to skim the satin skin but stopped as his mouth moved to the next finger and encountered the barrier of her rings.

The barrier of her rings. The sharp edges of her diamond, the smooth hard gold of her wedding band. The wedding band Michael had placed on her finger so long ago. The tiny insurmountable barrier of her rings. Confusion warred with frustration as Joe pulled back, drew her thighs closed, rested his forehead on her knees while his shoulders heaved with his hard breathing. Her fingers dug into his shoulders but they neither pushed him away nor pulled him back against her.

"Oh, damn, Sara, I'm sorry. I told myself to wait. I know you're not ready for this yet, but as soon as I touch you my intentions fly all to hell. I'm sorry." Joe's voice was thick and rough, muffled against her thighs. He pulled back, straightening and moving away from her. His face was dark.

His eyes avoided hers. It was on the tip of her tongue to ask how he knew she wasn't ready, but she didn't speak the words. She knew his response might very well be to make love to her. And she was afraid he might be right. "I wish..." she started, but her voice cracked and she stopped.

He'd lost control. She was so perfect, so passionate. He could still feel her, her mouth responding to his, her hands touching him, her breasts peaking, her thighs trembling against him. A man could die for a woman like Sara. Joe searched her face, read the confusion and hurt in her eyes. He felt worse. "Don't worry, Sara, I love you. I can wait for you." The words were out too soon. The confusion in her eyes blossomed. And he wasn't the least bit sure he could wait for her. His body was about to throb itself apart.

Joe forced himself to ignore his needs as he saw Sara safely home. He kissed her cheek at the door, but her eyes stayed enigmatic. Did she already regret their lovemaking? Had he left it too late or was he a fool? Would loving her ease the pain of the past and welcome her into the splendor of the future? Joe didn't know. He tried a cold shower, an exhausting run, a relaxing soak in the hot tub and a distracting novel, but nothing could erase Sara from his mind or answer the questions he had.

Sara was in much the same state, not knowing what was happening to her. Somehow she knew that making love with Joe would be different than making love with Michael. Joe would be passionate, fulfill her more completely, because he wouldn't be afraid of hurting her. Was that betraying Michael and the joy he had brought her? They'd been happy; she'd been content. Was this just the infatuated throb of hormones long in the need of release? Was she glad Joe had stopped? Relieved? Regretful? Angry? She didn't know. She couldn't relax, couldn't sleep.

She still felt jittery and confused the next morning when her mother called. She wished she could confide in her mother and seek her advice, but she couldn't. Agnes called several times a day, just to chat, but Sara couldn't tell her what had happened. She found it was almost impossible to tolerate her mother's worries and fears now that she thought she understood what motivated them. It seemed so silly for Agnes to be dominated by the past and her ridiculous fear of losing John. Sara wanted to scold her mother, to tell her to grab hold of what she still had and rejoice in it rather than fearing what she might lose. That love could be lost was only too real for Sara. Sara listened to her mother's chatter and gave snappish answers until she unexpectedly heard the answer to her problems.

Uncle Corny had called her father the night before, just to talk. As Agnes told Sara, "They have an empty room in the condo and said you're welcome to come down and visit. The weather's been beautiful. Your Uncle Corny said Gert has a lovely tan and that he feels great. He was making his silly jokes, you know how he is, about the sun aging some people, but making him feel younger. You should think about visiting them. It would make them very happy and you certainly owe them at least that much after living in their house for so long."

Despite her immediate resentment for her mother's attitude, Sara found the idea immensely appealing. If there was anyone in the world to whom she could tell her problems, it was Aunt Gert. And it would give her space, a reprieve from the temptation of running over to Joe's and demanding that he make love to her just so she would know how she'd react and could stop her endless speculating. "You know, Mom, I think I'll do just that. I wonder how soon Aunt Gert would want me."

"Oh, right away, I'm sure. I can't tell you how glad I am that you're going. You need someone to take care of you, and if you won't let me, at least I can trust

Gert and Corny. I just hate having you stay out in that
house all by yourself. You can be so foolish, letting in
stray dogs and whatnot. Why don't I call her for you?
And your father could make a plane reservation. He
knows just what to do. I'll call Gert and then talk to
him and call you back in a few minutes."

It was hopeless to tell her mother that she was a
grown woman fully capable of calling her aunt and the
airline herself. Maybe Aunt Gert could tell her how to
convince her mother. At the moment it was easier to
just agree, so Sara did. She left for Florida three days
later.

"LIKE MOTHER, like daughter," murmured Gert Van
Dyke, peering over her sunglasses at Sara, who was
stretched on a chaise longue at the side of the tur-
quoise pool sparkling in the southern Florida sunshine.

Sara frowned as she set aside the tube of sunscreen
after slathering another coat on her poor red nose. It
still hadn't recovered from her first day in the sun
when she had walked with Uncle Corny on the beach.
She'd just told Aunt Gert about Joe's theory regarding her mother's desire to keep her dependent. "She
clings to the past so desperately that she's wasting the
life she has left," Sara had concluded in sad frustration. Her frown deepened, and Gert pushed her sunglasses back up her nose, hiding from her niece's
wrath.

"Just what is that supposed to mean?" Sara demanded. "I'm not like my mother." She wasn't really
angry, just confused.

"How long has Michael been dead?" Gert asked rhetorically. "Three years. And you're still wearing his ring."

"Two and a half years," Sara interrupted defensively, not wanting to talk about wearing her ring.

"Closer to three."

"Two and a half."

"Either way," Gert continued defiantly, "you aren't still mourning him."

"I am. He was never really gone as long as I had Lala. She was just like him."

"No, Sara, that isn't the same thing. I know, Lala was like Michael, but a daughter isn't a husband in any way, shape or form. And I'm not saying you are or ought to be through mourning Lala." She paused to sip her tall frosted glass of fruit punch and consider her words. Sara listened silently, waiting to hear how she was like her mother, afraid of what her aunt might make her see.

"And I suppose, for that matter, that you'll always miss Michael with a part of yourself. But you aren't still mourning him. If you were, you wouldn't have been so distressed when you told me Joseph Fisher's in love with you. I saw the look in your eyes. You're glad he's in love with you and that makes you feel confused and guilty. If you were still in love with Michael you would have told me a hundred things that he would think or say or ought to see, but it's Joe who should see the sunset and Joe who would like the recipe for the seafood gumbo and Joe who would know what books Hemingway wrote when he was on the Keys. Frankly I think you're falling in love with Joe."

"Aunt Gert!" That was further than Sara had allowed herself to think.

"You're not still in love with Michael," Gert insisted.

"That's not the same thing as being in love with someone else."

"No, but don't you think there must be something special between you? Chemistry, unless you prefer love at first sight." Gert ignored Sara's protest. "That's how it was with me and Corny. I saw him and I knew he was the only man for me. Even his stupid jokes weren't enough to stop me from loving him. Although I must say, I did think I could break him of the habit eventually. It's the same with you and Joe."

"I don't see how. The first time I saw him he was helping Lala fly her kite and loving him was the absolutely last thing I was thinking," Sara said curtly, not wanting to think of those last days yet involuntarily remembering how wonderful Joe had been.

"But you told me you went over to his house on Thanksgiving. You weren't in any shape to be crashing a family dinner without some good reason."

"I was curious. His family is huge. And I had the pumpkin pie, and I told you all this before."

"Yeah, you were curious and you had the extra pie. They sound like excuses to me, Sara. There was already something special between you."

"Lala had just died. I wasn't falling in love," Sara insisted.

"Why? Would it be so bad? Your problem is that you feel guilty for not still mourning Michael. So you insist that you are. And that's how you're like your mother. You're clinging to the love that's gone and sacrificing the love that could be. For what?"

Sara sipped her fruit punch and didn't answer. Maybe, just maybe, Aunt Gert was right about Michael. But about Joe?

"I'm not trying to insist that you fall in love with Joe Fisher. It could, after all, just be a fling, a way of coping with the loss of your child. Maybe you need to reassert your sexuality and he's available, but it doesn't sound that way from here."

It didn't sound right to Sara, either. She wasn't using Joe. She lo...cared about him very much. "Well..."

"Just think about it, dear. I'm not asking for any commitments. Although I will say that Joe's not a half-bad man to fall for. If I was a few years younger and free, I might just go after him myself."

"Aunt Gert!"

"Tell me you don't think he's sexy. A little short, maybe, but that's not something two shrimps like us have to worry about. I've seen him on the beach in the summer and he's not bad at all. Not bad at all."

Sara couldn't restrain a giggle. She would never have said Aunt Gert was sedate in her retirement, but this was going a little far!

"You don't think so?" Gert demanded defensively, but with an undercurrent of humor. She might admire Joe, just like she admired Erroll Flynn and Robert Redford, but no one could ever replace Corny, whose body she knew as well as her own.

Sara cocked her head to the side, pretending to consider. It didn't take any thinking to know she thought Joe was sexy as hell. His athletic body, the intriguing texture of the hair on his chest. How she wanted to feel it rubbing against her breasts. She'd seen him in his swimming suit with the little trail of hair leading down from his navel. And then there were his shiny eyes and his dark hair that always looked a touch rumpled. "I suppose he's passable," she admitted grudgingly, teasing Gert.

Gert snorted derisively. "And I suppose you're not blushing, just suffering from instant sunburn."

"Okay, maybe I do think Joe is a little bit sexy."

"So you have good taste after all," Gert allowed condescendingly. "In that case I'll bring you another glass of punch." She got to her feet and picked up their empty glasses, calling over her shoulder, "After all, we'll need something tall and cold if we keep thinking about these handsome men."

"Are you talking about me again?" Corny asked as he stepped onto the patio carrying an armload of seashells.

"Yes, dear," Gert replied demurely, winking at Sara. She went past the screening row of potted plants and through the sliding doors into the condo to get their refills.

"Let me show you my treasures," Corny said as he eagerly began to display the shells he had found on his daily walk along the shore. Sara had gone with him on her first day in Florida and had been surprised to learn he walked nearly five miles a day, stopping sometimes to dig in the sand to find the buried shells or to talk with folks he met. Sara hadn't had the stamina to accompany him again, but now she oohed and aahed over the shells.

"Knock-knock."

"Who's there?"

"Conch."

"Conch who?"

"Conch you just say, come in?"

"Ugh!" Sara rolled her eyes. "That is so corny."

"At your service, my dear."

"I brought you a glass of punch, Corny," Gert said, handing it to him.

"Thank you," Corny said before he sipped it. "Mmm, you used pineapple juice this time, didn't you?"

"A little. And orange juice, too," Gert replied.

"I like this better than when you put in that darned grapefruit juice. If you want me to pucker up all you have to do is ask."

"Yes, dear."

Sara giggled.

"I'll yes, dear, you," Corny threatened. "Knock-knock."

"Who's there?" Sara answered when Gert failed to reply.

"Don't encourage him," Gert moaned, holding her head as if she had a migraine headache.

Corny snorted at his wife and turned to Sara. "Shell."

"Shell who?" Sara shrugged apologetically at her aunt.

"Shell we?"

"What?" demanded Gert. "That's not very good, Corny. I've heard you do much better."

"Shall we elect Gert to make our lunch?" Corny cackled gleefully at his wife's spluttering reaction and Sara laughed, too.

"I'll help," she offered but Gert shook her head.

"Corny will help," she ordered. "And you'll rest." Corny followed his wife into the condo, still chuckling to himself over the look on her face. And Sara remained beside the pool, soaking up the heat of the

Florida sun. Was she hiding in the past like her mother? Was she in love with Joe? She didn't know. But later when she went inside, she slipped off her wedding ring and diamond and tucked them into a safe pocket of her cosmetics bag.

"SO, JOE, my little bachelor brother, you got a hot date tonight?"

Joe laughed at Susan's avid curiosity. "Nope. Sara's still in Florida."

"That's good. Well, maybe for you it's bad, but for me it's good because I need a special favor from my favorite brother."

He should have known. If he would just engage his brain before he opened his mouth and let the whole world know he was sitting home alone on a Friday night. "What do you want now?"

"Don't sound so abused, Joey. No one's making you help me."

"I didn't say I would yet."

"Please? I want to tell David I'm pregnant again. That's not the kind of conversation you can have with three kids at the dinner table. I thought I'd take him out to a nice restaurant and break the news gently. You know how he gets about zero population growth. It's going to take him a few minutes to get used to the idea of being the father of four."

"Maybe you should have restrained yourselves."

"Joe," Susan complained. "Come on, what are you going to do tonight? Sit home and watch the Friday night soaps? You can do that here. I'll make it an early evening so you still have time to go hit the bars and get a lady for the night."

It was Joe's turn to complain. "Susan, I don't need a lady for the night. Sara'll be back in just a few days."

"Really? What about her suntan?"

"What about it?"

"Won't it fade?"

"Probably. What's that got to do with my need for her in bed? Or is that how you thought birth control worked? You've been trying the tanning booths instead of the pill? No wonder you've got another bun in the basket," Joe teased.

"Jo-ey. Why are you always so mean to me? It's not my fault your girlfriend wanted a perpetual suntan."

"Oh. That was Olivia. She's still in California. She's probably married to a beach bum by now. Sara went to Florida to visit her aunt and uncle. She was here at Thanksgiving, remember?"

"Oh, your little stray. Yeah, I remember her. She went to Florida, huh? Poor Joey."

"Why do you say that? Just because I love her doesn't mean I can't live without her for a few days."

"Yeah, well, it's too bad she doesn't love you enough to wait and take her vacation when you can get off from school."

"Come on, Suse, if you could get to Florida now, you'd go."

"Not without David."

Joe pulled a face at the phone.

"I just hope you don't get hurt. You're so hopeless about picking women, Joe. Bimbos and strays and..."

"Sara's not a stray."

"Don't be mad at me. I only want you to be happy, and I don't know how falling in love with some woman who's going to run off to Florida is going to make you happy. You ought to settle down and get married. You know you love children, and you're really good with them. That's why I want you to baby-sit tonight. Please, Joey. I'll do something for you someday."

"I'll believe that when I see it."

"I knew I could count on you. Thanks, Joe. If you can come by at about four-thirty, I'll pick David up from work and go from there. I'm sure the kids will be no trouble, and I'll set out something for you to make for dinner. You're the best little brother I have."

"I'm your only little brother and I don't know why I'm letting you talk me into this."

"Because I'm your big sister. It's your fraternal duty."

"You can take your fraternal duty and..."

"I'll see you at four-thirty, Joe. And bring along a book or something, it might be late."

"Whoa, what happened to making it an early evening?"

"Jo-ey! You wouldn't want to deny me the chance to go dancing with Davie before I get too fat to put my arms around him. I've got to go if I'm going to be ready on time. See ya, Joe."

Joe listened to the dial tone for a minute. How did Susan always manage to turn him into a malleable fool? Fraternal duty, hell! What about sisterly duty? There wasn't even a nice Latinate word for it. But he would do it for Susan because with Sara in Florida he didn't have anything better to do.

He had stiffened into an uncomfortable pretzel from lying on his sister's couch when he woke up to the sound of the toddler crying. Joe damned his sister and his fraternal duties and her early evenings and

damned couch that wasn't shaped for sleeping as he
ran up the stairs two at a time. He flipped on the light
and blinked against its glare before he slipped into
Junior's bedroom. "Hey, kid, what's wrong?" he
crooned, going to the almost-three-year-old's bedside.

"I want my Mo-o-ommy," wailed Junior loud
enough to wake the dead, although the two older kids
slept through it. Or at least weren't coming to his aid.

"Hey, Junior, it's me. It's your Uncle Joey," Joe
comforted, touching a cool forehead and cheek. "Did
you have a bad dream?"

"Mo-o-o-o-ommy," Junior sobbed. "Mo-o-o-om-
mee-ee-ee." Without ceasing the hiccuping sobs,
Junior climbed to his feet and held out his arms. Joe
wrapped his arms around the little boy and cradled
him to his chest, rocking him gently even after he felt
the wet flannel pajamas soaking through his sweatshirt. He silently cursed fraternal duty and swore that
he'd never fall for Susan's manipulative tricks again.
Early evening, hah! Even the bars were closed for the
night by now.

"Take it easy, Junior, it's okay. It's just a little
dampness, kid. We'll get you cleaned up and back in
bed before you know it." Joe wished someone would
tuck him into a nice soft bed that didn't leave him
feeling like he'd been tied in a knot. But there wasn't
anyone to do that, so he filled the bathtub with a couple of inches of water and gave Junior a quick rinse
before he wrestled his limp arms and legs into a dry
pair of pajamas. Junior watched him through heavy-
lidded wet eyes.

Hefting Junior's weight onto one hip, Joe searched
through the closets for fresh sheets for the small bed.

He couldn't find anything and finally made do with a sheet for Susan and David's king-sized waterbed. Let Susan worry about it in the morning. Fraternal duty only extended so far. Junior, for all his bawling for his mommy, was sound asleep by the time Joe tucked him under the makeshift covers.

Had he really thought he wanted kids? Joe touched Junior's soft chubby cheek with one finger and thought, hell, yes, he did. But only if he could sleep in his own bed with his own wife. He took the soiled sheets down to the laundry, added his damp sweatshirt to the load and turned on the machine before he went back to collapse again on the uncomfortable sofa. The word that ran through his head would have made five-year-old Mark cry out, I'm gonna tell my mom, I'm gonna tell, you said a naughty word. Joe yawned and scrunched his fingers through his hair. Where the hell was Susan, anyway?

Her Friday night had to have been better than his. Baby-sitting was okay when the kids were awake, but once they were in bed the evening stretched out long and empty. Not that it would have been much better at home. Sara was in Florida whether he was here or home. And he missed her.

He missed her, and he was afraid he'd blown it. She'd once accused him of getting in the way of her grieving by making her forget. If making her laugh was bad, what was making love to her? She'd wanted him just as much. Her body's reaction was undeniable. Her eyes had gotten confused and hurt when he had stopped. Hell, she probably would refuse to even talk to him anymore. Maybe Susan was right; maybe he did pick impossible women. He sure as hell had rushed it, telling her he loved her. That was the real clincher.

But maybe she'd give him another chance. She'd responded. She'd started it by petting his hair. He'd just have to try harder to control himself, to wait until she was ready. It wouldn't be easy with his body threatening to explode every time he touched her, but he could do it. She was worth the effort, worth the pain, worth the wait. If only she thought he was worth having, if only she gave him another chance.

He wished she wasn't grieving. Not just that he hated to see her hurting, although he did, but he wished, with pure selfishness, that she wasn't grieving. It was so difficult to compete with her sorrow. He needed to find a way to help her, a way to ease her pain and protect her. He still wanted to believe that lovemaking could be the answer, a way to forget the past and welcome the future, but that might be more selfishness on his part. He was more than ready to make love with her.

He shifted the laundry into the dryer and imagined making love to Sara. Imagined her eyes turning soft and dark. Imagined her body writhing against his. Imagined her legs wrapped around his hips. Imagined her fingers stroking...

"Hi, Joey! How'd everything go? Did the boys behave themselves? Where's your shirt?" Susan smiled happily and hugged him tightly. "David's coming. We had to go back and get his car from the parking lot at work. Thanks for watching the boys. You're a sweetie. I'll bet you want to get home and go to bed."

Joe gave her a crooked smile. "I take it zero population growth bit the big one?"

"Yup. David wants a girl as much as I do. The boys were okay?"

Joe plucked his still-damp sweatshirt from the dryer and slung it over his shoulder. "Junior wet his bed, but otherwise everything was fine. And you're right, I'm gonna go home and crash. You want me to wait until David gets home?"

"Nope, he's here now. And I want to be alone with him, if you don't mind."

"Have fun."

"We will."

Which was more than he could say for himself, Joe thought gloomily, closing his jacket as he left his sister's house. But somewhere between her door and his bed he remembered that Sara would be home that afternoon and everything felt a little better. It would work out. He loved her. She was the first woman he had ever really loved; fate wouldn't be so cruel as to break his heart now.

CHAPTER EIGHT

SARA PEERED through the small oval window at the modern brick-and-glass sprawl of the Kent County Airport, waiting until the covered walkway extended to the plane and the first-class passengers disembarked. Her parents would be waiting, her mother worrying that Sara might have missed the plane, her father being reassuring. Sara bit her lip and wondered about her trip to Florida. Was the measure of peace and happiness she'd found simply an interlude of unreality? Would her pain be waiting with her parents like something she'd forgotten to pack? She didn't push to beat the crowd but waited until the aisle was clear of people struggling with the overhead luggage carriers before she left the plane.

"Sara!" Her mother enfolded her in a fierce **hug** while her father took her carry-on bag off her shoulder. "Oh, baby, I missed you so much. It feels like you've been gone forever."

Sara smiled and hugged her mother. "I missed you, too, Mom. You ought to go to Florida. You'd love it. It was so warm and sunny, and Aunt Gert and Uncle Corny's condo is right on the beach. You can hear the waves at night. It was lovely."

"You look tired. Was the flight rough? Oh, and your nose! All those freckles. Didn't you use the sunscreen I gave you?"

"The flight was great, and I did use the sunscreen. I don't mind the freckles. It looked from the plane like you've gotten a little more snow." Sara kissed her mother's cheek and gave her father a brief hug before letting him lead the way to the luggage carousel.

"Well, it didn't snow all week, not until this morning," Agnes replied. "I was so worried that they'd cancel your flight. It wouldn't be so bad if you had to stay in Florida an extra day, but what if you had gotten trapped in some airport between there and here? Luckily it stopped after a couple of hours. I'm so glad you're safely home. Your father kept telling me not to worry, but I couldn't help myself."

Sara nodded. "Dad, you really ought to take Mom down there. Uncle Corny said to tell you to come and visit. He thinks you should take an early retirement and move down there. He can get you a good deal on a condo."

"He's been nagging me about that ever since I mentioned the possibility of retiring at fifty-five. Corny will still think of me as his baby brother when I'm ninety and he's a hundred."

"We're not ready to retire yet. And we're certainly not going to move away from here while you still need us. Sometimes I just don't understand your brother, John," Agnes complained. "Here come the suitcases, dear. Now you point yours out so your father can get it for you. Oh dear, look at that. What a shame! I hope *your* suitcase didn't pop open. I never liked those new ones you got."

"They're strong enough, Mom. Michael took them everywhere, and they never once popped open. He knew how to choose luggage. It's one of the prerequisites for surviving as an athlete. There it is, the blue one. Safe and sound.''

''No, no, let your father get it. He's still young and strong. I don't know what all this talk about retirement is, anyway. We're far too young yet.''

''That's the idea, Aggie, to retire while we're still young enough to enjoy it. I think it might be fun. I don't know that I'd want to spend Christmas in Florida, but January and February? It could be very nice.''

''Yes, but what about Sara? Are we just going to abandon her? She still needs us. It's too soon for us to retire and move across the country.''

''You know what's funny, Mom? I applied for a job while I was in Florida. I took along my résumé and portfolio to show Aunt Gert and Uncle Corny, just to get their opinion, you know, and one of Corny's golf partners knows a man who was interviewing and he got me an appointment.'' What Sara didn't tell her mother was that she had applied only to work the kinks out before she applied for real. And that Mr. Fromes, while not giving her a definite answer, had implied that she had two strikes against her—no previous working experience and unfamiliarity with the Florida climate and flora. Her chances of getting the job were slim, although he'd liked her work and suggested that she take a course in the native horticulture and then come to see him again. If she was serious about working in Florida he might be able to help.

''You'd move to Florida? You know Aunt Gert and Uncle Corny don't live there year-round. What about summer? Gert says it gets awfully hot and humid. I hope you haven't made a commitment without talking to us first. You shouldn't make these big decisions all by yourself, Sara.'' Agnes frowned, wrapping herself in her coat before going out to the car. Sara noticed her mother's hands trembling as she did up her buttons and felt guilty for not telling her the whole truth. No plum job was going to just fall in her lap. She didn't have any work experience. How could her mother believe that she would have already made a commitment to the position? But that's how her mother was.

"No commitments yet, Mom. They haven't even offered me the job. I was just saying you shouldn't let my location influence your retirement. I could end up going anywhere. Except maybe Texas. Marcus wants me to get a job there. Can you imagine me landscaping cactus?"

"I shouldn't have to tell you again that you shouldn't listen to that man."

"His name is Marcus, Mom," Sara complained as her father closed her suitcase in the trunk and asked if she was hungry and wanted to eat before they drove home.

"What?" Agnes asked helplessly. "I can't understand when you both talk at once.

Sara sighed. "It wasn't important. They served sandwiches on the flight...."

"Wouldn't you like something hot? Your mother and I didn't eat before we drove out here. There's a nice new restaurant on Twenty-eighth Street that I'd like to try."

"Okay," Sara agreed. "That will give me a chance to tell you all about Florida." She wouldn't let her mother's insecurities dictate where she lived or what she did or who she loved. Which sounded very good when Sara said it in her head. But she didn't tell her mother the job probably wouldn't come through or that she was seriously attracted to Joe Fisher, that she might even love him.

Did she love him or was it simply infatuation? The question remained in the back of her head all through the meal and the drive home, although she chatted about Florida and the weather. Agnes helped her unpack, protesting that Sara should be home instead of at Gert and Corny's beach house. As Sara waved to her parents and watched their car drive off, the question leaped forward in her head and demanded attention.

Was she in love with Joseph Fisher? She didn't want to be. She wasn't ready to risk her heart again. It would be so much wiser to play it safe and not fall in love again. She needed time to heal. But that was easier said than done, for Joe defied the rule, out of sight, out of mind. He'd been in her thoughts, as Aunt Gert had noticed, the whole time she was in Florida. But was that love? It could be infatuation. She'd have to wait and see. Aunt Gert advised taking him to bed to see if it was real, but Sara knew the sexual attraction was real. And making love with Joe would be a commitment. Michael was the only man she'd ever slept with before. Joe had already declared his love; she didn't want to hurt him any more than she wanted to get hurt herself.

It was all so confusing. She didn't want to think about it. She wanted to see Joe, to find out if he was as sexy and wonderful as she remembered. To see if the electricity still sparked between them. Sara called his house but he didn't answer the phone. She let it ring seventeen times. If the disappointment that swamped over her was anything to go by, her feelings for him hadn't faded while she was away.

Then she called Marcus to let him know she was home from her trip. He answered on the third ring, his voice sounding almost like Michael's. "Hello."

"Hi, Marcus! I'm home."

"Sara?"

"Right the first time."

"How was your trip?"

"Wonderful. The weather was marvelous the whole time. I have about a million freckles on my nose—"

"That's great, Sara," Marcus interrupted. "I want to hear all about it, but I'm with a client right now."

"But it's Saturday."

"That's the joy of being an insurance agent, you're not bound by traditional office hours but can work on your evenings and weekends, too."

"You didn't have to make the appointment. So what if you lose a sale? It's just money. Or are you one of those people who insists on eating every day?"

"Well, I do, as a matter of fact, but this isn't a sales call. I'm meeting with a woman who lost her husband in a fire last weekend."

"How awful," Sara sympathized, thinking of the widow. "I guess I better let you go, then. Why don't you come over for supper tomorrow night?"

"I can't get there before six-thirty."

"Okay. Try and take it easy, Marcus."

"Yeah, thanks. See you later."

"Bye." Sara hung up the phone, feeling sorry for poor Marcus. Every time she talked to him things seemed a little worse. His weary melancholy seemed catching. Sara called Joe again and listened despondently to the endless tolling of his telephone. Welcome home, she thought, and went for a walk on the beach to clear the self-pity from her head.

She'd hardly been on the beach long enough for the cold to turn her freckled nose red when Joe came back from the college library with a stack of research notes and a headache. He'd been a fool to try to work on an article after spending half the night on his sister's stupid couch. He tossed the papers down on the kitchen table and went to let the over-excited dog out the back door before he lost his temper with the yapping mutt. What a day. He was eager to see Sara, but he didn't know when her plane was due. So he'd driven to the library and tortured himself by searching for commentary on Jack Kerouac's literary influences for a sidenote to include in his article.

"Shut your trap, Roly Poly," he growled as he threw open the back door. The spaniel gave a last defiant bark to let him know who was boss and went tearing down the embankment, slamming through the drifts of snow, to make excited circles around Sara Davidson's feet. Joe wasn't too proud to admit that sometimes the dog was smarter than he was. He took off after Roly, just as eager to see Sara again. If he had a tail, he'd be wagging it, too.

How many times had he vowed to go slow, to give Sara all the time she needed? A thousand? A million? Not enough, apparently, for he couldn't stay calm and casual. He raced through the snow and grabbed Sara, twirling her around in a giddy circle that nearly landed them both on the ground. Which wouldn't be so bad; they'd fallen in the snow once before and kissed. He couldn't kiss her now, he was laughing too happily. Finally he forced himself to set her back at arm's length.

He wanted to kiss her, but some part of his brain was insistently repeating, go slow, wait until she's ready. She'd been distant when he talked to her before her trip, a reaction, he knew, to his declaration of love. She didn't look distant now. She looked better than he'd ever seen her, and it wasn't just the pink glow on her cheeks and the sun-kissed freckles on her nose. It was the welcoming smile that sparkled on her face. He wasn't about to jeopardize everything again, but he couldn't resist pulling her back into his arms and burying his face in the sweet-smelling hair that curled out from under the brim of her cap.

Her heart was pounding to beat the band, and she could feel the blood racing through her body. Joe had literally swept her from her feet. Sara laughed in dazed joy. Joe's ears were turning red because he wasn't wearing a hat. His spicy cologne clung to the blue-and-brown plaid flannel lining of his parka, which had covered her face during his bone-crushing hug. His chin was scratchy, and his laughter was sending vibrations through her bones. It felt good to be in his arms. Wonderful, in fact.

When she felt his lips against her temple she didn't even think before she turned her head and captured the kiss with her mouth. For a moment the kiss deepened dramatically, but then Joe pulled back and just moved his lips against her own. He turned his head away and gasped her name into her cap.

"Hi, Joe!" Roly bounced against her leg and yipped. Sara leaned over and smoothed his ears once. "Hi, Roly Poly."

Roly tried to steal her mitten.

"You look fantastic," Joe said with a huge grin. "I love your freckles." His eyes glittered wickedly. "Do you get them all over?"

"What a question! Most people start out asking about the weather," Sara complained while her mind conjured pictures of Joe kissing all her freckles. If only she hadn't smeared on so much of that damned sunscreen!

"I'm sorry, I didn't mean to ask you that." Joe pulled away with a dark frown, and Sara thought he looked awfully tired. The laugh lines around his eyes looked almost like wrinkles.

"Have you been sick? You look pale, and there are circles under your eyes. Or was last night just a wild night?" Talk about asinine questions! Sara thought.

"Nope," Joe said, laughing. "At least, not the kind of wild night your freckles make me think of. I was baby-sitting Susan's kids, Mark, Ryan and Junior. Junior's almost three, and he's almost toilet-trained." Joe shook his head and sighed with a crooked smile, but Sara laughed; she'd been through it all with Lala and understood perfectly.

Roly had found a stick that wasn't buried in the snow and dashed up to them now, begging for someone to throw it for him. Sara obliged, and they walked down the open beach with the dog.

It wasn't until Joe slipped for the third time and almost fell that Sara noticed that he was wearing flat-soled moccasins instead of boots. No wonder he was slipping and sliding. He didn't have mittens or a hat, either, and Sara realized then that he must have made a mad dash from the house when he saw her on the beach. It made her feel warm and tingly inside. Despite the feeling that was all womanly, Sara slipped neatly into her role as a mother. "Where are your boots, Joe? You're going to catch your death of cold," she warned, and turned them toward the houses.

"Let's go to my place," Joe suggested. "I'll give you a real Dutch welcome. I've got a pot of pea soup with lots of ham in it. And I can make some coffee—that's a Dutchman's version of nectar and ambrosia, isn't it?"

"Ah," Sara said with a smile. "Yes, and I think it sounds delightful. Let me run home and get your present while you go put on some dry socks."

"I'll come along and wait for you."

"You don't need to...okay." Arguing was useless when Joe had that stubborn expression on his face. "Come on in," she invited when Joe and Roly hesitated on the steps. "It'll take me a minute to remember where I put it when I unpacked."

"We're wet," Joe protested.

"At least stand in the front hall, not out on the stoop."

Joe agreed and leaned back against the door waiting while Sara dashed in to get his present. He felt like someone had carbonated his stomach. Little effervescent bubbles of joy were fizzling up through him. She was beautiful. He loved her. She had brought him a present. "Stay here, Roly," he warned and then hunkered down to rumple the disappointed dog's furry ears. "You're a smart dog, to want to follow her. She's one helluva woman." Roly wagged his tail.

"Are you telling that dog I'm like the poky little puppy?"

"Uh, no. Who's the poky little puppy?"

"Only the hero of one of the best children's books ever written. And you call yourself a literature professor! When she was learning to read, that was Lala's favorite story. She must've read it to me a hundred times. You should get it for your nieces and nephews.'' Sara scrunched her hat back down over her curls and slipped on her mittens. "Let's go.''

Joe led Roly outside and waited while Sara locked the door before walking with her down the driveway and along the road to his house. "They probably have it already. I can't keep up with all of them.''

"I'd feel sorry for you except I saw you with them at Thanksgiving and I know they all think you're the next best thing to chocolate chip cookies.''

Joe laughed and tweaked Sara's cap. He wondered if she knew that it was the first time she'd ever mentioned Lala to him without getting that horrible broken look in her eyes. He wanted to hug her. "So you really got me a present?'' he asked instead.

Sara help up the box. "Yup. I hope you like it.''

"You didn't have to bring me anything, you know.''

"What was it you said at Christmas about accepting gifts gracefully?''

Joe grinned. "Okay, how about, you shouldn't have but I'm glad you did?''

"That sounds better.'' Sara turned as Joe opened the door and called Roly. The dog looked at her and then saw the open door and came dashing over. Joe hid his delighted grin by bending over and toweling off the snowy dog. Sara was slowly healing, slowly becoming ready for the love he felt.

Sara watched while Joe stoked up the wood stove, made coffee and put the kettle of soup on the stove to simmer. She suddenly wondered if her present was appropriate or if he was going to think she was a stray again. In the store it seemed perfect, reminding her of Lala and the joy Joe's sand dollar had given her. And it would look good on the shelves in his living room where books shared their space with pine cones, an owl carved of soapstone, a bronze bowl of acorns, different rocks, and little vases of dried weeds.

Joe pulled two chairs over by the wood stove. "All right, let's see that package now." He patted the chair beside him.

"Don't look so excited. This isn't such a great present," Sara warned, hesitating.

"Hand it over. It's too late for second thoughts now," Joe ordered, laughter and excitement coloring his eagerness.

Sara gave him the box and sat stiffly in her chair, watching as he opened it and lifted the golden-brown starfish from its tissue-paper bed. "It reminded me of Lala, and her stupid song, and that sand dollar you gave her. You really made her happy, Joe. I don't know, maybe it's a strange present."

"I think it's just fine," he contradicted her. "I can put it on my bookshelves."

"That's what I thought, too," Sara admitted. "It doesn't hurt so much to think of Lala anymore. At first it seemed like I would never stop hurting. I guess that's good."

"Of course it is."

"I still miss her."

"I know you do. You always will. But don't let anyone make you feel guilty for how you deal with the loss, Sara. You need to mourn, but you need to heal, too. It's a balance, just like everything else."

"Everything?" Sara quipped, avoiding a heavy discussion just now.

"Sure, everything," Joe insisted, following her lead. "Like dinner. Pea soup, pigs-in-blankets—it's a good Dutch meal. The meat balances the carbohydrates.

With a healthy dose of fat on the top. Put some meat on your bones for sure.''

"When do we eat?" Sara asked. She'd eaten lots of fresh fruits and vegetables while she was in Florida. One Old Country meal wouldn't do her any harm.

Joe laughed at her eagerness. He went to check the pastry-wrapped sausage rolls baking in the oven. "The pigs need another fifteen minutes or so. Tell me all about Florida. How were the Van Dykes?"

So Sara told him about her trip and some of the things she'd seen and done, watching his reactions carefully. When she said Aunt Gert agreed with his theory about her mother's protectiveness, he only argued that it was her theory, not his. She didn't tell him Aunt Gert thought they ought to make love to see if what she felt was real.

She did tell him that Gert and Corny had liked her portfolio and had arranged a job interview. "I'm glad I did it, because I was scared silly and I didn't even want the job. It was good practice—to see what kind of questions I'll be asked and that kind of thing. I felt a little bad afterward because Mr. Fromes was so nice. He was pretty sure he wouldn't give me the job and he told me why. He said I didn't have any work experience and that I would find that designing gardens professionally was different than working for friends, but mostly it was because I'm not very knowledgeable about what grows well in Florida. He said if I took a class he could probably help me out. I felt like a creep then, for using him for practice. I almost apologized, but I chickened out and just thanked him.''

Joe smiled at her. He wasn't sure if he'd ever met a woman he admired more than Sara. She was honest and considerate; she was plain and simple, old-fashioned good. He loved her like crazy. And he was glad as hell that she wasn't serious about working in Florida because he didn't want to move and he didn't want to live without her. "Of course he'd help you out. Your portfolio is damned impressive. I think you ought to put one of those cherry trees in my yard."

"You would want a weeping cherry, Joe. It's no wonder you don't want me to see your yard. It'll grow about as well as that azalea by the front door."

"That thing! It had the most beautiful orange flowers when I bought it and it never bloomed again."

"Because you're torturing it. I'm going to move it to my parents' house this spring. It makes me want to cry to see it suffering."

"I told you I can't have a garden here. It's too shady and sandy," Joe complained.

"Just you wait, Joseph Fisher. You'll eat those words come summer. I'll give you the best garden you ever saw."

"With a weeping cherry?"

"With poison ivy if you don't watch it!"

Joe laughed and rumpled her hair and forced himself not to tell her he loved her. Instead, he got up to clear the table. Sara jumped up to help and ignored his orders to cease and desist. "So what have you been doing to keep your life exciting while I was lolling in the hot Florida sunshine?"

"Do you have to rub my nose in it? I was freezing my tail off up here and not doing anything exciting. Well, I'm working on an article that's going nowhere fast." Joe told her about it, and although she didn't know much about Jack Kerouac's literary influences and current resurgence of popularity, she sympathized with his research problems. Joe lapped up her pity, complaining, "And all that hunching over the microfiche machine at the library made my neck hurt even worse."

"Worse?"

"It was already stiff from falling asleep on Susan's couch last night."

"Poor Joey," Sara moaned in mock pity.

"Hey, I deserve a little sympathy."

"Hay is for horses." Sara ducked from Joe's bland look. "I could massage your neck if you want. I used to give Michael rubdowns sometimes. Not while he was playing ball, there were trainers then, but later. He was too exuberant. He'd always work out too hard and end up with sore muscles."

Joe was torn between resenting her mention of Michael and pleasure at the thought of the massage. He knew he shouldn't expect her to pretend the guy she was married to for ten years never existed, but he didn't want to hear about him. On the other hand, having her offer to touch him like that was more than slightly wonderful. And his neck was screaming for a massage. Automatically running his hand across the sore muscles, he agreed. "Where do you want me? These chairs sure won't work," he said, pointing at the high-backed kitchen chairs.

"We always did it on the bed."

He wished she wouldn't say things like that! Was she trying to make him crazy? "Wouldn't it be better to use the floor? The bed's kind of soft, and I always thought you were supposed to give a massage on a hard surface."

"Okay. We can use that sheepskin rug in your bedroom."

When had she seen that? Well, she had been in the house, changed for the hot tub and all. But if she didn't stop putting ideas in his head his body was going to explode in a million different directions at once. He led her to his bedroom, screaming at his body in an effort to maintain control. He started a fire in the fireplace with a match, although he felt sure he could've made it smolder with a single touch. Sara picked out a recording of Mozart's flute quartets and turned on the stereo. Joe flopped facedown on the luxuriously thick rug. This was supposed to be relaxing him? That had to be the biggest joke of the decade!

Sara knelt beside him. He waited. "Don't you want to take your sweater off?" He sat up and shed it, tossing it over on the bed. "And your shirt?" Joe didn't look at her as he stripped it off and tossed it aside. He laid back down and buried his face in his arm. He wanted her. Don't think about making love, he told himself. Relax. Relax. Think about something else, anything else. Just breathe in and out, nice and slow, inhale and exhale very slowly. Don't think about how good it feels, just inhale and exhale. Good. Inhale. Exhale.

Sara hesitated with the expanse of Joe's skin before her, but the urge to stroke his back was irresistible. She ran her hands over the smooth, firm planes of his shoulders, his muscles becoming pliant under his skin, slightly tan and speckled with a few dots of darker pigmentation. He wanted to kiss her freckles? Not half as much as she wanted to dip her head and kiss his!

The muscles in his shoulders and neck were reluctant to loosen and relax under her ministrations but Sara couldn't bring herself to straddle Joe's muscular torso. She leaned awkwardly over him and was tired by the time his muscles softened. When he was relaxed she continued with less vigor to stroke the length of his back. His spine made a straight furrow between the symmetrical sculptures of flesh. He was beautiful, masculine and strong. His skin was warm and smooth against her palms. She never wanted to stop touching him.

The stereo clicked and the music ended. Sara leaned over and whispered a kiss onto each of Joe's freckles. She sat up on her heels. Joe didn't move, didn't react; Joe was sound asleep. Sara didn't know whether to sigh in relief or shriek in frustration. Why lie to herself? She wanted him to shiver when she kissed him, to roll over and take her into his arms and make her his. Sara sighed and eased down onto the rug next to Joe. The fire jumped merrily in the grate, reducing the wood to ash, sending tendrils of smoke climbing the chimney. The fire inside her was more of a smolder, unable to leap into bright satisfying flames because she wasn't bold enough to seduce Joe.

Did she love him? She reached out and touched a silky dark curl of hair at the back of his neck. It was ridiculous to let herself fall in love so soon. But this wasn't just infatuation. She did more than lust after Joe's body. If only she could be sure. If only there was a litmus test for love, with a pretty color change indicator to tell if it was the real thing or not. Instead she had to rely on her own perceptions, battered as they were by the loss of Michael and Lala. She didn't trust herself anymore.

Joe had said she should, that condemning herself was a way to pretend she had control. Maybe it was the same with love. Maybe she was only pretending to be uncertain because it gave her the illusion of controlling her emotions. Maybe she already loved Joe. A log split and settled in the fire with a shower of sparks. Joe didn't move. Sara sighed. She felt a little like that log, splitting into two, uncertain whether she loved Joe or not, whether to make love to him or wait. It seemed inevitable that someday they would make love. Maybe that was supposed to tell her something.

Joe's body was rising and falling with the rhythm of his steady breathing. She ought to wake him up and send him to bed, Sara thought, but she didn't. She gave in to the temptation to rest her head on his back while she stared at the shadowy ceiling and felt every breath he took with every cell of her body.

If she turned her head, would she be able to hear the steady thumping of his heart? Sara didn't know where the idea came from, but she tried it. Her own heart was pounding so loudly that she wouldn't have heard a drum corps over its beating. She looked back up at the ceiling and contented herself with making her breathing match Joe's. It was easy. Did that mean something? The fire died to a glowing bed of coals. Sara grew drowsy. Roly woke up from wherever he'd been napping and came looking for companionship. He mistook the mellow mood of the pair on the sheepskin rug as an invitation to join them.

Sara sat up to avoid his quick-draw tongue. Roly turned his attention to Joe's ear. It was probably a good thing Joe's voice was sleep-muzzy, Sara thought, trying to repress a smile. Roly didn't mind. He waited while Joe sat up and then attacked again. Joe pushed him away and then swept him back into a brief embrace that left the dog on his back looking deliriously happy as Joe scratched his belly.

"How's your back?" Sara asked.

Joe shrugged his shoulders and stretched, making the muscles on his chest and sides flex intriguingly. "Better," he smiled and then yawned widely.

"You fell asleep right away."

"I didn't mean to."

"The whole idea of a massage is to relax you."

Or excite you, Joe thought. "It worked," he said. "What time is it, anyway?" He felt like he'd slept a week.

Sara shrugged. "Maybe eight."

"Give me a minute and I'll walk you home," Joe said, scrubbing his face with his palms. "I'm really zonked."

"I know." Sara watched while Joe stood up and raked through a dresser drawer until he found a threadbare sweatshirt with the neck slit. Did he want to get rid of her so badly? "Do you ever wear new sweatshirts?"

"Only if I have to. They're more comfortable when they're broken in."

"Broken down is more like it," Sara teased. Joe loomed over her, ruffling her hair before he pulled her to her feet. Roly scrambled back when she moved, and Sara felt something soft beneath her foot. He yelped, and she took a hopping step forward in an effort to keep from putting her weight on his tail. She collided with Joe instead. His arms steadied her. The electricity arced between them again as if someone had flipped a giant switch somewhere.

He wanted to pull her even closer, to press the whole length of her body against his, to kiss her until they fell breathlessly on the bed. What he did was take a step back.

"Joe?" Her voice was tentative, slightly breathless.

Slow the hell down, Joe screamed at his body. "Yeah?" Did she have to look at him with those smoky blue eyes? With her lips parted like she wanted a kiss? Didn't she know what she was doing to him?

"Did you mean it when you said you loved me?"

Panic sent the neurons in his brain on vacation. Did he say yes? She wanted him to say yes because she loved him. She would run like a scared rabbit if he said yes. Accuse him of getting in the way of her grieving and say she needed time and space, for him to leave her alone. He'd die. Lie? Say no? What if she did love him and he hurt her? "Yes," he blurted out.

Sara took a deep breath. That took long enough. Or was she panicking? Did he regret his declaration of love? "Will you kiss me?" She couldn't think straight while she was wanting to be in his arms so badly. After the kiss, then she'd decide what to tell him. Why had she brought this up, anyway? Was she a fool in love, an idiot, a moonstruck, lovesick, besotted fool?

Joe took a deep breath and gathered her into his arms. He was frightened but overjoyed at the same time. She did care. She did want him. She wasn't going to run. She was going to kiss him. Maybe this was the right time to make love, to show her how perfect it would be between them. Yes, that's what he'd do. He'd love her until she couldn't deny her future lay with him.

Sara slid her arms around Joe's neck. That Joe was hesitant and gentle didn't bother her. She found it more richly masculine than the blatant machismo that often passed as masculinity. A man should be frightened of love; it was a very powerful emotion. But if he reacted to his fear by being savage and punishing, then he wasn't really strong at all. Joe's embrace was fierce, but his mouth was utterly gentle as it brushed her lips.

He pulled back and their eyes met. She read vulnerability and joy in the love shining from his dark eyes. He saw the confusion that lingered in hers, mingled with excitement. She licked her lips nervously, and his eyes were riveted. She could feel the heat of his gaze making her lips dry. Before she could wet them again, he leaned forward and did it for her. Sara felt like she would faint with the sudden rush of erotic pleasure that raced through her.

Her lips parted, and he slid his tongue slowly into her mouth, exploring the delicious sensations. His body was waking up fast, warming up faster. He deliberately tried to hold back, afraid his passion would overwhelm Sara and send her skittering away for shelter. Instead, she dueled with him, forcing him to intensify the kiss. Joe used every ounce of determination he could find in order to force himself to pull back. He urged himself to wait, wait, wait. Don't blow it by rushing now! Sara took a deep gulping breath and dropped her head onto his shoulder. "I want to make love with you, Joe," she said. Her breath was steamy against the hollow of his shoulder. Joe's body seconded the suggestion.

Wait, his mind screamed. "Are you sure, Sara?" His voice sounded funny, almost squeaky. He couldn't breathe. His hands gripped her sides, keeping her close but holding her a little bit away at the same time. "I think I'd die if you regretted it in the morning. I'd rather wait until you're sure of what you want."

Sara tried to pull back and think, to make a responsible decision. All she could think about was touching Joe's body and being touched by him. How could she decide now if this was a mistake when she could slide her palm under his sweatshirt and feel the coarse silkiness of the hair that whorled on his chest? His stomach jumped under her touch, and his muscles grew tense as his breath hissed from his lungs. "You want me."

"I know that," Joe said, closing his eyes. He'd read the confusion, seen her split second of hesitation. "I know how to take a cold shower. I wouldn't know how to live with your regret. I love you, and like you said, I want you. But I can wait, Sara." If her hand slid any lower she was going to make a liar out of him. A cold shower wasn't going to do much good for him tonight.

"I took my rings off," Sara insisted, but part of her was already pulling back. Maybe Joe was right, maybe she wasn't ready for this yet. Could she say for sure that she loved him? As much as she had loved Michael? There was a sinking feeing inside her when she realized she still wasn't certain what she felt. Lust, yes, and love. But how much of all this was just a stockpile of hormones built up during the three long years since Michael died?

Joe threaded his fingers through Sara's. "I know," he sighed. "You also had a long day. You woke up this morning in Florida. Lord knows it's not that I don't want you, Sara, but I don't want to take advantage of you, either. It would hurt both of us. Give me a minute and I'll take you home, and if you still want to make love tomorrow, I'll be more than happy to oblige.''

He let go of her hands and caressed her cheek, running his fingers back through her hair. ''I love you so damned much.'' He sighed and kissed her, then pulled away and disappeared into the bathroom before she even had a chance to respond. Sara glared at the closed door. How could he be so damned cool about it? Her body was in a state of rebellion. If he really loved her so damned much how could he stay rational? Her brain had turned to mush. She was so damned confused, so tired. He was right, she'd woken up in Florida. The day was already too long and too full. She was going to go home and crawl straight into bed and sleep for twelve hours. And then...

And then she'd decide what would happen next. Sara left Joe's bedroom and pulled on her coat and hat. She was about to leave when she heard Joe call her name. ''I'm going home,'' she called back.

''Wait a minute,'' Joe growled, storming into the living room. ''I'll walk you.'' He started yanking on his boots.

''I can walk by myself, Joe. I'm not scared of the bogeyman.''

''Don't be an idiot. Don't you ever read the papers? A woman shouldn't go out walking along a deserted road after dark. You sure as hell aren't walking home from my house alone.''

''I can walk along the beach. It's safe enough. I'm not going to spend my whole life behind locked doors just because there are a few sick men in the world. Women get raped during the daylight hours, too, you know.''

"Come on," Joe snarled and ripped open the front door, letting Roly and Sara precede him. They stormed along in silence until the end of the driveway. Joe turned back and ordered Roly to move it.

Sara stopped in her tracks. "You're the one who stopped everything. Don't you be yelling at Roly. He's just an innocent dog!" Her eyes flashed with anger; her finger wagged at Joe's chest.

Joe managed to turn his obscene reply into a noise that was somewhere between a growl and a primal scream. The noise echoed along the empty road.

"Feel better?" Sara asked with supercilious disdain.

Joe roared again, much louder. "Now I do." And to his surprise, he did.

"Well, I hope you didn't wake up too many of the neighbors."

"No one heard. Who's out here? The nearest neighbor who isn't in Florida or Texas or Hawaii is Bart DeBoer, and he's deafer than a doornail. The closest people to hear would be the Ryersons, and they're a quarter mile away. If anyone could hear you scream it wouldn't be so dangerous for you to walk alone."

"You sound like my mother. You could hear me scream."

"Yeah, well, I'd rather walk you home than sit around and listen for you to scream. This way I know you're safe. Give me a break, Sara. Taking out our frustration on each other is kind of stupid, don't you think?"

"You started it." Sara wanted to bite back the words as soon as they left her mouth. She turned to Joe to apologize, but it was too late. He'd scooped a handful of snow from the top of the Van Dyke mailbox and was about to wash her face. "Joe," she screeched, but he didn't stop.

While she spluttered and wiped her face, he laughed. "You know, you ought to learn to control your temper when there's all this snow around just begging me to help cool you off."

"You're the one who was yelling at the poor puppy. Maybe you should take a roll in the snow, Joe."

Joe rolled his eyes at the little rhyme. "I'd rather take a roll in the hay." He sighed heavily. "Forget I said that, okay? How about brunch tomorrow? We could walk down the beach to the restaurant. I think they serve Sunday brunch from ten to two."

"That sounds—" Sara's voice deepened "—great."

"But . . ." Joe prompted when she hesitated.

"I can't. I'm supposed to go to my mom's for dinner after church. She'll have a purple fit if I stand her up after being gone for so long. It'll probably take half the afternoon. How about I call you when I get back, okay? If it wasn't Mom, I'd say forget it, but . . ."

"It's okay, Sara. We'll do it another time."

"Promise?"

Joe smiled. "Yeah, I promise. Get a good night's sleep, okay? I'll see you tomorrow."

"Yeah, you, too. Good night, Joe."

"G'night."

Sara hesitated. "Bye."

Joe grinned and finished unlocking the door for Sara. He opened it and flipped on the hall light. "Good night, Sara. Go to bed. We'll talk tomor-

row." He kissed her, a brief, hard kiss. "I love you."
The door closed.

Sara stared at it. "I love you, too, Joe," she whispered, but of course he couldn't hear. She sighed. Tomorrow...

CHAPTER NINE

SHE'D COME FROM CHURCH an hour ago; if ever her prayers were going to be answered, let this be the time. Please, Sara thought, let the couch open up and swallow me whole. I can't stand one more minute of this...this farce. Just let these cushions split open and swallow me. Slurp. Gone. Because I cannot stand this. I'm going to kill Mom and Dad or die myself. She wanted to give a primal scream twice as loud and three times as frustrated as the one Joe had let loose in the silence of the woods last night.

"Oh, yes, Mr. Vos, Sara has done some landscaping, haven't you, darling?" Agnes called Sara back to the elegant living room with its delicately cabriole-legged furnishings. Sara nodded. Couldn't they change the subject?

No, of course not. She'd met her parents at church and gone home with them for Sunday dinner as they planned. But the plan had a new twist. Burt Vos, the owner of Vos Landscaping, and as Agnes had mentioned more than once, a widower for fifteen years now, had been included for the family dinner. Sara could understand her parents wanting to invite a lonely man to their table after church; after all, Burt Vos had been a member of the congregation for years and years. But why was he here today, only the day after she mentioned getting a job elsewhere? Could it be because he owned the second-largest landscaping company in town? Or was she just being suspicious? Sara asked herself sarcastically while her mother pulled out the photo albums to show Vos her gardens.

The poor man had come for Sunday dinner and was paying dearly, having to listen to Agnes give an endless, breathless sales pitch for her daughter. He seemed to consider it a fair bargain, three helpings of pot roast for an hour of his time. "Isn't Sara lovely in this picture?" Agnes asked. Sara cringed, not wanting to lean over and look, yet drawn to see just which one it was that Burt Vos was nodding and smiling at. It was a nice picture of her in a dusty-rose-colored evening dress, taken on the night she and Michael had gone out for dinner and dancing after he'd been named salesman of the year for the real estate company, three months before his life was taken by the drunk driver.

"And this is the garden Sara designed for her late husband's sister. I would have made it perfectly symmetrical, but Sara says that would be bad. Now how did that go, Sara?"

"The design is basically symmetrical, balanced, which is peaceful and stately, but static. The slight asymmetry draws the eye, gives the viewer a plan, so to speak, for seeing the garden. Just your basic formal gardening guidelines," Sara stated factually. Maybe she ought to try to impress Burt Vos—she did want to stay in the area if she could—but somehow Sara just couldn't bring herself to take advantage of her mother's machinations.

"Very well done," Burt said, nodding ponderously, his heavy jowls flushed from the full meal.

"Oh, and you must see the photos of our garden. Sara worked so hard on it." Agnes paged through the album. "You know Sara has a degree, don't you? In landscape design. It was a very innovative program, and she was one of the first graduates. The man who set up the program, what was his name, Sara?

"Henry Black."

"Ah, yes, Professor Black, he still keeps in touch with Sara."

"Not really, Mom. I wrote to him and mentioned that I was attempting to enter the job market and asked for any help he might be able to give. He hasn't answered yet. That's hardly a major correspondence."

Agnes gave her a cold look. "Oh, well, here we are. This is the backyard. Isn't the rose arbor lovely? It was all Sara's idea. I do love to sit out there on June mornings. It's just like, like sitting inside a rosebud." Agnes almost shivered with the remembered pleasure.

"Lovely," Burt agreed, but he seemed to Sara to be looking at her mother and not the pictures. She wanted to sink into the couch all over again. She didn't realize how far she had pressed herself back into the cushions until Burt Vos turned to her. Suddenly she felt foolish. She should have either gone along with her mother's plan or put a stop to it; this sitting and cringing was for the birds.

"You're quite talented, my dear. If you're really interested in working, you ought to stop by my office sometime," Vos urged. Sara was quite sure she was the only one who heard the reserve in his voice, and she might have just imagined it.

"Why don't you set a time now?" Agnes urged. "Then you won't be missing each other. I know you aren't always in your office, Burt. You have all those big greenhouses and fields to oversee. John's the same way, running the showroom. Lots of times, when I call, I have to leave a message because he's back in the service garage or out on the lot. If you make an appointment, it just makes it easier, don't you think?"

"That's a good idea, Agnes," John put in from his armchair.

"Hmm, how about a week from Monday, just before lunch, say eleven, eleven-thirty?" Burt offered.

"Fine." Sara wanted to tell him she would never settle for a little something that was arranged out of charity, but now was not the time or place for that kind of declaration of independence.

"Great," he said much too heartily. "Now I do have to get home. My son's supposed to bring my grandson by this afternoon. The pot roast was scrumptious, Agnes, just like my Elaine's. You've got a good woman here, John, better keep a hold of her. And I'll see you, Sara, a week from tomorrow."

Sara smiled and nodded, standing back while her parents ushered Burt Vos out the front door. Her smile turned to a dark frown once the door closed. "What's wrong with you, Mom? I've never been more embarrassed in my life. I don't need you to get a job for me. I'm not a poor helpless widow. I can get a job by myself, based on my merits. I don't need charity."

"Sara." Her father's voice held a deep note of warning. "Is that any way to talk to your mother?"

"Sara, darling," Agnes said tearfully, "I know you don't need charity. I'm very proud of you, and if I embarrassed you by bragging, then I'm very, very sorry. You were so rude to poor Mr. Vos. I invited him to dinner because he's a widower, a lonely man who always has to eat his Sunday dinner alone. After all," she reproved, "the Bible does advocate charity, whether you approve or not."

"Mom," Sara complained, knowing it was hopeless. "You wanted him to offer me a job. You practically crammed the idea down his throat."

"I never did. And I never meant to. Your landscaping is simply something we have in common with the man. Did I ask him to offer you a job? No. I think you're overreacting, dear. Maybe you want to reconsider working. You say you don't need the money, and the idea doesn't seem to make you very happy, does it?"

"Your mother does have a point there, Sara. You're not worrying about money, are you? If you change your mind and want me to help you with a budget, you only need to ask."

"I don't need a budget and I do want a job. I just want to get it myself, to know that I can do it. Is that so hard to understand?"

"No, of course not, but I don't see what it has to do with you being so rude to poor Mr. Vos. He's a nice man who's very lonely. Do you know he gave the church all the Christmas decorations, even those huge wreaths on the front door? And he didn't even want his name in the bulletin."

"Your mother's right, Sara. Burt Vos is a good man. And I think you might need to take a little time and consider your actions today. You were quite rude."

"Don't be afraid to change your mind about working," Agnes hastened to reassure her. "I know it sometimes seems as if everyone else in the world works, but there is nothing wrong with staying at home. There are women who think I'm worthless because I don't have a job, but I feel that supporting John is my job. We're a team. Women shouldn't have to work. If they really want to, okay, but they shouldn't be made to feel like they have to.''

But she didn't have anyone to be a team with, Sara thought sadly. She did need a job, something to fill up her horrible empty existence. ''Maybe you're right,'' she said with a sigh. ''I think I'll go home. I've just remembered Marcus is coming by for dinner and I need to make something for us to eat.''

''You seem tired. Why don't you call and tell him to come another time? You mustn't push yourself. You might have jet lag.''

''I'm okay. I'll have time to rest once I get dinner in the oven. And I can't have jet lag—Florida and Michigan are in the same time zone.''

''You know what your mother meant.''

She knew exactly what her mother meant, but she hadn't necessarily said what she meant, Sara thought darkly, taking her leave. Her head was throbbing by the time she got home. She didn't know she wanted to talk to Joe until she drove past his house and saw the extra car in the driveway and knew she couldn't; then it was suddenly the only thing she wanted. Instead, she put together a big casserole of the tomato-based beef stew that Marcus loved and set it in the oven. She wasn't hungry, and after the big noon meal, didn't know if she'd ever want to eat again. But Marcus ate like Michael, like a starving bear. Sara made a gelatin salad and set out the ingredients for homemade crusty rolls. Then she ducked out the back door and took a walk on the beach.

She hoped Joe would see her and come running down to bump into her. He'd done that before, pretending their meetings were accidental. What a sweet, silly, wonderful man he was. She was going to have to tell him she loved him and wanted to make love with him. But how did you say that to a man? Joe was too damned responsible, too conscientious. Men were supposed to get hot and forget everything but having their wicked way; instead, Joe pulled back and told her to be sure, that he could wait. He was, Sara thought with a frustrated smile, a man in a million. She really did love him. If only she'd been as certain last night.

The January beach was bare—drifting snow and pale sand, naked logs and gnarled branches like frozen fingers stretching toward a nonexistent sun. The ice had built up along the shore so that the lake was white except for a narrow line of black water at the horizon. The sand dunes were wooded with dark trees and green pines. At the side of the channel Big Red stood as an oasis of color in the midst of the achromatic landscape. Like Joe in her life. Sara stood for a minute, a little shaken by the thought. Then she turned and walked home, slowing down as she passed Joe's house, but he still didn't appear.

The climb up the embankment seemed exhausting. Sara laughed bitterly under her breath. She wasn't physically tired, just disappointed and emotionally drained by the dinner with her parents. And not all that enthusiastic about seeing Marcus. She loved him like a little brother, but she'd bet dollars to donuts that he'd be depressed and withdrawn. It was going to be a long night. Maybe she should call Joe and ask him to join them. But that would be unfair to Marcus, who deserved to hear about her trip and have someone to tell his troubles to. She pushed open the back door and screamed.

The sound echoed in the entryway while her heart stopped and then resumed beating at three times its normal pace. She couldn't seem to draw the air back into her lungs even though she knew now that the man in the house wasn't a stranger but Marcus. It was amazing what a split second of fear could do to a body. She was shaking with the excess adrenaline coursing through her.

"Sara!" Marcus turned on her with startled eyes. "You scared ten years off my life!"

"What are you doing here?" She took a deep breath and exhaled slowly.

"You invited me to dinner. Don't tell me you forgot," he scowled.

"I didn't forget," Sara defended, wondering why he was so mad at her. "It's not six-thirty yet, and you never came walking in the back door before."

"Sorry," Marcus said with a sigh. "I was supposed to go to Melanie's this afternoon so I could go over her insurance, but she forgot and had other plans. So I came out early. And you didn't answer the door so I came around back and checked the back door. I figured you were down on the beach, but I wasn't wearing boots and I thought if I could get inside I'd wait for you where it was warm."

"Makes sense," Sara conceded. "I didn't mean to yell like that, but I was surprised to find a man standing in here. I think you took *at least* ten years off my life."

"I'm sorry."

"Me, too," Sara chuckled. "At least it helped me remember that I have a box for you. When your mom and dad moved to Arizona they gave me a couple of boxes of stuff, and I was wondering if the one wasn't a mistake. It's right here." She'd been using the stack of boxes as a mitten rack for weeks now.

"Mom and Dad gave you stuff?"

"Yeah, a few boxes. It's mostly stuff like Michael's high school trophies. I don't know exactly what I'm going to do with them, put them in the attic, I guess." Sara heaved a couple of boxes aside. "Here," she said, shoving one sagging box across the floor toward Marcus. "Your mom said no one else wanted it, but I just couldn't believe you didn't. It's the old crèche," she added, misreading his hollow look for confusion.

Marcus knelt down and flipped open the box, staring at the worse-for-wear straw roof on the little stable building. Tissue paper blanketed the tiny figures of the nativity scene, protecting them until another Christmas season came around. "Mom said no one wanted it?" he asked tonelessly.

"Yeah," Sara said, frowning. "But you collect all those antique ornaments, so I couldn't believe you didn't want it. If Lala was still alive I wouldn't want to give it up, she loved it so much. I can close my eyes and see her and Michael acting out the whole story. But it seems like you should have the Davidson family treasures, not me. I know Mary and Melanie won't want it. It's too old and battered and they like everything just right, but..."

"Just right," Marcus said, sneering bitterly and cutting off Sara's chatter. She was nervous and she didn't know why. Marcus should be happy, should be thanking her, not just staring at the crèche. "Everything always has to be just right," he informed her, pulling himself to his full height and smashing his foot into the small stable.

"Marcus!" Sara shrilled in shock as she scrambled back, climbing the small step up toward the kitchen as if it would offer her some sort of protection.

Marcus kicked the box again and again, until the cardboard and thin wood broke down and spilled the tiny ceramic figures onto the cement floor of the entry. Sara cringed, watching in horror as he deliberately stomped on each little lamb and cow, on the donkey and the shepherds, crushing everything into splinters and dust. He hissed and growled under his breath, cursing violently. When everything was broken Marcus collapsed heavily against the wall in a slump. His breath came in harsh gasps that filled the little room.

Sara approached him hesitantly, afraid of him for the first time in her life, afraid of the fury that had possessed him, of the savage intensity that had driven him to destroy what he loved. She touched his back with one hand, as gently and uncertainly as she would touch an injured dog, ready for him to turn on her, ready to jump back and seek safety.

Marcus shrugged against her hand, shaking off her touch. "Leave me alone. She never even asked me if I wanted it. She never even asked me."

Marcus slowly slid down the wall to kneel in the remains of the crèche, his knees crunching against the debris with a noise that shuddered down Sara's spine. Still leaning against the wall with one arm, resting his head against his forearm, Marcus watched as his other hand sifted through the debris in a meaningless search.

Sara stood helplessly, aching to ease the desolation that remained in the wake of his rage, aching to help, yet repulsed and angry that he had indulged the dark emotion.

"She never even asked me," Marcus repeated again in a broken voice. "They hate me because I'm alive and Michael isn't. If they could have chosen they'd rather have me dead and him alive. He was special and I'm just a poor copy, that's what they think."

"Marcus," Sara protested, "you know your parents don't wish you were dead. No one wants you to be a copy of Michael. Don't you think you're being a little melodramatic? Your mom probably just forgot that she hadn't asked you if you wanted the Christmas stuff." She put her hand on his shoulder again and he let it remain.

"No one wants a copy." Marcus sneered. "Coming from you that's rich. You tried to make love to me and had to stop because I wasn't a good enough copy. You're not Michael, you said, and you never will be." He twisted under her hand, moving to sit slumped against the wall with his head buried in his arms. "I tried, you know, I really tried." His voice was muffled, but not so much that she couldn't hear the raw defeat in it. Sara didn't know how long she stood next to him, rubbing his shoulder in a tiny comforting gesture, waiting. She didn't know how long they might have stayed like that if the oven timer hadn't shrilled.

"I'm supposed to bake my rolls now," she told Marcus over the thin, grating screech. "Come in the kitchen. It's chilly out here. I can sweep up the mess later. Let's get warm now." She held out her hand to help Marcus up, and he took it and used it to pull himself to his feet, nearly dragging her down in the process. She led him through the kitchen, pausing for a second to turn off the annoying buzzer, and gestured him onto a living room couch. "I'm going to make us some hot cocoa. I'll be right back."

Sara spilled sugar and cocoa powder in her haste to make the cocoa. Somehow cocoa seemed necessary right now—how many times had she given Lala a comforting mug of the drink? Marcus seemed to need the same kind of care. But what could she say to make it all better?

When she returned to the living room he was slouched on the sofa with his long hands dangling between his legs. He raised doleful eyes for a moment and then stared back down at his limp hands. Sara worried that he was as destroyed emotionally as the crèche was physically. Could he really believe that his parents—Vivian, warm and tall, Greg, a gentle giant—wanted him dead?

"Here you go," Sara said and set his mug of cocoa on the table near his elbow. "I didn't have any marshmallows."

Marcus didn't reply, and Sara didn't know what to say or do. She sipped her cocoa and burned her tongue. Marcus just sat, and when she looked over at him again, Sara saw the tears sliding silently down his cheeks.

SHE HADN'T CALLED YET. She said she would call, as soon as she got home from her mom and dad's house. It was almost dinnertime. He had an extra serving of chicken. If she'd just call he could offer it to her. Maybe she forgot, Joe rationalized.

But, hell, how could she forget? Almost making love had short-circuited his brain; all he could think about was Sara. He'd gone to bed thinking of her, dreamed wonderful dreams of her, woke up with thoughts of her, spent the whole day with her filling his head. He'd barely been able to converse with his brother when he was over. How could she possibly have forgotten to call? This was asinine. He was a grown man, a mature adult, not a besotted teenager making cow eyes at the very thought of a girl. He wasn't going to let her dominate his whole day. He didn't have to spend the day staring at the phone. She'd call.

Or would she? Joe asked himself as soon as he got down on the beach with Roly. Did she feel rushed? Regret last night's lovemaking, regret her arousal? She wouldn't be able to deny that she had been aroused; her body had been screaming for his lovemaking, only her eyes had questioned him. Those blue eyes, smoky with passion, blinking open and revealing fear, like some phantom glimpsed in the flames of a fire. Joe turned and followed her tracks through the snow to the back door of the Van Dykes' beach house.

Damn it! She'd left the door not only unlocked, but unlatched. Like a fool, she was heating the great outdoors and, worse, endangering herself. Joe scowled fiercely. When he opened the door and stepped inside, his irritation was vaporized by the bomb of fear that exploded inside his stomach, mushrooming up and choking his lungs, leaving his head disconnected from his body with its strangely echoing heartbeat. Splinters of broken wood and dusty clay rubble littered the floor; from inside the house came the sound of sobbing.

He moved without thinking and found himself in the living room staring at Sara over the wide set of heaving shoulders on her lap. Her eyes were wide and very deeply blue. "Joe!" she gasped, then continued with an incredulous look, "What in the world are you doing?"

He couldn't seem to find his voice to answer. Sara wasn't in any danger. She was sitting on the couch with another man's head in her lap. Joe was suddenly aware of the heavy marble rolling pin he was brandishing and let his hand drop to his side. "Your door was open and there was a big mess. I heard someone crying. I thought..." His voice stumbled over the strangled sob that came from the man on Sara's lap. "I'll go close the door," he finally said and left the room to give the guy a chance to get a grip on himself. He hoped to hell and heaven that no one ever found him in that much misery; there were some things a man ought to do only when he was alone. Crying was one of them. He was sweeping up the mess in the entry, unable to leave and unwilling to return to the living room, when Sara found him.

She stood on the step and watched him sweep. Roly scampered in and bounced against her. She rubbed his head. Joe glanced at them and then concentrated on the job. Why did he feel embarrassed and in the wrong? He took the dustpan and swept the remains of the nativity scene into it, dumping the pieces into a convenient cardboard box, waiting for Sara to say something. If she sneered at his protectiveness he was going to lose his temper, Joe thought, and say things he'd end up regretting. One of the lumps of clay was bigger and he flicked it with the broom. It rolled, unbroken, into the pile of litter.

He picked up the manger holding a tiny baby Jesus. It was, miraculously, unbroken. There was still hope.

He handed it to Sara. "I guess it was more solid than the others, capable of resisting greater stress." Whatever the stress was, it had to be deliberate. Dropping from the top of the Empire State Building might make a mess like this, but not dropping from someone's arms. He felt confused and shaky in the aftermath of his panic.

Sara turned the manger over in her hand. "Marcus was very upset." She finally looked up and met his eyes. "The man in the living room is Marcus, my brother-in-law."

"I know. I met him the day I brought Lala that sand dollar."

"Oh."

Joe waited for her to say more, but the silence stretched. He scooped the last of the debris into the box and carried it out to the garbage can in the garage. Sara wasn't in the entry when he returned. He left Roly in the entry and stepped into the kitchen. She was mixing ingredients in a bowl. Marcus stood awkwardly by the kitchen table, gazing out at the icy lake, his hair damp with the water that had failed to wash the blotchy tearstains from his face.

"Marcus," Sara said calmly, almost gently, "this is Joe Fisher. He lives next door. He's the . . . a friend of mine." What had she been about to call him? Joe swallowed his question and shook hands with Marcus Davidson, both of them pretending that everything was fine. It was a show of bravado that enabled them to get to the dinner table, Joe simply assuming he was included when Sara set three places. No one mentioned the ruined crèche, Marcus's tears, or Joe's dramatic entrance. In fact, very little was mentioned in the stilted conversation until the middle of the meal when Sara asked Marcus about the client he had seen the day before. "Marcus sells insurance," she added in an aside to Joe.

"She's still mad as hell, but as long as the police and fire marshall are still investigating the fire, I can't pay. I don't have any choice in the matter, and I told her that over and over. It's the way the policy's written. But she's screaming and shouting and threatening to sue me. Heck, I figure she's probably the one who started the fire."

"Marcus!" Sara chastised him, although it did seem as if her pity for the recent widow might be misplaced.

"Sounds like a sticky situation," Joe observed. "I don't think I could handle your job."

"No, you'd want to take care of all the poor sad people who came through your office," Sara teased. "Joe's the original pushover for babies and strays," she told Marcus.

"Gee, thanks," Joe responded, hiding his real hurt in sarcasm.

"Your mother said it first," Sara pointed out. "And I should know, I'm one of your strays."

"That isn't how I think of you at all."

"Just what do you do, anyway?" Marcus demanded, suddenly exchanging his role of tormented little brother for the much more palatable one of protective big brother.

"I teach modern literature at the college," Joe explained casually. Part of him was sitting back, observing the interrelationships in the triangle. Sara was hiding behind a shield of teasing jokes. Why? Was she afraid Marcus would object to their love or was she trying to tell him to cool it and give her space? Was

Marcus Sara's little brother in need of comfort, or a rival? Or was that only his own insecurity's jealous raving?

"Sounds cushy. I guess the only problem you have to handle is coeds who want better grades."

"Marcus!"

"Unfortunately that hasn't been my experience," Joe mock-mourned. "Except for a few baby-faced freshmen who gush about my years of experience, I've yet to meet any of these nubile coeds ripe for the plucking."

"Sure, Joe," Sara laughed. "You wouldn't notice even if a ripe one fell in your lap, you goof. Seriously, you're just too nice."

Marcus frowned. "I don't think you'd make a successful insurance agent."

Joe lifted a shoulder. "I wouldn't want to be a successful insurance agent, so I guess that's okay."

"What a person wants out of life rarely has anything to do with what he gets." Marcus ripped open one of the crusty rolls Sara had made and stabbed a knife of butter into the soft center.

"I disagree."

Sara looked from Joe to Marcus and back to Joe. She was tired. If they fought, she thought she'd just go quietly upstairs and hide under her pillow. Or bean them both with the rolling pin.

"Are you doing exactly what you want, what you always dreamed of doing?" Marcus asked. "Sara's not. She graduated with this fancy degree in landscape design and got a job changing diapers and coddling a seven-foot-tall baby. And I'm sure as hell not doing what I want. People don't get what they want out of life."

Sara frowned and considered setting Marcus straight.

"Again, I disagree. I'm doing exactly what I want, and I think Sara must have made a choice or two. To the best of my knowledge no one forced her to get married and have a child, or even to stay at home with Lala. Getting what you want isn't always easy, but it's usually possible."

"Maybe no one was holding a gun to her head, but Michael didn't exactly encourage Sara to get a job. He was a spoiled brat who demanded what he wanted." Marcus turned to Sara. "You threw away your dreams for the sake of Michael's ego. He's been dead three years and you still pretend it was what you wanted. Don't you ever get sick of kissing his..."

"Marcus!" Sara's voice cracked through his words like a whip through the air. "Don't talk about Michael like that. I know you're hurting and I want to help, but I'm not going to sit here and tear Michael apart just to make you feel better. I chose to give up my career, and yes, it's what Michael wanted, and at times I resented it, but it was always my choice. And you chose to become an insurance agent. No one forced you to do it."

"Like hell, Sara! What do you know **ab**out it? You've had your parents falling over themselves to make you happy all your life. All my parents wanted was for me to be like my damned brother. You got to choose what you wanted to study. I would have killed for a chance like that, but even with Michael dead I don't get it. I'm still supposed to be just like him. And I'll tell you something, I hate it. I'm damned sick and tired of following in his footsteps."

"So don't," Joe suggested a touch coldly. He didn't want to hear about Michael, and he especially didn't want to hear Sara forced to defend him. Michael was Sara's past; he was her present and he was going to do his damnedest to be her future. "Who's forcing you?"

Sara had to force back her tears. She was exhausted, and these two idiots were determined to start a fight. "Stop it," she pleaded. "Please, just stop it. Maybe you did feel forced into insurance, Marcus, I don't know. Emotional blackmail is a way of forcing people to do things. On the other hand, I never knew you didn't like your job, so maybe it's partly your fault. Joe managed to rebel against his family, and he had a lot more footsteps to follow in. So I guess it's possible. Right now I just want you to stop arguing about it."

There was a very long moment of silence. Marcus picked crumbs from the table and dropped them into his soup plate. Joe reached out and touched Sara's arm very gently. She rested her forehead in her hand and tried to calm the pounding in her head. "So what do you really want to do, Marcus?" she finally asked.

He swallowed hard. "I wanted to sculpt. For as long as I can remember I wanted to sculpt. But I was always supposed to be like him. To play basketball." His voice was flat, utterly calm. "To be a great salesman. What a joke. I can't make a basket to save my life, and I hate selling. I wanted to study art, but Dad wasn't going to pay for that. No security. Impractical. Anyone with brains can see that business is smarter. Hell, why bother with the degree, just get a job."

"You always did like art classes," Sara recalled. "You were good."

"Yeah, well, not good enough for a scholarship."

"You should have asked us for help."

Marcus laughed bitterly. "Michael said I should listen to Dad, and all Dad ever said was that I was lucky to have Michael to bail me out, and why can't I be more like Michael. You think I'm being a jerk, but they really do wish it was me." His eyes glittered with tears again.

"Oh, Marcus," Sara said and went around the table to hug him. Joe watched, feeling like he got left out somewhere along the way, wanting only to hold Sara the way she was holding Marcus.

"I'm sorry," Marcus muttered into her arms, sniffling back his tears. "I'm being a jerk. It's just when I saw the crèche it was like everything I ever buried came up all at once, you know."

"I know. It's okay," Sara soothed. "You'll never make it trying to be Michael. You're just too different. You're going to have to stop trying and start being yourself. I'll bet you've got enough money to go to school if you give up the apartment and office and fancy suits and all. Go back and start over. He could do that, couldn't he, Joe?"

How the hell was he supposed to know? "I don't see why not. It probably won't be easy, but the path to happiness isn't always paved in yellow bricks."

"Joe," Sara chastised, but she knew from his tone that he was serious. She wondered how hard it had been for him to become something different from everyone else in his family. And admired him even more than she had before. She was glad he was here tonight. For whatever tonight was worth. At least it was all out in the open now, so the whole terrible evening was probably for the best. She gave Marcus one last pat. "If you need money, Marcus, I could lend you some from Lala's insurance."

Joe wasn't too sure that was a great idea. Maybe sacrificing and working for what he said he wanted would be good for Marcus. The guy had it hard, but he hadn't exactly stood up to his problems and faced them. Making it too easy would be a mistake. He had to be responsible for his own future or ten years from now he'd be in the same boat, crying because he didn't really want to be a sculptor. Joe didn't figure it was his place to say anything, though, so he kept his mouth shut.

"I've got money," Marcus admitted. "I guess I just never had the guts."

"Maybe you just needed a little encouragement," Sara suggested.

"That's sometimes all it takes," Joe agreed. He wouldn't mind a little encouragement himself right about now. It was pretty obvious that he wasn't going to make love with Sara tonight. She'd had another rough day. But a little encouragement, just something to tell him he hadn't blown it all to hell last night, that would be more than welcome. He sighed.

Marcus yawned. "Hell, Sara," he complained, "having nervous breakdowns all over your house tires a guy out. I need to get home and hit the sack. I guess you'll have to tell me about Florida some other time. Why don't I give you a call tomorrow, when I've got my calendar handy?" There was a thread of something dark running through his determined cheerfulness.

"Okay. If you wait a couple of days you can see the pictures Uncle Corny took. He promised to send copies up as soon as he got them back from the photo shop.''

"Sounds good. I'll talk to you tomorrow."

Joe stood up and shook Marcus's hand. "It was nice to meet you," he said, inflecting the polite phrase so it sounded wry enough to let Marcus know he didn't pity him.

"If you're a friend of Sara's, I'll probably be seeing you again. Preferably under better circumstances."

While Sara walked Marcus out to his car, Joe cleared the table and loaded the dishwasher. What a night, he thought. Sara needed time to get used to his love. She needed time for her grieving, time and space. With her life like this he'd probably be old and gray before he got a chance to make love to her. And holding back was hell. He wanted to sweep Sara into his arms and make everything better. And he knew just how he'd do that, too.

Sara had some ideas of her own. When she returned to the kitchen Joe was scrubbing the tomato-encrusted casserole in the sink before adding it to the load in the dishwasher. Having him pitch in and help was special. Michaël never had. There was some truth in the things Marcus had said; Michael had squelched some of her dreams so that she would be his perfect wife. But since it was too late to change what had happened, Sara thought it best not to dwell on his failings. There were good things to remember. She'd remember them. And welcome the differences in Joe.

She wrapped her arms around Joe's waist, pressing her cheek against the scratchy wool of his sweater, smelling the faint spiciness of his cologne mixed with the clean, masculine scent that was all his own. He was warm and strong and solid. She needed him to make love to her tonight. Too much had happened. Unless he held her she was going to spend the night awake, remembering, feeling progressively worse, until she was once again crying because Lala was gone.

Joe's wet hands closed over her own, dripping suds on the floor. He loosened her grip and turned around to wrap his arms around her. "Tough day?" he asked, laying his cheek against her silky curls. Sara nodded. She tipped her head, wanting his kiss. Joe reared his head back and looked into her eyes. "Maybe tomorrow will be better. You look like you could use a good night's sleep." She nodded again, staring at his lips, wishing he would kiss her.

Smoky blue eyes and pink parted lips proved too much for Joe's resistance. He bent and kissed her, just once, gently, just a kiss to make things better. No passion. He wasn't going to give in to that temptation. He wasn't going to make love to her. She wasn't ready.

He wasn't going to kiss her. Sara wanted to scream. Was he being noble or did he not want to make love to her when she was not at top form? She realized she didn't care which it was. She needed Joe tonight. If only they had an established relationship; she felt like a virgin, wanting only for the first time to be over with so that she could enjoy their relationship. Tonight she needed him. She tried being subtle, parting her lips for his kiss, then went further, running the tip of her tongue against the swell of his lower lip. Joe pulled back and tipped her head against his shoulder with a hand at the back of her head, buried in her curls.

Was she trying to kill him? Didn't she know what she was doing to him? A man could only take so much, and with Sara he couldn't take much at all. She only needed to look at him for his head to fill up with tantalizing images and his body to leap to attention, ready to make them real. Joe pulled her tight against his body and buried his face in the sweet-smelling curls. "I love you, Sara," he whispered under his breath. And I'll wait for you, somehow, he added in his own head.

Sara pulled back out of his tight embrace. She looked straight into his eyes, and it felt like she was seeing inside, into the depths of his soul. "I want you to make love to me tonight," she said. "I know it's selfish. I know I should wait until I'm in better shape. But I need you now. Please, Joe, I need you."

Sara waited for him to pull back, to say no, she might regret it. He didn't. His eyes flared and grew dark and fathomless, deeper than the nighttime sky, sparkling with crystalline stars. She felt something swell in her throat. She loved him so much, loved him for being willing to wait and loved him for not waiting now. Now she waited.

He stepped back. "Hold on," he ordered. Something started to wilt and die inside Sara's chest. He took a deep shaking breath. "Let me finish this up a minute." What had faded inside her suddenly brightened again. Joe was going to make love to her. Now. Tonight. She reached past him and grabbed the half-scrubbed casserole. Shoving it into the dishwasher, she pushed the starter button and wiped her hand on the seat of her jeans.

Joe smiled. He loved her so much he thought his heart would burst; he could feel it swelling, cracking, breaking into new territory inside his chest. He hadn't felt this nervous and uncertain about making love since the night he lost his virginity back when he was a freshman in college. He wiped his palm on his jeans and took Sara's small fragile hand in his.

The walk to the bedroom took forever, through the dark rooms and up the steps, Joe's hand warm around hers as he half led, half followed her. She could barely walk. It felt like her insides were about to vibrate into a million pieces.

It took about two seconds to get to her room. Joe felt he needed more time. Time to tell himself to slow down. Time to regain control of his heart before it beat through the wall of his chest. Time for Sara to be absolutely certain this was right. Tonight had to be splendid so that Sara would see the glory of their future together. So that the past would dim into yesterday while tomorrow dawned.

Sara flipped on the light and hesitated. Was it too bright? Maybe she should turn it back off. What was she supposed to do now? Strip for him? Strip him? Joe dropped her hand and turned on the bedside lamp. He turned off the overhead light. She just stood there. She had to do something or Joe was going to think she was scared. But what?

Before she could move, Joe stepped in front of her. She knew what he was going to say. But he didn't speak, he just brought his hands up to her cheeks and pushed gentle fingers through her curls, sliding them back from her face. "I love you," he said. His mouth covered hers. Something exploded inside Sara. She pulled closer to him, pressing against the firmness of his thighs and the wall of his chest. Her fists clenched on the fabric of his sweater. His kiss was deep and passionate but slow, so slow. Her blood roared through her veins like a freight train; she could feel the throb of the engine in her abdomen, could hear the echoing whistle in her ears.

For a second he'd thought of asking her again. But she wasn't frightened, just shy. Why was that so sexy? Her kiss wasn't shy. Joe had to take a step back in order to suck air back into his lungs. Her fingers were tangled in his sweater. He smiled as he pulled it over his head and paused so she could let go. When was the last time he'd made love with a woman who wasn't almost cool in her expertise, making him feel as if he was dancing a formally choreographed routine? Sara was as wild and sweet, as sexy and pure as rock and roll. She was a rocking screamer with hot guitar riffs and pounding drums; she was an easy-rolling ballad of love. She was everything he ever wanted in a woman. She was his.

Her hand reached for his chest, then dropped. He ran a fingertip along her jaw, down her neck, across her collarbone. She shivered. He unbuttoned the top button on the long lambswool cardigan. Slowly he opened the whole length of the sweater. She stood utterly still. She wasn't wearing a bra. Just smooth skin, silkier than any fabric could ever be. He didn't touch her. He picked up her hands and put them on his shoulders. Then he touched her, touched her perfect breasts, touched their perfect rose-colored tips. He pulled her a half step forward so her breasts touched his chest and let his hands touch her smooth back. He bent his head to whisper a kiss onto her perfect mouth.

Explosions never whisper, and the kiss that exploded between them was no exception. It was out of his control in a split second, raging hot and passionate. Her hands were touching his chest, loosening the top button of his painfully tight jeans. He reached down and yanked the fabric so the buttons all popped open one right after another. His sigh was lost in her mouth. Her hands touched him through the cotton of his underwear; every muscle in his body went instantly rigid. His breath hissed out.

It worked. She broke his control. Joe stripped off her pants, flipped open the bed covers, laid her down on the cold sheets, blanketed her with his warm body, kissed her—her mouth, her neck, her breasts—until she was hot. She ran her fingers through the lovely unfamiliar tangle of hair on his chest. She kissed his neck, ran her tongue along the ridge of his collarbone. She ran her fingers down his sides, over his wide ribs, past his tapering waist, to the firm muscles of his hips, pulling him against her. Her thighs welcomed him.

He reared back, catching her eyes, waiting until she finally looked into his eyes. He was going to ask her again if she was sure. "Sara," he said in an almost breathless voice, husky with passion, "this is as slow…as I can go. You're…so damned perfect. I love you, Sara." Her name turned into a deep groan as he slowly entered her. He paused, breathing hard; her body adjusted and her hips rose. He took her past the stars to the place where nothing mattered but their own tiny world of hot exploding light.

Afterward, gathered in his arms, warm in a cocoon of covers, Sara listened as Joe told her how wonderful she was. She felt like molten gold, thickly liquid and glowing warm. "I love you," she whispered to him, easing toward sleep in the cozy embrace of his body.

CHAPTER TEN

JOE BLINKED against the brightness of the bedside lamp. Time had stopped, and the world had continued spinning. Had he just closed his eyes for a moment or slept soundly? He couldn't tell. Beside him, deliciously warm against his chest and thighs and delicately solid under his draped arm, Sara was breathing in the constant measure of deep sleep. A lazy smile touched his mouth as contentment enveloped him in its soft embrace; if he never moved again he would be perfectly happy.

The same could not be said for Roly, who was whining with increasing urgency. The poor guy was still locked in the entry, Joe recalled with a touch of guilt. He had to get up. He couldn't just lie here and let his dog wake Sara up, and he couldn't enjoy his blissful cloud of contentment when he felt guilty. He eased himself from the bed, bending over and waiting to see if Sara would wake. A soft swelling of sweet tenderness filled him. He loved her.

He slipped his parka over his jeans and opened the back door to let Roly out, waiting with freezing feet while the dog took his own sweet time. Should he go home now or wait until morning? It wasn't really a question: he had no choice. To leave Sara now would be to pull his heart from his body, impossibly painful. He scowled at the cold black sky studded with more stars than seemed possible. To fit that many stars in one sky, you'd have to overlap them. And yet the endless dark sky held them all and remained empty. The distant lake was even darker than the sky, black beyond the ghostly whiteness of the snow on the beach and the coastal edging of ice.

Joe shuddered and whistled for Roly. The dog scampered into the house wagging his tail and shook, showering cold snow onto Joe's bare feet. After a last long look at the heart-breaking beauty of the night-time sky, Joe turned back into the warmth of the house. He locked the door and turned off the light, let Roly in to sleep in the kitchen, then returned to the bedroom and turned off the light that had illuminated their lovemaking.

Sara was so still, so distant. He had to gather courage to slip back into the bed and cradle her against him. She moaned under her breath and turned toward him, moving closer. He felt inexplicably desperate as the tiny seed of melancholy that had split open with the piercing light of the stars now grew within him. It felt like a vine twining around his vital organs. He wanted to clutch Sara against him as tightly as he could, as if with the fierceness of his embrace he could somehow possess her. Even as he felt a stirring in his loins Joe knew that possessing Sara physically wouldn't be enough.

He needed more than that. It wasn't enough to share a single night with her. He needed to share her life. Without her he was incomplete, as incomplete as he had always been without his twin. No! How had he come to be so damned vulnerable? What if Sara didn't really love him? What if the words she had murmured hadn't been for real?

He knew his love was real; it was utterly unlike anything he had ever felt for a woman before. Love was no fairy tale; it was a vast, enormous, all-powerful thing that had captured him. An emotion? It was more than that. Whatever he had labeled love before had suddenly been given an extra dimension, making a circle into a sphere, into something mind-bogglingly different. The geometric analogy that popped into his head was mildly comforting—he was, after all, a Fisher. And all Fishers ended up married with kids.

Would Sara marry him? How long would he have to wait before she was ready to explore that possibility? Lala hadn't been gone long. Not long at all. Had they gone too fast? Would she regret this in the morning? How could she? It had been wonderful . . . dazzling. . . .

Joe touched Sara's hair gently, running his fingers over her curls. He touched the smooth skin on her forehead and temple with the feathery tip of one finger. Would she mistake his love for compassion? Her love for grief? What a person clung to in the middle of a tempest-tossed sea wasn't necessarily what they wanted to cling to for life. Would she be too cautious, mistake him as someone who just happened to be available?

If he were as intelligent as he pretended to be when he was lecturing his classes, he would've erected a shield around his heart. But it was already too late. He already loved her. He couldn't protect himself. He could only hold her small body close in the dark under the covers and soak up her warmth for as long as it lasted. Only love her and hope it would last forever. Earlier he had imagined that he could show her the splendor that could gloriously be theirs, now he was afraid to love her, knowing he would reveal too much. Maybe in the morning, when the sun had obliterated the stars from the sky, it would be safe again.

For now he just eased his frame close to Sara and felt her heart beating, listened to her breathing, knew that for the moment she was his to hold. The contraction of fear eased; the deadly feeling of vulnerability faded. Sara moved, rolled over, and Joe loosened his grip on her. She wrapped an arm around him, squeezed against him, muttered his name, went limp again. Joe relaxed and finally drifted back to sleep.

When he woke again the room was still dark, but he knew it was morning. He scrabbled on the nightstand for his watch. Sara sat up in the bed and blinked. Joe held his breath. She looked at him for a long minute. He reached out and pushed a curl off her face. She lay back down beside him. "Good morning," he murmured and waited to see what she would say.

"Time's it?" Her voice was thick with sleep.

"Six-oh-two. I've got to get up. I've got my eight o'clock this morning." Joe arched his back in a muscle-popping stretch, groaning with satisfaction. They'd gone to bed so early that he was well-rested. He relaxed again, casually running his hand down Sara's side, waiting for her reaction.

She yawned.

He waited, touching her hip, pressing her subtly against him.

She yawned again and ran her hand across the mat of hair on his chest, back and forth. She stretched and collapsed against him. She wasn't withdrawing. "Skip."

"What?"

"Why don'tcha skip?"

It felt like electrocution, excitement buzzing through his body at a million miles an hour. She sure as hell wasn't withdrawing. He propped himself on an elbow, kissed her collarbone, touched her breasts, smiled at the sudden gulp of air she needed to take. He kissed the suddenly peaked dusty-rose tips of her breasts, caressed her hips and thighs. A muscle jumped in his groin. "I can't skip class."

She stiffened a little bit. Joe rolled on top of her, keeping his weight on his elbows, trapping her between his body and the mattress. "But I could skip breakfast," he offered. Her smile answered all his questions. He hadn't been able to go as slow as he wanted last night, and he didn't have time now. But Sara didn't seem to mind. She was as eager as he was, and rose rapidly toward the culmination of their ecstasy, her release triggering his.

He ended up collapsed half next to, half on top of her. Three deep breaths and he was pushing himself off the bed. If he didn't move right this instant, he was going to give in to the temptation to stay in her bed half the day, to fall into a blissful post-coital daze, to make love again and again, until he got it right, until he went as slowly as he wanted to. Instead, he marched himself off to the bathroom and stepped into her shower for two long cold minutes. She was climbing out of the bed when he came back into the bedroom.

"Stay in bed. I'm going to run home and shave and then leave for school. You wouldn't believe how temperamental students get when they show up and the professor doesn't."

Sara frowned and pulled the sheet and blankets around her. Joe felt sick at the sign of her regret. He didn't have time for this right now. Hell! How could he not have time? Sara was a million times more important than a classroom of half-asleep freshmen lit students. He went to the side of the bed and took her face in his hands, kissing her thoroughly. "I love you," he whispered afterward. He looked into her eyes.

"I . . . breakfast is the most important meal of the day. Aren't you going to eat?"

"What I did was more important."

"Joe."

"Sara. I love you, honey, but I really should get to school."

She just looked at him. "Right now?" He nodded. "Okay. Will I see you later?"

He grabbed her and crushed her in a bear hug. "Just try and stop me. I love you. Like crazy. I'll be pounding down your door as soon as I get home."

She hid her face against his shoulder. "I'm being silly."

"You're being incredibly tempting."

"You better go."

"I know." He pulled back, and she slowly released him, watched him reluctantly leave.

"Joe."

He turned in the doorway. "Yeah?"

"I love you."

Somehow he managed to drag himself away from the kiss that followed. He went home. He decided he must be either insane or an idiot: only a fool would walk away from a woman like Sara in order to go to work. He spilled dog kibble all over the kitchen when he fed Roly. He buttoned his shirt crooked and put his sweater on backward. And when he had it all straightened out, he realized he hadn't even shaved.

Tucking a towel in his collar, he took a deep breath; thank goodness for safety razors! He opened the medicine cabinet and smeared shaving cream on his beard. Shoving the can back on the shelf, he knocked a box and two jars into the sink. As the foil-wrapped contents spilled from the box, Joe felt suddenly sick. How could he have been stupid enough not to take precautions before making love to Sara?

Going to class had been stupid, too, Joe decided later in the morning, his normal dedication flying out the window. No student ever learned anything from hearing a distracted professor read his lecture notes out loud. He'd ducked most of their questions and dismissed class early. And now he was supposed to have office hours, to sit here and let his students come and pour out what seemed today to be their trivial problems. He considered pretending he wasn't in his office when the fist person knocked. But he hadn't locked the door, and the blasted jerk turned the knob and pushed it open.

"Hey, Joe-boy, how's life treating you? Have you looked at your budget for next year? They want to cut the math department by twelve percent. We're not glamorous anymore. We're just supposed to train math teachers. I'm going to take the next offer I get and leave this place to stew in its own juice." Tim plopped down in one of the chairs in front of the desk and propped his feet on the other. "You wanna Danish or a cinnamon roll?"

Neither sounded good, but he was hungry. Joe shrugged. "I'll take the Danish." His brother passed him the pastry and a huge cup of take-out coffee. Joe took a bite and wrinkled his nose. It would be a prune Danish. He sighed. He should have stayed home and talked to Sara. He should have restrained himself until he was sure of Sara's love. Or at least used protection. "What the hell am I doing here, anyway?" he asked himself.

"I dunno," Tim responded irrepressibly. "Is this a test?"

"Tim."

"Aw, don't sigh, Joey, everything will be okay, just tell your big brother all your troubles."

"This is serious."

"So's a twelve percent budget cut. I suppose the English department fared better. People are all riled about maintaining the standards of a liberal arts education. And they forget that arithmetic and geometry are two of the seven traditional liberal arts."

Joe sighed heavily and turned to stare out the window at his view of the campus, where everyone seemed to know where they were going. How many of those baby-faced kids down there would forget to use protection in this day and age?

"Okay, Joe, I'm being serious and listening." Tim dug into his waxed paper bag and pulled out a second Danish. "You wanna doughnut?"

"No." He was only halfway through with his lovely prune Danish. Joe sipped his coffee. "This tastes like swill."

"I wouldn't know. I guess you've had a broader education than I have. Probably because I went to a college that appreciated mathe..." His voice trailed off as Joe turned back toward the window. "Spill it, Joe." Tim was suddenly serious.

"I think I blew it. I think I really blew it." He spun his office chair back to face the desk and saw the demand for more information in his brother's eyes. "My

chance with Sara. Davidson. You met her at Thanksgiving.''

''Big eyes? Blond? Her kid had just died?''

''Lala.''

''What?''

''Lala. Her daughter's name was Lala. Michella.
Lala. Get it?''

''Oh. How'd you blow it?''

''It was way too soon. She needed more time and I
rushed her.''

''I take it we're talking about sex?'' Tim raised an
eyebrow and spoiled the effect by picking yet another
pastry from his bag. ''What'd ya do, come on too
strong?''

''No.'' Joe stood up and faced the window.

''Then what the hell's the problem, Joe? Somehow
I just can't see you pressuring a woman into your bed.
It's not your style. And if she went willingly, it's her
problem. It's practically the twenty-first century.
Women are responsible for deciding whether to jump
in the sack with a guy or to stay out.''

''Sara's still mourning Lala. She's not ready for a
full-blown relationship yet.''

''And are you?''

''I want to marry her.''

Tim took his feet from their perch on the chair and
set them on the floor. He took a big gulp of coffee. All
the Fishers had been waiting for this for a long time.
''We're talking the big L word?''

''Yeah. I love her.''

''And you made love last night, and now you're
worrying yourself sick over nothing.''

''It's not nothing. I should have told her to wait,
and if I was going to take her to bed the least I could

have done is remembered to protect her!'' Joe sank back into his chair and pulled it close to the desk, letting his face sink down into his arms. He sighed. He'd blown it.

"All this fuss because you forgot? What about her? Joe," Tim said, shaking his head, "what's the worst thing that could happen? She ends up pregnant. You marry her and live happily ever after. Why don't you go buy her some roses and tell her you love her? Women like that kind of romantic stuff. Sitting here worrying sure as hell isn't going to help your relationship any, now is it?"

Joe raised his head. "She said she wasn't going to ever have any more children because it hurt too much to lose them. What if...?"

"There's a difference between saying that and actually getting rid of a kid that's growing inside you," Tim pointed out. "And you don't even know if she's pregnant. I think you're borrowing trouble. My prediction is that you'll end up marrying her. Fishers fall once and they fall forever. You might as well plan to make the best of it. I better tell Betsy to dig out the old monkey suit. You want the last one?"

Joe shook his head at the proffered bag. Tim stuck the doughnut in his mouth, showering his shirtfront with powdered sugar, and wadded up the bag and aimed for the wastebasket. "Damn!" He got up and retrieved the bag. "I've got to go, Joe, got a class to teach. You ought to get out of here."

"I've got office hours till noon."

"Skip it, just leave a note on the door. See ya." Tim shrugged at the obvious answer and turned in the doorway to toss the bag back toward the wastebasket. "Damn!"

Joe frowned as he got up and put the bag in the trash. He should have followed his instinct earlier; he should have skipped. He was a fool to put work above Sara.

"Oh, Dr. Fisher, I'm so glad you're here." A boy who looked as if he ought to be too young to shave, yet sported a three-day stubble, rushed into the room. "It's about that paper that's due tomorrow. I think I need an extension, 'cause, you know, I wanna do a really great job and I haven't had time. This is, like, the fourth paper I had due since the start of the semester and..."

Joe waited until there was a break in the rush of words and calmly explained the extension policy he'd already outlined in class. He shooed the boy off, finally, and wondered if he'd ever been that young himself. And then he took his big brother's advice and left a note on the door before he headed downtown to the jewelry store where he struggled to choose a diamond ring that would be good enough for a perfect woman. The expensive rings were gaudy or too big for Sara's delicate hands. And the small diamonds reminded him too much of the ring Michael had given her. But finally he found the perfect ring. Maybe Tim was right, and everything would work out just fine. He loved Sara, like a Fisher. Forever.

WHEN JOE LEFT HER, Sara sank back down on the crumpled sheets and smiled goofily at the ceiling. She felt warm and glowing, alive with the special joy of love. She loved Joseph Fisher. And he loved her. Everything was coming up roses. Her life was turning around. She had a job interview in a week. She was in love with a new man. A wonderful new man. Who made love like a dream. Or had it all been a dream? Sara smiled again and stretched on the bed. When the phone rang it didn't even disturb her. She reached out a languorous hand and drew the receiver to her mouth. "Hello," she drawled.

"Sara? Is that you? Are you all right? You sound sick."

She felt sick, with disappointment. What had made her think Joe would be calling? He was in class, lecturing his students. "Hello, Mom. I'm fine."

"Are you sure, dear? You sounded awful hoarse, and there is a lot of flu going round. I knew you should've canceled your little dinner party last night and gotten your rest. You're pushing yourself too hard. Why don't you come home for a few days and let me take care of you?"

"Mom. I'm fine. Really. So, what's up?"

"Does something have to be up for me to call you?"

"No, I just thought maybe you had something you wanted to talk about." Besides making me your little girl again, Sara added silently.

"I just wanted to see if you were less tired today and to ask how your dinner went. I was thinking about you all evening, wondering if you were okay. You always push yourself so hard, and it isn't good. A person needs to listen to her body when it says to rest. And I thought it might be nice for you to come home for a few days. I missed you while you were gone, and you'd have a few days to relax and let someone take care of you."

Sara ignored the invitation. "My dinner was good. Well, I don't know, it was okay, anyway. Marcus is a little mixed-up right now. He's thinking of quitting the insurance business and going to school. He wants to be a sculptor, but it's a pretty big decision to have to make.''

"Well, I hope he hasn't roped you into taking care of him! You're in no shape to be babying that man.''

"Mom," Sara complained, "he's my brother-in-law and I love him. Of course I'm willing to help him...."

"Love him? You listen to me, Sara Jane. You are not in love with that man." Agnes stopped and softened her voice. "Baby, you were close to someone and you lost him. Thinking you're in love with someone else is a normal reaction. I understand that. And you've had a bad time since then. But, Sara, you mustn't..."

"Mother." Sara struggled to remain patient with her mother while an ugly little doubt crept out from its hiding place in a back corner of her mind. Was her love for Joe...? "I'm not in love with Marcus. I meant I love him like I would love a brother. He needed someone to talk to, and Joe and I were here to listen. It was nothing more than that.''

"Who's Joe?"

"Joe lives next door. He's..."

"To Gert and Corny's summer house?"

"Yes. He's a nice guy.''

"What does he do?''

"He teaches English at the college. Dr. Fisher?''

"I never heard of him.''

"He's been there for years. And living next door to Gert and Corny. Aunt Gert knows him, she mentioned him while I was visiting her." Sara didn't say that Aunt Gert told her to bed him. "He lives in the stone house south of Gert and Corny's.''

"Hmm..."

"It was his dog that was here on Christmas Eve.''

"Oh."

Oops, Sara thought, admitting that was a mistake.

"And he knows Marcus?"

"Not really," Sara admitted.

"Well," Agnes huffed, "that's certainly a strange guest list! Are you seeing this man, this professor?"

Sara nearly provided the name, but she caught herself up shortly. She had to learn to stand up to her parents. Her silent resentment and their redoubled efforts were only making the situation worse and worse. "I don't see how that matters."

"Really, Sara, you sound very defensive. You're seeing him, I know you are. And it matters because I'll be the one who has to pick up the pieces after you break your heart by fooling yourself into believing that you love him. Your daughter's only been dead two months. Do you really think you're ready to engage in a serious relationship?"

Sara didn't say anything. If she opened her mouth at all something horrible was going to pop out, and she wasn't even sure what it would be. Her mother hadn't done much to help pick up the pieces after Michael— her beloved husband, not "someone she had once been close to"—had died. And she was little help after Lala died. Since when was Agnes willing to talk about Lala? And she was tempted to ask, who said it was a serious relationship?

Agnes let the silence stretch for a long moment and then sighed delicately. "Sara, darling, please don't do anything silly. I love you, and I don't want to see you hurt. Why don't you come home for a few days like I suggested? It will give us a nice chance to have a good mother-daughter talk."

"I'm kind of busy, Mom, getting ready for this interview with Burt Vos and whatnot. I think I'll pass." Sara thought her voice sounded dead. She felt like something bright and beautiful had died inside her. "In fact, I ought to get going now."

"Oh, Sara, you're mad at me now." Agnes sighed. "I only say these things because I love you."

"I know you love me. I love you, too," Sara stated, and ended the phone call. It was true: she did love her mother despite her flaws. Was it also true that her relationship with Joe was just a psychological trick, a reaction to Lala's death? Lala. She'd only been dead two months, just like her mother had said. That wasn't very long. What had happened to that horrible sadness that had threatened to overwhelm her, that had sent her dashing out into the night to stand frozen at the edge of the lake because she couldn't stand being in the empty house?

Joe.

Joe had happened to her that night. But that wasn't why she fell in love with him. Was it? Although she had once accused him of getting in the way of her grieving. He did make her forget the pain. He filled up the empty spaces that Michael's and Lala's deaths had caused. Did that make their new love false?

Sara felt like tearing her hair out in the rage that her confusion caused. She wanted an answer, something solid and certain. She got off the bed and took a long hot shower, letting the steaming water pound the questions out of her head. Only when the water turned cold did she step from beneath the spray and wrap herself in a towel. And by then she had an answer.

Maybe not a complete answer, but something nonetheless. She was determined not to be like her mother. She wasn't going to cling desperately to the past, pretending it could be recaptured, paying the price of a sacrificed future. The past was done. Michael and Lala were gone. She had loved them and she missed them. Joe said she would always miss them. But that didn't mean she had to spend the rest of her life trying to figure out some way to recapture them, to bring them back to life. That wasn't going to happen.

Sara wasn't completely satisfied with the answer. She pondered the whole situation, trying to figure out if there was a proper way to grieve, a proper timetable for these things. She ignored the phone the next time it rang. She wasn't ready to talk to her mother again, especially since Agnes would conveniently forget the earlier conversation if it suited her purposes. Instead, Sara went through the other boxes from Vivian and Greg Davidson. A few of the things she would keep, but most of it she didn't know what to do with. She would never have any use for Michael's high school trophies, and yet she couldn't just dump them. Luckily her parents had a big attic. She'd put them there.

She was going to have to do the same thing with all of Lala's belongings soon. And decide if she would keep the apartment or find someplace else to live. But it was nice to be so close to Joe. It was nice to walk on the beach and know that if he saw her he'd come running out of his house and accidentally bump into her. She didn't want to move from the beach house, although she would have to come summer. But that wasn't for a long time yet.

Sara had washed the dust from her hands and made a half of a peanut butter sandwich for lunch when the phone rang again. It suddenly occurred to her that if her mother couldn't reach her by phone she'd come for a visit. Sara answered the phone.

"Sara? Is that you?"

"Uh-huh."

"You sound funny."

"Thanks, Marcus." She took a big gulp of water. "I had peanut butter stuck to the roof of my mouth."

"A likely story."

"Marcus."

"Sara," he mocked. "How are you today?"

"Good enough, if you ignore my mother and her invitation to spend a few days at her house to renew the mother-daughter relationship. What about you?"

There was a silence. "I still want to quit and go to art school, and I'm still scared."

"You can do it."

"How do you know that?"

"Well—" Sara hesitated "—I guess I don't. But look at it this way, Marcus. Most art students don't know if they'll ever make it big or not. At least you have the advantage of knowing you'll never actually starve as an artist. You can always go back to selling insurance if you have to."

"That's true."

"Go for it, Marcus. You'll regret it if you don't."

"That's true, too."

"So?"

"Well, actually, I did call a couple of art schools this morning to find out about how I went about getting in. They mostly want portfolios, and when I said I hadn't done any sculpting since high school, they got kind of cold. But what about a university? I could get in easy enough and then declare an art major."

"That would be worth checking out. And you could always transfer to a school with a strong sculpting program after a couple of years."

"Yeah, that's what I was thinking. So anyway, are you going to tell me all about Florida?"

"Now?"

"Well, I'm sitting in my office with an hour to kill before my next appointment, and my only companions are a dying philodendron and a ham on rye. Do you want me to just sit here and worry about getting sued for doing my job?"

"No, but this is a long distance call."

"So? I'm paying for it. I'll put it down as a business expense."

"Marcus."

"Have you decided who you want to change the benefits on your life insurance policy to? The way it stands now, since the listed beneficiaries are deceased, your parents would get it."

"I..."

"There, now we're officially a business call. Tell me about Florida. Or better yet, tell me about that guy. How come he came running into your house with a rolling pin ready to protect your virtue? The man's in love with you. So what's the scoop?"

"He lives next door, and he came over to talk to me. He saw the mess and thought someone had broken in. He grabbed the nearest thing and rushed in. He'd do it for anyone he thought was in trouble."

"And I was born yesterday."

"Marcus! I already had this discussion with my mother this morning. Joe's just a friend."

"Okay."

"No, he's not." Marcus remained silent. "I think I'm falling in love with him."

"So tell me about him."

So Sara did. She told him about how Joe had helped Lala fly the kite and how he had brought her the sand dollar. About how he had rescued her from the beach, and about Thanksgiving with his family. About Christmas. About meeting him on the beach and sharing his hot tub after the blizzard. About all the articles he'd written that she'd read. About his theory regarding her mother's behavior. About how she desired him and how she worried that it was too soon since Lala had died. "Do you think it is?" she asked in conclusion.

"I can't tell you that," Marcus replied. "It does kind of worry me that you met him right as Lala was dying, and he was so nice to her and all. It kind of sets him up as a hero, you know what I mean?"

"I guess." Sara felt leaden. That wasn't what she wanted to hear.

"On the other hand, he reminds me of Michael."

"How? They're nothing alike."

"Yeah, they are. Michael was kind of a hero, too. And he had that same protective streak. Michael was okay finding people houses to live in—make 'em happy and all. He would've starved trying to sell insurance. Can you imagine him predicting disaster? *What if you die? Who's going to take care of your wife and children?* And handing out the checks to people who just lost their house or something? No matter what my father might think, Michael would not have made it. Just like your Joe said he wouldn't."

Sara felt a momentary pang at his example. Michael had never predicted that disaster for himself.

They had bought insurance because his kid brother was selling it and for no other reason. Her mind vibrated when Marcus called Joe hers. Her Joe. Like her Michael? She was silent, considering. She did agree that there were similarities between the two men. It probably made sense. Any man she fell in love with would have some similarities to Michael, the first man she'd loved. It was only natural.

"Seems to me, you ought to let it ride," Marcus said after a moment. "You don't have to be making any major commitments to him this afternoon, right? So keep seeing him for a while and see if it's for real. Live with him, even. Bet your Mom'll love me for that advice, huh?" Marcus and Sara laughed together, neither suspecting she would be asked to make a major commitment that very afternoon.

Sara took a walk on the beach after the long phone call. It seemed that she and Marcus had truly put the disastrous attempt at lovemaking behind them and had restored their old relationship. The day was pleasant with a rather watery sun adding blurry blue shadows to the white ice and pale sand. It was cold, but there wasn't any wind. Joe didn't come running down from his house to join her. She tried to remember his schedule for Mondays, but it was always changing, it seemed, as he met with this professor or that student. She ought to get him to write down his class schedule, she thought, feeling a bit proprietary.

Marcus was only partially right about Joe, she decided. He didn't have Michael's exuberant high spirits. He didn't celebrate at every excuse. Time with him was more likely to be quietly happy. Michael liked active competitive sports, ones that usually left her in the stands playing cheerleader. Joe had enjoyed the one time they had read together: she reviewing articles, and he checking his students' essays. It had only been for an hour. But it was nice. And he liked to talk. And he wouldn't always want her to laugh her troubles away. So he wasn't really very much like Michael at all.

Except, like Marcus said, they both were soft-hearted and slightly heroic. Would Joe want to protect her as much as Michael had? That wasn't a pleasant thought. She wasn't going to give up her chance to finally get a job and use her talents. And she wasn't going to always do things his way. She'd been happy with Michael, but living alone and caring for a dying child had strengthened her, given her a new independence that wouldn't be easily surrendered. If Joe had some stupid idea about keeping her all safe and wrapped up in cotton batting, he'd better think again! As if she wasn't getting a little ahead of herself!

Sara laughed out loud in the cold air. The lighthouse was gleaming scarlet in the thin sunlight. But today she noticed the bright blue rails that lined the channel, and the gleaming nuggets of color in the parking lot at the state park across the channel, and the sky was a thin blue, the trees and dune grass all sorts of browns and grays and tans and greens. Even the sand was colored—grains of white and black and tan and brown and garnet—if only she looked close enough. She turned and walked back the way she had come. Even if Joe wasn't the only color in her life, he was a beautiful bright spot.

And this time he did come running down from his house to meet her, with Roly circling around him and jumping at his legs. Sara impulsively spread her arms wide and waited for him to run into them. She was laughing. She loved this man who spread his arms and ran toward her, sweeping her into another of his silly twirling hugs, laughing as much as she was. They were breathless when he stopped and set her down. And he hadn't even kissed her yet! That's what he did next. And then they were really breathless. Sara scooped up some snow and tossed it at his face. "Cool off!" she laughed. "I'm not about to get passionate with you down here in all this snow."

Joe looked taken aback. Sara laughed. "Now you behave or I'll put that snow where you need it most and you won't like that at all."

"Threats already? Give a woman one inch and she takes a mile!" Joe blustered. Sara just laughed, and he threw his arm around her shoulder and pulled her against his side. "How far did you walk? You want to walk some more or go inside?"

"I'll walk with you a little way."

"Okay." Walking with their arms around each other was awkward in their big winter parkas on the uneven sand and snow. Joe took Sara's hand in his and then tucked them both inside his mitten.

"You're going to stretch it all out of shape," she warned.

"So, I'll just always take you with me when I want to walk in the cold."

Sara glowed. Joe was such a romantic, such a sappy, corny, delightful romantic. They walked south along the beach, away from the lighthouse for a way and then turned back. Roly had left a zigzagging trail along both sides of their straight track. It looked silly, Sara thought, like some electric buzz of excitement traveling beside the set of lovers' footprints. "Your

place or mine?'' she quipped as the houses came into
sight.

"Mine." Sara thought Joe sounded a bit tense. She
glanced up at him to see if he looked grim, but he had
his head swiveled around as he whistled for the dog.
Roly came barreling past them and turned so fast he
almost lost his balance. He danced around Joe's feet,
begging for praise. Joe leaned down and rumpled his
ears. "Come on, dog, let's go home." Sara glanced at
him again. He caught her looking and gave her a very
cheerful smile. Almost too cheerful, she thought.

When they had peeled off all their outdoor clothes,
Joe waved Sara to the living room. "Make yourself
comfortable. I'll just make some coffee." He needed
a minute alone; he was nervous as hell about this.

Sara followed him into the kitchen. "Let's sit in
here. I like it. It's cozy." She pulled two chairs in front
of the wood stove. Joe frowned. The champagne was
chilling in the freezer and he had to move it down into
the refrigerator, but he didn't really want Sara to see
it before he proposed. Maybe she wouldn't notice.

"Ooh, champagne!" Sara took the bottle from his
hand. "Wow! This is good stuff. What'cha celebrating?''

"You."

Sara bit her lip as tears filled her eyes. Joe was the
sweetest man on the face of the earth. And he loved
her. "I love you, Joe," she whispered and hugged him
as hard as she could. She tried to kiss him but he
turned his head away. She stepped back. "Joe?"

He took the champagne from her hand and set it on
the counter next to the steaming coffee maker and two
crystal champagne flutes he had dusted off in prepa-

ration for the celebration he hoped would come to pass. "I have to talk to you."

"You sound so serious. Is something wrong?" Sara let him lead her to the chairs by the wood stove. She sat down, but he didn't; he knelt on the hearth rug by her feet. She felt something cold touch her spine. What was wrong?

"No. Well, maybe. I don't know." Joe took a deep breath and looked into her eyes. "Last night . . . I love you," he said with such fervor that Sara was frightened by his intensity.

"What's wrong?"

"Nothing. I never did this before. I'm screwing it all up."

"Never did what?"

"Sara," Joe said quickly, "last night we, I, forgot to use protection. I never thought to ask. And if you're pregnant, well, I want you to marry me." The words were out before he could stop them. And they were not the right ones. What he'd meant to say was he loved her and wanted to marry her. Nervously, he dug his hand in his jeans pocket and handed her the ring box.

Sara stared at him. That explained the champagne, anyway. And why he was on his knees.

"Sara?"

"Give me a minute," she said very softly. "This is a little out of the blue for me." She knew she wasn't pregnant; her doctor had put her on the pill to regulate her when the stress of Lala's illness started to affect her body. But Joe's proposal was something else. She was tempted to say yes. She loved him and he loved her: what else mattered? That he was only asking because he thought she was pregnant? That he was playing hero again? And would be as overprotective and stifling as Michael? That it was the same reason her mother had married her father and now lived in fear that his love wasn't real?

Sara closed her eyes. "I can't marry you." She didn't see the agonized look that fleetingly crossed Joe's face to be replaced by determined composure.

"You don't have to decide now," he said calmly. She hadn't even opened the box and looked at the ring he had picked. He swallowed the bile that rose in his throat. "Take your time and think about it. I'm not trying to pressure you. I love you."

A cold anger gripped Sara, a protection against the pain of saying no to the man she loved. She wished he had just asked her. But no, he had to play the big hero and protect her. And she couldn't stand for that; it was the one sure way of guaranteeing that they would never be happy together. "Take my time? You're damned right I'll take my time! My daughter died two months ago. Two months! And now I'm supposed to fall into your arms and live happily ever after? Fat chance, buddy."

She handed him the ring box and took a deep breath. She shouldn't lose her temper she thought. "Joe," she started and then stopped and continued in a gentler voice. "Joe, I love you. Or at least I think I do. But my mother thought she loved my father, and she married him because she was pregnant and look where she ended up. I don't want to be like my mother, never knowing if you really love me or if you just married me because you felt guilty. That would be stupid. I think maybe I need some time by myself to think this through."

"You're being stupid," Joe burst out. "I told you I loved you before we ever made love. And I meant it.

Hell! I'm not some eighteen-year-old fool, Sara. I know the difference between love and lust. And I wouldn't ask someone to spend the rest of her life with me if I didn't love her. Because that's how I view marriage, as a commitment to spend the rest of our lives together, until one of us dies. I think you're more like your mother than you want to admit. This has nothing to do with Lala. It's Michael you can't say goodbye to. Just like her, clinging to the past because you're too damned chicken-hearted to take a chance on the future. Whoever told you life came with a gilt-edged money-back guarantee? It doesn't work that way. Now take it or leave it. Will you marry me or not?''

Sara's eyes were an opaque blue. She felt removed from the situation, as if she were sitting outside herself observing it. ''I'll leave it, thank you.'' She stood up and walked to the front door, where she began pulling on her boots and coat. Joe followed her, but she spoke before he could. ''I am not like my mother. You're the one with the problem. You want to marry someone who doesn't exist. The Sara you met two months ago was weak and helpless. She needed you to protect her, like a child or a stray. But that isn't the real me. You're going to have to find someone else. Goodbye.'' She left, shutting the door solidly behind her, and walked home along the road, wanting to double over with pain.

CHAPTER ELEVEN

JOE HEARD SOMEONE knocking on the door and dragged himself off the couch in front of the fire to answer it. He knew it wasn't Sara; she never pounded in that noisy way. Tim and Betsy were standing on the stoop arguing with each other.

"I told him," Betsy informed Joe, "that we shouldn't just stop by, that you might not be alone and would value your privacy, so if we're interrupting anything lovely, it isn't my fault."

"You're not."

"Joey," Tim said, patting his shoulder, "are you still brooding? I thought I told you, give her roses and tell her you love her. It always works. Women are suckers for that romantic stuff."

"Ah, my husband, the guru of the lovelorn. What do you know about love? I'm the one who seduced you and then proposed. You were just a dumb Fisher, swallowing my lure and getting reeled right in. Now, Joe, what's all this Tim's been jabbering about you getting married?"

"I'm not."

"I'm not," Tim mimicked. "He's all upset because he made love to her and forgot to use protection. He'll marry her, he loves her."

"Tim," Betsy instructed, "go make some coffee. I guess I better have herb tea," she complained, patting the increasing roundness of her belly. "There are caffeine-free teabags in my purse. I want to talk to Joe without all your caterwauling."

"Caterwauling! I don't get any respect. First the school cuts my budget by twelve percent, and now my wife gets on her high horse and treats me like a slave," Tim complained dramatically as he left the room.

Betsy rolled her eyes, but she turned serious when Joe didn't grin along with her. "Chances are she's not pregnant, Joe. A lot of women panic without real reason. Do you want me to talk to her?"

"I don't know," Joe said with a sigh, slumping back down onto the couch. Sara wasn't the one who panicked, he was. He'd run around like a chicken with its head cut off, buying a ring and squawking stupid things. A real featherbrain.

"Hey, Joe-boy! You got champagne. That's a step in the right direction! So how come you're sitting here all alone tonight?" Tim came back into the living room brandishing the foil-wrapped bottle.

"Because," Joe said, enunciating each word very clearly, "she said no."

"No?"

Didn't they believe a Fisher could be resisted? Joe wondered, staring at the subtle herringbone texture of his wool pants. "No."

"You asked her to marry you?" Betsy asked carefully.

"Yes. And she said no."

"Oh, dear."

"You poor dumb idiot!" Tim sympathized, less delicately than his wife. "You proposed to her just like that? I forgot, so let's get hitched? That was stu-u-pid! I told you, roses. You need that romantic stuff."

"Go check the coffee, Timothy."

Joe looked up as Tim left the room. Maybe he was right. What had Sara said, it was out of the blue? He sighed and went back to staring at his lap.

"Joe, there might be a grain of truth in what Tim's saying. That does sound a little abrupt. Are you just going to sit here and take no for an answer? Sara didn't seem like the kind of woman who would jump in bed with someone unless she loved him. She's not weak. I really admired her at Thanksgiving. I think you found a good one, the right one. Now we just have to convince her. Maybe Tim's right, maybe it's time for the roses and, to quote the expert, romantic stuff."

"I don't want to pressure her. She said Lala died two months ago. It's more like ten weeks, but what's the difference? It's too soon. She said she loved me. But I blew it all to hell by losing my temper. First I insulted her, and then I told her she had to decide right that very instant. Tim's right. I'm a stupid, dumb idiot."

"You never lose your temper."

"Sure he does. Here's your tea." Tim sat next to Betsy on the other couch, stretching his bony frame out into a disjointed sprawl. "You should have seen him when he was a kid. When he was about twelve he had this special rope he bought for climbing trees, and Drew used it for some fraternity project. Ol' Joe just about took on the whole fraternity to get it back. Spitting nails and fire, he was."

"I was assuming he'd matured a bit since he was twelve," Betsy informed her husband. "Ultimatums rarely work. Forgiveness, understanding, love— they're a little more effective."

"Yeah, well, it's a little late now. I already gave her the ultimatum and let her walk away. What can I say? I'm a jerk."

"Well, you're pretty damn good at feeling sorry for yourself," Betsy commented a bit acerbically. "If you love her so much, how come you don't want to try to change her mind? Or at least restore something of your relationship? So she doesn't want to rush head-long into marriage. Does that mean you can't love her anymore?"

"I do love her. I'll always love her!" Joe nearly shouted.

"Good!" Betsy approved with a big smile. "Now we're getting somewhere."

It took him almost two hours to get rid of them. Only by promising to buy roses first thing in the morning and to beg for Sara's forgiveness had he been able to get them to leave. If he carried out even a third of Tim's wild plans Sara would have him locked away in a mental institution somewhere, if not in a jail. Kidnap her for a weekend? Sure, she'd love that, and her mother would probably call the FBI in on the case. Send her a dozen dozen roses every day till she said "Yes"? That would certainly make paying off his mortgage an impossibility for the year. Serenade her? Where was he going to get a musician to come out and stand in the snow in the middle of the night? Maybe he would see her on the beach tomorrow and go running down to pretend to accidentally bump into her.

SARA WALKED HOME stiffly, refusing to admit the pain that was clenching her stomach. Pride kept her spine straight and her eyes dry until after she had reached the bedroom. Then she curled up in the bed that still smelled faintly of Joe and their lovemaking and cried. She cried until there weren't any more tears, and she didn't even know if she was crying because Joe had proposed to her or because she had said no.

When she woke up the next morning it took about two minutes for her to realize crying her eyes out had been a vain exercise; the pain was still there and now her head was stuffy as well. She'd only managed to make things worse. That seemed to be all she ever did. She wanted to crawl back under the covers and cry.

Sniveling self-pitying idiot, she ruthlessly labeled herself. She got up and took a shower. Yesterday she'd stood under the streaming water and decided not to be like her mother, not to cling to the past. Her whole life seemed to be unfolding before her, starting over. She wasn't going to let Joe Fisher's machismo ruin it for her. If he needed to play hero and ride around on a white charger rescuing damsels in distress, that was his problem. Not hers. She wasn't a damsel in distress. She was a capable, independent woman who had welcomed a helping hand over a particularly rough stretch. Now she no longer needed him; she would go on by herself, get her job, move someplace else, make a new life. Without Joe.

She refused to let the tears fall until just before noon when the roses arrived, a dozen long-stemmed roses of a red so rich and dark they hardly seemed real. Sara thought her heart might break as she ripped open the envelope to read the card. "I love you." It was so classic, so elegantly eloquent, so like Joe. She missed him so much. Tears poured down Sara's cheeks; she had to mop her face when the doorbell rang.

She looked tearstained, but it didn't matter. Joe wouldn't care; he'd just pull her into his arms and hold her until this hurt disappeared into the past.

Only it wasn't Joe at the door. It was a florist's deliveryman with another box for her. Another dozen red roses, as exquisite as the first. But why two bouquets from two different florists? The card. She ripped it open and read it. "I love you a billion ways, Joseph Fisher." A billion ways? That was overkill, and it didn't even sound like him. What the hell was he trying to do to her? He ought to know she needed time and space to consider what had happened, what he'd accused her of. He was just going to pretend it hadn't happened? Send roses and more roses and . . . and what? She was supposed to fall back into his arms? All he really wanted was for her to fall back into his bed! And he was a fool if he thought these two schizophrenic bouquets were going to do the trick.

Sara went shopping and bought a nice new dress to wear to her job interview next Monday. The silk camisole and tap pants she bought were solely for her own pleasure, to make her feel good about herself. She never once imagined Joe's hand sliding the spaghetti straps from her shoulders so that the scallop-edged silk would slide down and hang for a breathlessly provocative moment on the hard tips of her breasts before falling to reveal her to him. She never thought that his hands might slid up her thighs and right under the scalloped hem of the pants. Not for a split second. And she wasn't crying now.

Certainly not because there was yet another delivery of flowers only five minutes after she walked in the door. Another dozen roses from the first florist, with the same simple card, ivory linen with black ink declaring his love. It wasn't his handwriting. Why would he have the florist sign the cards if he really cared? Why couldn't she make sense of this? Or at least enjoy his romantic extravagance? She hoped no more bouquets would come because the third one used the last of Aunt Gert's big vases. She didn't want his stupid flowers. And she'd tell him so, too.

Sara wrote Joe a little note and tore it up. The next attempt was scuttled as well. Finally, after a dozen notes had ended up wadded into crumpled balls and been tossed at the wastebasket, Sara decisively put her pen to paper and wrote *the* note that she would give him. It was short. Very short. Maybe she should sign her full name. Maybe she should use a salutation. Maybe…no. This is how it was going to be. She pulled on her coat and walked over, in the dark, not the least bit scared of the bogeyman, and tucked the note between the storm door and the big front door.

She hurried home and waited for him to call her. He didn't. Finally she went to bed. She missed knowing someone cared. Wasn't that funny? she thought, not even pretending to laugh. She'd told Joe she needed time to grieve, and now she had time and she missed him, not Lala. She was so confused. She had to remember why Joe was wrong for her. He wanted a damsel in distress. He'd been surprised by her talent when she showed him her résumé. But she'd been surprised, too, by how good it looked, a little voice reminded her. No buts, she shouted back. He didn't think she was capable. She'd show him!

Only how would he know if he never called? Knowing she'd regret it in the morning, Sara cried herself to sleep again.

JOE FOUND THE NOTE in the morning, when he was already running ten minutes late. He thought about waiting and reading it after class. But he was already reading it before he finished wondering if he should. "The roses are nice, but I can do without the pressure. S."

He felt like sinking down into the new snow on the steps and crying. He hadn't even sent her any roses. Yesterday he'd walked the beach until his feet nearly fell off and she never joined him. Today he'd planned to call. To apologize for his stupid temper tantrum, for acting like a thwarted five-year-old in the candy aisle at the grocery store, and to offer her as much time, space and understanding as he could give her. To tell her he loved her with all his heart and would always be waiting no matter what. To give her the gilt-edged guarantee that he'd shouted didn't exist. She didn't sound exactly receptive.

Tim. It had to be Tim. He was going to die for this. Die deader than a doornail for screwing up his admittedly faint chance to get back together with Sara. Never mind that it was his temper that got him into this whole mess in the first place; that just made it all the more likely that it would get him out. Didn't it?

THE ROSES CAME shortly before the phone call. The same bouquet of twelve dark red, long-stemmed roses. With the same ivory linen card with the same black scrawl. She didn't cry this time, just set the roses in a quart canning jar she found in the back pantry. The scent of roses was filling the house. What would Joe say if he knew it reminded her of the hospital, of the roommate Lala had once had whose parents had sent in dozens of roses from their flower shop in a vain effort to get rid of the medicinal hospital smell?

"Sara Davidson?" The voice was familiar. For a second she thought it might be Joe's, but it was a shade off. She wasn't really surprised when the caller identified himself as Tim Fisher, Joe's brother.

"Yes?" She hated the tremble in her voice. What would she do if something happened to Joe? What was wrong? He'd been hit by a drunk driver? He was in the hospital somewhere? Dead? *Oh, God, no!* Sara screamed inside her head. "W-what . . . ?"

"Joe informed me that if I wished to retain my masculinity, I must call you immediately and apologize for sending you the roses in his name. I am, as he so accurately put it, an interfering, meddling, buttinsky with my nose stuck way too far into his business for comfort, both his and now mine. I humbly offer my sincerest apology and beg your forgiveness, and while you're at it, why don't you give Joe a break and cut him a little slack? He waited a long time for you to come along, and now that he's finally in love you can't expect him to have it all perfect the first time around, so how about it?"

Sara heard something that sounded like a roar of rage in the background, and then Tim's voice continued. "Well, hell, Joe, what'd you expect me to say? Go ahead and rip his heart out, it's fun to see him suffer?" The words that followed probably did irreversible damage to the phone lines. Sara quietly hung up the receiver.

Was Joe really hurting or was that just Tim's obvious flair for drama? He was probably hurting, Sara admitted. If he hadn't sent the roses then he was probably hurting as much as she was. Because he did love her, and she had known all along way in the back of her head that he wasn't just trying to bed her. There were lots more fish in the sea for a Fisher like him, and she wasn't the biggest or the brightest or the best. So he really must love her. And she really loved him.

But that was a fine kettle of fish. Because they were all wrong for each other. She wasn't ready for a new relationship, a new commitment. And she didn't want a man to protect her. She wanted a man who considered her his equal. And Joe needed a woman to take care of. He needed someone to fill his house up with kids and laughter. Someone who didn't require a gilt-edged guarantee.

It hurt to know she was wrong. She would love to carry his children inside her, to grow big as they did, to suckle them. Boys with his strong compact body, learning to climb trees. And little girls with his big dark eyes tagging right behind them. He thought marriage was a forever thing. From what the papers said, that wasn't the most common attitude anymore. Joe was special and she loved him. She just couldn't live with him. The little voice telling her that she could was wrong.

Despite Tim's apology, if it could even be called that, there were two more bouquets on Wednesday. And on Thursday three more bouquets and a gentle lecture from Betsy urging her to talk to Joe. Later the phone rang again. "Yes?" Sara asked after Vera Fisher had identified herself. This time she wasn't afraid that something had happened. At least not as much. Perhaps because Vera sounded so crisp and in control.

"If Joe knew I was calling you he'd be very upset with me," Vera admitted. "He's still quite furious with Tim. He says you need time, that you feel it is too soon after your daughter's death to commit yourself to a new love. And no, I'm not going to argue with you, my dear." Vera took a deep breath and continued, sounding less formidable. "You know I lost a child?"

Sara made an assenting murmur; she'd been expecting another protective lecture, like the inadvertent one Tim had given her, like the very understanding one Betsy had given her, urging her to talk to Joe, to tell him she needed time but admit she loved him.

"Jeremiah. That was my son. That pregnancy was like a special present after we thought there would be no more babies. I was so happy, and so was Robert. We were always busy, but the kids made it worthwhile, you know, not the silly honorary degrees and awards. They were just icing on the best cake in the world. Everything was perfect, and then the doctor told me there were two heartbeats and perfect suddenly got better.

"Then, two weeks before I was due, I got mugged. We went to Chicago for a lecture and I was impatient to get back to the hotel afterward. I went down to the car. I was still very proud of having beaten all these men in their own field. I guess I thought I was invincible. A man tried to take my purse and I tried to fight him." Vera's strong voice almost broke. "Robert came out and the man ran off, but I went into labor. Jeremiah only lived a few hours, not even until morning. I felt guilty for being a fool. And Robert blamed himself for not leaving when I wanted to. We were both selfish, hurting because we lost one baby instead of taking comfort from Joey. Every time I looked at him I thought of Jeremiah. I think we neglected him. Oh, he was fed and had his diaper changed, but I think we failed to love him enough. The older kids sometimes thought he should have died like Jeremiah did. Or that by surviving he proved he didn't need anyone.''

"But that's not true," Sara protested in a raw whisper.

"I know. But children don't always see things rationally. Maybe no one ever does. I didn't mean to tell you all this. I never told anyone before. It's just that Joey needs someone to love him, and I think you're the right person for him, and I wouldn't want you to do something in the pain of your daughter's death that you would regret for the rest of your life.''

Sara couldn't say anything past the lump in her throat. Vera didn't seem to expect anything. She didn't even say goodbye before she gently hung up and left Sara to listen to the hum of a dead phone. She hung up her phone, too. She wanted to walk on the beach and let the cold, clean air blow through her head and sort out her thoughts, but she was afraid she would bump into Joe and she wasn't ready yet. In her pain she'd been very selfish. Was she very wrong?

Joe. Was he really all that overprotective? He must have had it drummed into his head from birth that men should never allow a woman to walk alone at night. So maybe he didn't really doubt her ability to take care of herself. Maybe he hadn't been surprised that she could manage to put together a decent portfolio, but impressed. In a way, maybe he was right, maybe she was clinging to the past. Not to Michael, but to Lala. Was she going to regret throwing away this love for the rest of her life?

She didn't have any answers by the time she turned out the light and crawled into bed. Just nine bouquets of roses and an ache in her heart that should have told her everything she needed to know.

What would she have done if she had known that beyond the dark tangle of woods Joe was standing in the window watching as the last golden glow of light went out and left her house and the night bathed in darkness?

He sighed heavily and leaned on the window jamb. What was he doing up here, anyway? Standing in one of the guest rooms watching her shadow move behind the curtains. Had there ever been a man more foolish than he? He'd thrown away the most precious gift in the world; he'd thrown away love. Sara was his sunshine, the light of his life. Every sappy cliché a lovesick poet or singer had ever written seemed appropriate. And now he was doomed to darkness.

Only a few nights ago he'd stood, warm from Sara's bed, and shuddered at the beauty of the stars. Then he had seen the stars and reacted with childish dislike. The same sky of stars curtained the heavens tonight over the same stretch of inky black lake. Now he knew how greedy he had been.

When he was eight he had read that a person who died became a star in God's heaven, and he had immediately planned to become a spaceman and visit Jeremiah. When a teacher had debunked his fantasy in class by mathematically demonstrating just how impossible it would be to travel, not to a distant star, but even to the nearby moon, he'd wanted to die himself, of embarrassment. And he had hated seeing the impossibly distant stars since then. Like a child who'd never grown up. He'd accused Sara of clinging to the past, but wasn't he worse?

He'd seen the beauty of the stars and turned away and never noticed the utter darkness of the lake. Did he really want the sky like that? So black that even hope became impossible? How could he be sad about Jeremiah when he was sharing his bed with Sara? Like the sunlight, she obliterated the stars and turned that black lake of hopeless despair into a glittering blue mirror of all the happiness in the world.

All she had asked for was time. Time to finish saying goodbye to Lala. Was that so very hard for him to grant? How often had he told himself to go slow and give her just that? Joe rested his forehead on the cold smooth glass and sighed again. Even Lala knew more about life than he did. She at least had her song about reaching the starfish on the beach. He was too dumb to manage to hold onto a star that fell into his lap.

He had accused Sara of needing a gilt-edged guarantee, but wasn't that what his ultimatum had demanded from her, the guarantee that she loved him more than anything else in the world? He'd been an utter fool, and tomorrow he was going to fix it. Betsy was right when she scolded him, when she said he was good at self-pity. Moping around would get him nowhere. Tomorrow he would tell Sara he loved her and would give her all the time she needed. Tomorrow he would give her a gilt-edged guarantee.

SARA OVERSLEPT and woke to the sound of the telephone ringing. She rolled across the bed and nearly slid over the side in her haste to answer it, but before she even said hello she realized that her hope that it would be Joe was silly. It was probably her mother. No, it was a man's deep voice saying hello. Her heart leaped in her chest. It was Marcus. Her heart sank like a heavy stone dropped into a deep, still pond, radiating endless circles of pain.

"H'lo, Marcus."

"Did I wake you up?"

"No." Sara made the automatic lie and then corrected herself, "Yeah, I guess you did."

"I'm sorry, Sara. I should have guessed you'd sleep in today."

"Why?" Was she still asleep or was he not making sense?

"To…hide, I guess, I don't know. You want me to come over tonight? I tried to get the day off, but I've got a big meeting about a group policy that I really can't blow. It'll pay my tuition for…"

His voice trailed off into silence, but Sara didn't understand why. What was he trying to say? "Sure," she agreed a touch skeptically, "come over whenever. You know you're always welcome."

More silence. "What are you going to do today? I mean, anything special? If you want, I'll call in sick and we can go see her grave or something."

Sara frowned. "What are you talking about?"

"It's Lala's birthday, isn't it?"

The silence took on a whole new quality. Sara couldn't speak. She'd forgotten. After condemning Joe for getting in the way of her grief. With all this time on her hands. She'd forgotten her baby's birthday. Sara wanted to die.

"Sara?"

"I forgot," she admitted hoarsely, willing back her sobs.

"I'll come over."

"No!" Sara almost shouted. She couldn't stand having someone else around her now, someone who knew just what a terrible, selfish thing she'd done. "No," she continued in a more controlled voice. "Go to your meeting, Marcus. I'm okay." She swallowed hard. "I knew her birthday was coming. I just hadn't remembered yet this morning. Call me tonight, okay?"

"If you're sure that's what you want. I'll forward my calls so you can get me any time today just by calling my office, okay?"

She nodded and then realized she needed to speak. "Yeah, okay, Marcus." She said goodbye and hung up the phone.

Lala would have been eleven today. Sara went through her aunt's house to stand in the kitchen windows and look down over the beach just as she had months before when she watched Lala fly her kite with the strange man, the professor, Joe. Today there wasn't any sunshine, just gray clouds from an unseasonable warm front leaking gray drizzle onto the compacted banks of snow. The lake was the color of emptiness and sorrow, a dark gray-green murkiness beyond the fencing of dirty ice. It looked as ugly and dismal as she felt inside.

A year ago she'd been driving Lala to school with a batch of chocolate cupcakes with chocolate icing. They'd been decorated with sugar-cube dice that added up to ten. It was the same birthday treat Lala had brought to school each year, since she turned six in kindergarten. And now Sara would never again have to paint all those terrible little dots onto cubes of sugar. Not for Lala. Not ever for Joe's babies, not now that she'd thrown him away.

She rolled her forehead back and forth on the cool damp glass and squeezed her eyes tightly shut as a feeling of overwhelming emptiness grew inside her chest. It was as if her insides had all disappeared, leaving her nothing more than a hollow shell, as disappointingly empty as a chocolate Easter rabbit that even a child's thumb could easily puncture. How was she going to celebrate Lala's birthday?

To Lala, celebrating had come easily, from her simple joy in being alive. Each year they had celebrated much more than the traditional holidays. There was the first day it smelled like spring, and the first day it was warm enough to swim in the big lake, the first strawberries of the season, and the first peaches, the first corn on the cob, the last day they swam before winter. A midwinter thaw like today's might be celebrated with a barbecue. Her favorite picture of Michael was of him grilling hamburgers in his winter parka and a six-foot-long stocking cap that Lala had given him for Christmas. And when the snow came back with a vengeance, they'd celebrated the cancellation of classes with an afternoon marshmallow roast. After Michael died and they moved to the apartment, they had to roast the marshmallows over the burner on the stove. But they'd celebrated anyway.

Sara's weak smile of remembrance dissolved into tears, and she slumped down in one of the kitchen chairs and buried her head in her arms, sobbing. Her sobs welled up out of the emptiness inside her and echoed in the emptiness of the house. It was as cold and empty and lifeless as she was.

It hadn't been like that when Lala was alive. Even when she was so sick, her tiny presence had been enough to fill the house, to make it warm and welcoming. But now it was only empty; now she was only empty. Now she would never celebrate again. Sara tried to ignore the uncomfortable pokes her mind was giving her. Not the memories of Lala. She missed her, but the memories didn't hurt. They made her smile. What hurt was knowing there would be no more memories. But it was thinking that she was clinging to the pain of the past to avoid facing the future that made her uncomfortable. Joe had said she was more like her mother than she wanted to admit. And she was proving him right.

Lala was gone. The memories remained. Sara had been changed by Lala's presence, and those memories were a part of herself. There would always be those memories in her heart, those traces on her soul, to...to what?

Not to prove that Lala had existed once and was gone. Not to serve as a memorial to her. To what? To celebrate; there were traces on her soul to celebrate Lala's life. Like everything she had done, Lala had turned Sara's memories into a celebration; she had left Sara an infinitely richer person, with a treasure store of happy memories and a thousand lessons on how to make her own happiness.

To remember Lala's birthday by sitting at the kitchen table, in the half light of a rainy day, sobbing, was a travesty. Sara thought of how many times she had vowed not to deal with her loss like her parents had dealt with her growing up and away from them. She wiped at her face angrily with a paper towel and flipped on the kitchen light to make the room cheerier.

It helped a little, but Sara didn't know what to feel if she didn't feel sad and empty. Except maybe guilty about her fight with Joe when she should have understood what he meant, said yes, taken his ring and welcomed him into her life. She got up and wandered through the house, looking out the windows at the gray rain. In the end she went into the room that had been Lala's for the last few weeks of her life.

It was just another empty room. It captured nothing of Lala. Her own room captured more; there were her favorite photos and the sand dollar on the dresser. And in the chair by the window sat Lala's oft-repaired teddy bear. Sara thought of all of Lala's things sitting in the apartment across town, and for the first time since she left there, she felt compelled to return.

THE APARTMENT FELT strange. It was cool and musty-smelling; it wasn't home anymore. She had never realized how small and isolated this little encapsulated space on the third floor was. Without Lala and without her plants, the apartment was pitifully shabby and drab. Her bedroom was the worst room in the apartment. Without the pictures of Michael and Lala that had stood on the dresser and nightstand, the room was colorless and lifeless. Compared with Joe's room with its simple pale wood furniture and the voluptuous luxury of the sheepskin rug and fireplace, her room was a nun's cell. She couldn't imagine making love with Joe on this bed.

Sara turned and went into Lala's room. There were toys spread around the room on shelves, and it seemed as if at any moment Lala might come running in to pin another drawing on the tackboard or to place another stuffed animal with the rest of the zoo on the bed. And yet the room seemed static, lifeless, frozen into place in a way it never had before. Sara knew then that the room couldn't capture any of Lala's exuberant spirit;

it couldn't keep her alive any more than a jar could capture the wind.

A jar could hold air, but it could never capture the wind. Wind had to be free in order to exist. Just so, Lala's things could be preserved forever and Sara would have nothing, for Lala's essence was her spirit, her joy, and that could only be experienced and lived in the present. The only fitting memorial for Lala was life going on. Why did she only learn that after she'd refused Joe's proposal?

Sara sat on the edge of Lala's bed and picked up a stuffed lion with tufted ears. Pulling gently on the fluffy ears, she thought about what to do with Lala's things. She could give them away. To Lala's friends, to Joe's nieces and nephews? She shrugged. It didn't seem right.

Once, when her school had a charity toy drive before Christmas, Lala had brought her best stuffed animal, a giraffe with long curling eyelashes. It had been her favorite next to her teddy bear, and Sara had tried to talk her out of giving it away. Lala, she recalled, had argued that if some kid was only going to get a secondhand toy for Christmas, then it ought to be a good one. Lala would have wanted her toys to go to the Salvation Army, for kids who really needed them, Sara decided.

She drove to the closest grocery store to get some boxes and had to smile at the stock boy's helpfulness. He dug through a stack of boxes until he found the ones he thought would be the best, the ones that had held the expensive oranges and apples in trays. He was quick to point out the double bottom and the carrying handles in the sides. Sara was still smiling as she thanked him and drove back to the apartment. He reminded her of Lala.

It took a long time to sort through everything—Sara remembered a thousand details of Lala's life that she had forgotten. She kept a few more of Lala's favorite toys and the photos and drawings she found, but most of the things she packed up and took to the Salvation Army distribution center. The woman on duty there helped her carry the boxes inside, telling her how wonderful these things were. It was exactly what they needed for a family whose house had burned down the week before. There were two little girls who needed clothes and toys the family would be hard-pressed to afford since they hadn't adequately insured the house.

To Sara that made it seem as if she had done exactly the right thing. She was glad that Lala's possessions wouldn't wait in a storeroom for months and months before they were used.

Instead of returning to the apartment—it would never be her home again—she drove to the beach house. It was late afternoon, and the gloomy day was moving toward an early evening. Sara was tired and hungry and wanted a hot shower and a good meal. More than that she needed to talk to Joe, to tell him how she felt, what she had discovered about missing Lala, and how she had missed him.

Would he want to talk to her? After the way she'd turned him down? And wrote that nasty little note because she didn't understand the roses? Come to think of it, she still didn't understand the roses.

SHE WASN'T the only one. Next door Joe was puzzling over them, too. He'd come home from class late, having cornered a professor from the art department and talked the bemused—or was it amused?—man into drawing him up a fancy-lettered, gilt-edged guarantee. And he had stopped on the way home and taken Tim's advice the way it was best taken—watered down. The single red rose he bought was beautiful. Perfect.

Exactly like the three dozen the florist's van had delivered, asking him to hold them for his absent neighbor. If it wasn't for Sara's absence and the florist's solution to the delivery problem, he might not have learned of Tim's duplicity. The delivery boy thought it worth mentioning that his neighbor had already received eight bouquets of red roses. And to think Tim had been back in his office slurping coffee and eating cinnamon rolls that morning, giving him more unwanted advice for winning Sara back.

Five minutes later he was still puzzled. Tim swore up, down and sideways that he had nothing to do with the roses, apart from one bouquet. Who the hell was sending her roses then? Her brother-in-law, the golden boy with his extraordinary height? Hell, Sara didn't need to get mixed up with him just now. The boy—and Joe thought he was more boy than man yet—needed a big sister, not a lover. He glared at the three fancy boxes.

What the hell? Joe asked himself and ripped the ribbons off one of them and found the card nestled among the baby's breath and deep green ferns. It was one hell of a bouquet; it made his single rose look scrawny and cheap. And he recognized the handwriting, too. Matthew. The second-oldest brother. Just how many of his obnoxious siblings were involved in ruining his life? It was just one of the questions he intended to put to his brother as soon as he answered his phone.

"Hello, Matthew."

"Uh, hi, Joe. I, uh, thought you might be calling."

"I am."

"Yeah, well, uh, Joe." Matt gathered himself, threw back his shoulders with a who's-older-here-anyhow? forcefulness, and explained. "I take it you found out about the roses? You're not going to threaten to take away my share of the family jewels, are you? I heard poor Tim's treading the straight and narrow. But do you really think that's fair, to berate him for trying to help?"

Matt didn't give Joe a chance to reply. "You know, I didn't like your Sara, at Thanksgiving. Thought she was giving me the eye. But as one member of the family pointed out to me recently, she probably simply mistook me for you. So, feeling a bit responsible for putting her off the family by giving her a disapproving look, I thought it appropriate to do something to help you out."

"How many?"

"A dozen." Matt's dignified tone grew slightly sheepish.

"A dozen, as in twelve?"

"That is what a dozen means, Joe."

"Okay. So who else is involved in this racket you have?"

"There is no racket, Joe. No need to be paranoid. Except for Betsy calling Sara and..."

"Betsy called Sara?" His voice was colder and icier than the February drizzle falling outside.

"Yeah. Tim was talking to me on Monday night, and he happened to mention that he thought a dozen

dozen roses would be the perfect gesture of your love for Sara, but that he knew you weren't going to send them. And he said he couldn't stretch his teacher's budget that far. So I ordered them for you. Sort of to make up for glaring at your girl at Thanksgiving. And only because I love you, Joey. We all want to see you happy. It's time you settled down and had some kids. Samantha's thirteen. She needs someone to baby-sit on Friday nights, otherwise she'll end up at concerts with her friends. Her favorite band—I forget the name— has five men with long hair sticking out in all directions and pants so tight they can't think about taking a deep breath without threatening their own well-being!''

It was a ploy that didn't work. "A dozen dozen?" Joe asked.

"A dozen dozen. That's one hundred and forty-four, Joey. I got the best they had, blood-red, long stems. Damn nice. Bought a couple for Deanna while I was at it. You should hope your girl rewards you like my girl rewarded me. Or maybe not. A hundred and forty-four times might...''

Joe hung up the phone. A buzzing feeling of irritation filled him. He paced back and forth across the living room. How the hell was he supposed to handle Sara with his whole family jumping on the bandwagon and sending her flowers and calling her. No wonder she asked him to to stop pressuring her! What the hell was he supposed to do now? His stupid single rose was going to look pretty damned sad next to his brothers' outrageous bouquets.

Should he bring her the three bouquets from Matt and explain who they were really from? Joe sighed and looked at the little certificate he'd had drawn up. All his solemn promises. His grand plan. To roll the guarantee and slip it in the band of the diamond-and-sapphire ring, to wrap it with the single perfect rose, to present it to Sara with the promise of his love and all the time she needed. Now it seemed like just another corny gesture. Empty and silly. He put his coat back on and picked up the three boxes of roses.

He should have chosen to walk along the road, as the path through the woods had puddled with the day's rain. Now the air had turned colder, and the puddles had thin ice surfaces that crackled and broke under his feet. The roses were bulky and awkward to carry. He stopped at the edge of the yard to hitch them up in his arms.

There was a dark sedan in Sara's driveway. Joe stood for a long time, the cold seeping into his bones, and then turned and walked home again. He felt he'd never be warm again. It didn't help that he spent the whole evening in the guest room where the heat was turned low to save energy, but where he could watch the lights in Sara's house through the trees. When the lights blinked out he stood in the dark and shivered.

He was going to have to do something. He couldn't live without her. Love might not be a fairy tale, but it was no bed of roses, either, not even with his brothers' excessive help. What if she didn't take him back? What if she couldn't forgive his tantrum and ultimatum? What if she decided he'd been part of her grieving and now she needed to move on? He wanted to be her eternity, her happily ever after. The sky was dark, the clouds shielding the stars from view. Would they blow over, or had the stars disappeared? Was there any hope? Would Sara ever love him like he loved her? And what would he do if she didn't?

"I THINK I MADE a terrible mistake," Sara said sighing into the silence after telling Marcus the story of her day.

"By giving Lala's stuff away?" Marcus asked with a puzzled scowl. She had just finished telling him how good it had felt to know the things were needed and would be put to good use. All this wind in a bottle stuff, which made sense, in a way, he supposed.

"Oh, no, that was right. I could feel it." She gnawed the inside of her lip. "My mistake was turning Joe down. He asked me to marry him." She glanced at Marcus through her lashes; he was just looking at her, waiting for an explanation. "You said to take my time and wait, and Mom said it was this elaborate psychological trick that my mind was playing on me as a reaction to Michael's death."

Marcus's comment was short and disgusted.

"You don't agree?" Sara asked.

"Come on, Sara, if you were going to fall in love with someone as a reaction to Michael's death, don't you think it would have happened three years ago, when he died? Give me a break! Your attempt to pretend you were in love with me might come under the heading of elaborate psychological tricks. You gave me a hundred reasons why you think you're in love with Joe Fisher. And you never mentioned sex, and I think that's there for the two of you." Sara gave him a look. "I saw how the two of you were looking at each other the other night. I might have been bawling like a baby, but that didn't mean I forgot everything I ever knew about being a man."

Sara sighed. "It's there."

"And he proposed?"

"I said no, I needed more time to grieve for Lala. And he said that I was a lot like my mother, clinging to the past to avoid facing the future."

"That doesn't sound like him, but I guess I don't know him very well. Are you sure you love a man who's that unsympathetic? I mean, what's his big rush?"

"He thought I might be pregnant."

"Sara."

"I'm not. I know I'm not, okay. And I said I wouldn't marry him if I was because it would be just like my mother marrying my father, that I would never know if he loved me or not."

"That's a little different. And the floral effect? That's his doing?"

"Yeah. And I think that's not much like him. Kind of overpowering."

"Have you talked to him about giving you more time? There's no rush if you're not pregnant."

"No."

"No, there's no rush, or no, you haven't talked to him?"

"I haven't talked to him. Some of the roses are from his brother. And his mother called me. Oh, Marcus, I think I really hurt him," Sara said, surreptitiously wiping away a tear.

"Talk to him, Sara. You love him. He loves you. Don't go and screw it all up by doing what you're supposed to do. And listen, you are not like your mother. You went on after Michael died, and you've amazed me since Lala died. I know how much you hurt and how brave you were. Braver than your mother would have been if you had died! Tomorrow morning I want you to march yourself up to the guy and tell him. You love him, he loves you, and you'll get married as soon as you're good and ready and not before. And then give him a big smackeroo!''

''Marcus,'' Sara chastised him, unsuccessfully hiding a grin, ''you're acting like my big brother. I'm supposed to be giving you advice.''

''You can love him and miss Lala at the same time. Don't make my mistakes, Sara.'' Marcus met her look and seemed more confident than she had ever seen him. Sara reached over and hugged him. He was absolutely right, and in the morning she would take his advice and plant that kisseroo on Joe's smacker. Or whatever.

CHAPTER TWELVE

JUST HOW DID ONE DRESS in order to march over and
plant a big smackeroo? Sara felt she needed all the
help she could get. The bubble bath that was supposed to relax her hadn't done its job. All those fragile little bubbles popping like illusions in the light of
reality made her nervous. What was she going to say
to him? Would he understand? Of course he would;
Joe was sensitive, insightful and intelligent. He loved
her. She loved him. Once she decided what to wear,
she'd go tell him just that. Trying to live without him
had been a mistake.

What had all her anger and explanations been but
a way to hide? She had been scared, and she still was,
but it was a fear she would have to live with. Yes,
something might happen to Joe someday: she might
lose him just as she had lost Lala and Michael. But to
live without him for that reason hurt too much. She
was missing his presence in her life almost as if he were
dead. To suffer that pain unnecessarily was stupid. A
way to control her own destiny so that she didn't have
to admit that there were things in the world that were
stronger than she was. Like blaming herself for Lala's
death. Joe was right, she wasn't responsible. Pretending she was wouldn't protect her from another loss.
She would just have to take her chances.

She might as well go over and give him his kiss. And deciding what to wear wasn't that hard. She put on the new lingerie, no longer pretending she hadn't imagined his reaction to the lovely, sensuous, stimulating camisole and tap pants. She pulled on her faded jeans and the beautiful sweater he'd given her for Christmas.

She was about to go out the back door when someone arrived at the front. Joe? Sara ran through the house and threw the door open.

"Hello, Sara."

"Mom. Dad." Her voice sounded flat.

"Aren't you going to invite us in, dear? It's cold out here today! Your father shoveled these steps so you wouldn't have to. I don't suppose Aunt Gert thought of hiring someone to do it. She's used to Florida in the winter, after all."

Sara held the door open wide and let her parents in, hanging their coats while they stomped the snow from their feet. There had only been about four inches of snow overnight, and the man who plowed the driveway had already come through. Her father hadn't worked too hard. Sara wished she hadn't come running back through the house and thrown the door open like that. She could hardly tell her parents to get back in their car and go away. Especially since she hadn't talked to her mother yesterday, even though it had been Lala's birthday.

"What's cooking?" her father teased. "Maybe we can get a free lunch out of this visit, huh, Aggie?"

"John! We couldn't possibly put you out, my dear."

Sara tried to speak, to say that she wasn't planning on sticking around long enough to feed them lunch.

"Speak for yourself, Aggie. I can put her out for a cup of tea if nothing else."

"I'll go put the water on," Sara agreed reluctantly. "But there's nothing for lunch, I'm afraid. I've got other plans, so..."

"So do we, baby. I was just teasing you. Your mother and I are going to the home show at the Civic Center and then out for lunch. I want to show her those travel trailers. I think that would be a great way to retire. Not that Corny agrees with me. He was trying to sell me on that condo again last night. Wasting his money, I told him, calling long distance to talk about that."

"Come on in and sit down," Sara urged. "I'll get that kettle on and be right back." She led them into the living room.

"Where did you get all these roses?" Agnes asked. "There must be—" she paused to count "—five dozen roses here. What in the world is going on?"

"Oh, them," Sara said, dismissing the issue. "Let me put the kettle on and I'll tell you the whole story." She took the time in the kitchen to try to think of a story, but nothing the least bit plausible came to mind. She'd have to settle on honesty and hope it proved to be the best policy.

"Here you go," she said as she carried the tea tray into the living room. "It'll need to steep a minute yet."

"Did I see roses in the kitchen, too?"

"Yes, Mom, you did. You see, I had a little misunderstanding with Joe Fisher—you remember I told you about him, he teaches literature at the college?"

"Yes," Agnes agreed, frowning slightly as she concentrated on this story. No one sent roses like this over a little misunderstanding.

"Well, Joe must have told his brother about it and his brother thought we needed help getting back together, so he started sending me all these roses in Joe's name. But then Joe found out and made Tim call and apologize. So you see, the roses don't really mean anything. Where's the first place you want to go after you get your travel trailer, Mom?"

Agnes didn't speak as she concentrated on the task of pouring the tea.

"I'd like to see California," John remarked. "All my life I wanted to see sunny Cali-forny."

"We certainly haven't decided to buy a trailer yet, Sara," her mother assured her. "We'll be here to take care of you for a long time yet."

"Don't stay here on my account."

"I told you, Aggie, she's a grown woman. From the looks of all these flowers, she's already found someone else to take care of her. She doesn't need us anymore."

Sara smiled at her father.

"Don't be ridiculous, John. She's not going to just up and get married. We haven't met any special young man yet, have we? You're just trying to throw her off on someone else so you won't feel tied down anymore."

"Actually, Mom, I have thought about getting married again." Sara tried to rub the tension from her forehead. They might as well get used to the idea. If she ever got rid of them and got over to Joe's, marriage just might be in her immediate future.

"Well, of course you've thought about getting married again someday."

"I mean soon. To Joe Fisher. He's a wonderful man."

"Sara! You see what you're doing, John? She's just saying these things to protect us. What if she actually marries him? Do you want that on your conscience?"

"I think if Sara decides to marry someone to protect us, she's a fool and will get what she deserves. If, on the other hand, she loves the man . . ."

"All you care about is your adventure. What if I don't want to travel?"

"Don't be silly, Aggie." John tried to calm her. "You'll love it."

"I doubt if you want me along at all. You ought to go on a nice fishing trip with a couple of the guys and I'll stay here in case Sara needs me. We settled down early, and I suppose it's normal for you to want a boys' night out once in a while to make up for everything you missed when you married me."

Sara nodded slightly at her mother's words; Joe was right about her mom, she was clinging to the past.

John chuckled. "Me, fish? Come on, Aggie, you know me better than that. We worked hard when all our friends were still playing. We deserve to play while they're still working."

"At the price of our only daughter's happiness?"

"I'm not planning on getting married for your sake," Sara informed her mother a touch coldly. "You're not responsible for my happiness."

"I'm not responsible for your happiness. I'm not supposed to care that my husband wants to go traipsing all over the countryside in a little trailer. I guess it's my day to get told, isn't it?'' Agnes said forlornly.

"Agnes, would you stop fretting?" demanded John. "You'll love traveling."

"What if I don't? You just toss me out at some rest stop and go on?"

"We don't have to sell the house until after we've tried it! And you know damned well I wouldn't chuck you out at a rest stop. I'd at least drive you to a gas station!"

"Dad!"

"Well, come on, Sara, have you ever heard such drivel? I love the woman. What would I be doing chucking her out at some rest stop? Who'd be there to make my dinner and keep my feet warm at night?"

"You could find someone fast enough," Agnes accused.

"I guess," John agreed, "if I wanted someone else, I could find someone else. But I only want you, Aggie, and you know it." He sounded fierce, but his eyes shone with love.

"I still say we need to take care of Sara," Agnes argued, but she wasn't quite as adamant now.

"No, Mom, I can take care of myself."

"What if something happens?"

"We're not going to be on the moon, Aggie! And there's always my brother to help her out."

"He's right, Mom, and really, I can take care of myself."

"Anyone would think that two months ago you weren't staying at our house under a doctor's supervision," Agnes observed.

"Almost three months. It's a long time." Sara didn't know what more to say. She could point out that yesterday was Lala's birthday, and she hadn't gotten any help dealing with the day from them, but what was the use of making them feel bad? At least they were talking about traveling, about moving away from their empty nest.

"Speaking of long times, we've been here a long time. We better hit the road if we're going to get to the home show before lunch. Come along, dear."

Sara was up and getting their coats before her mother could disagree. They had been there an awfully long time. At least half an hour, and she had plans. She didn't have all day to sit around while they fussed with their teacups and her mother debated whether or not she was obligated to help wash up. She wanted to march them out the door like a Marine drill sergeant: hup, two, three, four! Double time! Move! Move! Move!

And after they had put their coats on, kissed her goodbye and chatted about the weather and seeing each other in church tomorrow and everything in the whole world; after they had strolled out the front door and down the steps and talked about the icy conditions and scattered salt; and after Agnes had already gotten into the car, her father bounded back up the steps and caught Sara as she was going inside. "Do you think it worked?" he asked. "Corny said she doesn't think I really love her. Do you think I convinced her?"

"Dad," Sara said with a smile, "you did good, but you're going to have to convince her every day, not just once."

He sighed. "Oh, well, it's a lucky thing I love her then."

"Yeah."

"This Fisher, he must think something of you to send so many roses?"

Sara smiled again. "Yeah. I think he loves me." She waited, half expecting her father to echo Marcus's advice and tell her not to let him get away.

"Don't you marry him before we have a chance to meet him."

"Dad," she protested.

"All right then, we'll see you tomorrow," her father stated, assuming his wish was her command. He hurried down the steps to close Agnes's door for her.

Sara watched them drive away and sighed heavily as a delivery van turned in. At this rate it would be midnight before Joe got his kiss! And where was she going to put more roses, anyway? Thank the good Lord that at least tomorrow was Sunday, and the florist wouldn't be making any more deliveries. Maybe some of the first ones would die by Monday. Or maybe she could convince Joe to stop sending them.

She didn't rush over to Joe's house immediately. Seeing her parents again made her wonder if she hadn't been right before, if marrying Joe mightn't be a big mistake. Was he only interested in taking her to bed? Sara chewed on the inside of her lip as she washed and dried the fragile tea things. She didn't really know much about him. She didn't know, for sure, if he had sent all these roses or not. It didn't seem right, but what if she didn't really know him at all? Then what? Maybe her father was right and she ought to slow down and have her parents inspect Joe before she said yes.

Inspect him? For what? Sara banged the teapot on the edge of the sink and almost broke the spout off as she started laughing. She was a poor silly goose if she thought her parents could tell her more about Joe than she knew herself! All her angry accusations were so much tripe, stock doubts she'd culled from TV soaps. What could be more ridiculous than accusing Joe of only wanting to bed her? She'd practically had to tie him down and swear on a stack of bibles that she knew what she was doing and she wanted to make love to him. And not respecting her talents? Isn't that what women were supposed to complain about? Joe had only been acting like the decent man his mother had brought him up to be.

He was a decent man who was about to have his socks knocked off with the very best smackeroo she could manage.

If he ever answered his door, Sara amended a little later as she pounded on the front door again, sending Roly into a renewed spasm of excited yipping. His steps weren't shoveled yet, and no cars had come or left. Unless he spent the night somewhere else or was walking the beach without Roly, he was inside. She pounded louder and wished he had a doorbell. That would be one of the first things she changed when she moved in! Sara caught herself up and blushed.

Joe groaned a couple of dark words and buried his head under the pillow. Between Roly's yapping and the pounding on the door, a guy couldn't even sleep in on a Saturday morning. And if whichever one of his interfering, busybody, pain-in-the-butt brothers it was thought Joe was going to get up and let him inside just so he could hear how his family were trying to ruin his love life, the jerk had another thing coming. He was going to stay right here and sleep.

The bed seemed to vibrate with the pounding. Joe moaned and groaned and muttered curses as he rolled to his feet and pulled on a misshapen pair of sweatpants and a faded sweatshirt that didn't match. He scowled at the dog and threw the door open to turn his scowl on whichever sibling had dared to darken his doorstep.

Only it wasn't his brother. It was Sara. Standing on his doorstep. And she smiled at him. He scrunched his fingers through his hair trying to get his sluggish blood flowing to his brain. It had snowed last night, and the whole world was clean and white. The storm was past, and just at that moment a ray of feeble sunlight broke through the remaining clouds and sparkled on all the pristine snow. He waited a moment, half expecting the roiling clouds and brilliant rays of sun to be accompanied by a heavenly chorus singing alleluia. He must be dazzled by the sun in his eyes, he thought a moment later, stepping aside to let Sara in. Roly dashed out and began leaving crooked trails through the snow, following the tracks of birds and squirrels and mice over the drifts.

"These are for you," she said, handing him a florist's elegant cardboard box. "I really have no room for any more. Could you please stop sending them?"

He scowled at the box as he opened it and plucked up the card. "These are from Matt." If he wasn't such a fool, he'd toss them in the trash, but somehow he couldn't bring himself to throw them out. So he would

set them with the three bouquets he'd never delivered. And stare at them with the same malevolent
glare, hoping all the petals would fall off. "Did you
get the others? He said he sent a dozen dozen. I'm
sorry. I didn't know he was doing it until last night,
and you had company so I didn't apologize right away.
They delivered three of them here because you weren't
home."

He couldn't look at her, so he led her into the
kitchen, where he plunked these roses into his very last
juice container. Too bad if he wanted juice for breakfast—there was no place to make it now. Sara was
chattering on about the roses, but he wasn't really listening. He ducked into the bathroom and rinsed his
face and mouth. He still felt half asleep, and he was
caught in some misty world that was neither dream nor
reality. He'd wake up soon enough and stop imagin-
ing that Sara was smiling at him.

"Are you even listening to me, sleepyhead?"

Joe blinked at Sara. Her hands were on her hips, but
she was grinning at him. Or the water running out of
his hair was getting in his eyes. He started to make a
pot of coffee. Sara came over and bumped him with
her hip. He froze and stared at her.

She almost laughed at his owlish look. The poor
dear would probably have a heart attack if she kissed
him now. "I'll make the coffee, Joey. You're still so
sleepy that you're practically snoring." She reached
for the scoop to measure out the coffee, but he didn't
relinquish it. She took it from his fingers, and he almost jumped out of his skin. As if he didn't want her
to touch him. Sara set the coffee to brew and caught
his hand. He stared at her fingers. Sara wanted to

laugh. She couldn't resist. She leaned over and kissed him. It took him a while before he unfroze, and then he jumped back like someone had just dumped cold water on his head.

"Give me a minute," he demanded and left the room. Sara looked after him. Had he changed his mind? Would he stick by his now-or-never ultimatum? She bit her lip and started cleaning mushrooms and grating cheese so she could make him a nice omelet for breakfast. The way to a man's heart and all that. When he returned to the kitchen he was wearing the same disreputable sweats, but he'd shaved and there was a heady combination of mint and spicy woods scent about him.

"I'm sorry," he said in an awake voice, "about my family hassling you. Tim apparently convinced Matthew to send you those roses. Only Tim would think of sending a dozen dozen roses. And I heard Betsy called you. I tried to tell them you wanted time, but I guess they figure a Fisher's not to be resisted. I hope it didn't bother you too much."

He sounded so formal that Sara wanted to shake him and muss his carefully combed hair. He'd been easier to talk to when he was vulnerably sleepy. "The roses were a bit much," she said lightly. "Do you like green pepper in an omelet?"

"No."

"Onions?"

"If you want, I don't care."

There were so many things she didn't know about him. She said so and admitted, "That's one of the things that scared me when you proposed so fast. I don't know anything about you. I don't know what your favorite flavor of ice cream is, or your favorite movie, or even your favorite color. I was afraid I didn't know you at all.''

Joe was silent. ''Vanilla. I don't know, I read more books than I see movies. And I like the color your hair glows when you stand in the sunshine like you're doing right now. It's like sunshine and fire.''

Sara turned and looked at him in surprise. He had seemed so remote, and now he was…flirting with her. He examined the tablecloth in front of him. Sara smiled to herself. She poured him a cup of coffee and added cream, just as he liked, and brought it to him. ''I decided it didn't matter,'' she commented easily. ''I mean, does it matter what kind of ice cream you like when I know you'll dig in your attic for a starfish for a little girl? Or what movie you like when I know you'll invite a stranger in to help stuff your Thanksgiving turkey? That was my next problem. I didn't want to be just another one of your strays.''

''You're not. I never thought of you as a stray. I wish you'd stop saying that.'' Joe sounded furious, and Sara retreated, hiding in the business of stirring up eggs and milk and melting butter in the pan.

''Well, I got past that, too,'' Sara said, carefully pouring the egg mixture into the pan. ''After your mother called I realized…''

''My mother called you, too?'' Joe demanded.

''Uh-huh. Where are the plates?'' She didn't really need to ask.

''On the left. I can't believe my mother called you. Don't they think I can do anything by myself? I'm not the baby anymore!''

"You'll always be the baby, Joey," Sara said, biting back a smile.

"Don't call me Joey. You're starting to sound like them!"

"They love you, Joe. Maybe that's why I sound like them. I love you, too." And she slipped the omelet onto two plates and set them on the table, sitting down and taking a bite. After a minute she met Joe's eyes. "Eat your eggs before they get cold."

He waited and then, finally, picked up his fork and lifted a bite to his mouth. He couldn't taste anything. What had Sara come over for? Did she know what she was doing to him? Making him hope for everything in the world. Making his heart do back flips. He wanted to scoop her into his arms and kiss her until she was breathless and he knew what she really felt. Instead, he took another bite of the eggs.

And threw his fork down. "Come here," he commanded, standing up and pulling her against him, letting her feel what she was doing to him, threading his fingers through her soft golden curls, tipping her head back and watching as her eyes turned that dark smoky blue that he decided was his favorite color. He would have told her, but his mouth was busy, rubbing against hers like a floating feather, pressing little kisses onto the corners of her mouth, capturing her gulp of astonishment or pleasure and working, gently, suggestively, until her lips parted and she moaned deep in her throat, asking for more than a kiss.

He didn't pull back until he couldn't take a second more without his lungs bursting or his heart exploding from all its gymnastics in his chest. He closed his eyes and sucked in the air he needed. Had he ever thought he could live without this? Without Sara? He must have been crazy. This was as necessary to him as breathing. More. "I love you, you know," he stated. "I didn't mean any of what I said to you on Monday. That was some of the most foolish twaddle I've ever come up with in my life. And I'm sorry. I should have told you that right away. I had no right to say those things or to give you an ultimatum."

Sara smiled and pulled his head down for another kiss. Joe took control, running his tongue along the inside of her lower lip and then thrusting it into her mouth. He wanted to be in control. Sara pulled away. They were going to get this straight once and for all.

"I'm sorry. I'm rushing you again. But you don't know how tempting you are." Joe pressed his hips against hers, demonstrating just how tempted he was.

"Let's make love," Sara urged. Forget the eggs! Who wanted eggs when they could have this?

"Sara. I can give you all the time you need."

"I don't need time. I need you."

"If you're sure," Joe agreed, giving her plenty of time to change her mind.

"I'm sure! Are you going to need an engraved invitation every time we make love?"

Joe frowned. "No. I just don't want to pressure you. If you want to wait a while..."

"I want to make love to you right now. I don't even care if we do it here or go in the bedroom."

"The table's already a mess. We'll go in the bedroom." Joe took her hand and led her through the house. Sara followed, shaking her head. The man was going to drive her crazy. She'd be gray before she was forty. And she'd love every single minute with him.

Just when she thought she knew what he would say, he said something completely unexpected or changed his mind.

Joe wished he could magically straighten the bed and get the dirty laundry off the floor and into the hamper. He had been so depressed last night that he had just collapsed into the bed. Which reminded him. "I have something for you," he said, kicking aside the clothes and flipping the sheet and blankets back up on the bed so they would be within reach afterward.

"Later, okay? There's only one thing I want right now."

Joe felt every muscle in his body go rigid. Did she know what it did to him to hear that...lust in her voice? He turned and touched her cheek. "This time I want it to be perfect for you. I went too fast before. I want to go slow. To make it perfect for you." He brushed his fingertips along her cheekbone and bent to kiss the edge of her jaw. His arms scooped her against him and laid her back against the sheets. He followed, not yet letting his body touch hers but hovering above her, willing himself to go slow.

"Joe," Sara protested and tried to push him, but her hands couldn't resist the feel of his chest. She pushed his sweatshirt up and ran her hands across his flat stomach and over the delightful texture of hair and muscle on his chest. She strained upward, trying to catch his mouth.

"No," he said. "Don't. I want to go slow." He pulled back and touched her gently. Like he was afraid to really touch her. Or he needed to be in charge. He stood back up and waited until she sat up and then lifted the hem of her sweater and eased it over her head. Like he was undressing a child, Sara thought. If she let him, he'd make it perfect for her, wondrous. But she didn't want him to make love to her; she wanted him to make love with her. With a full-fledged, whole, independent woman. When he stepped back to gaze at the unexpected camisole, Sara slid across the bed and stood on the other side.

"You want to wait?" Joe asked, just as if it wouldn't kill him to stop. If Sara hadn't been able to see—his sweatpants were awfully flimsy—that stopping was the last thing he wanted, she might have felt ashamed of her own ardor.

"No. You're not listening to me. I want to make love. I want to make love, not be made love to." Joe was frowning at her, running his hand through his hair, looking confused and uncomfortable. "Don't you see? You're treating me like a fragile piece of china or something. I'm not fragile. I'm strong. You keep trying to protect me. You keep taking responsibility for everything. You make me feel like a kid. I'm just as responsible for what went wrong on Monday as you are. I shouldn't have gotten irrational and run away. I should have stayed and talked. You want to control everything," she complained, stepping out of her jeans just in case he was getting the wrong idea. "You once told me that I wanted to blame myself for Lala's death so I could believe I was in control. Now you're doing the same thing.

"You are not in control here, Mr. Fisher. I am. So you do what I say. Got it?" Her eyes dropped and caressed the start of the trail of hair that led down from his navel, caressed the droopy bow that held up his sweatpants, caressed him through the fabric. She raised her eyes to his, demanding an answer.

Joe swallowed. His feelings of foolishness and embarrassment, of rejection and resentment, were being vaporized in the heat of her gaze. No one had ever said anything like that to him as long as he had lived. He wouldn't have forgotten. He'd never forget this. If someone had asked him ten minutes ago what he thought of sexually aggressive women, he might have responded coolly. Now he knew, there was nothing in the world like having the woman you love say she wanted you. He felt wanted and desirable and loved and sexy as hell. And that underwear she was wearing! He didn't know what you called it, but it was something special. He'd never seen panties like those, with the wide legs, so wide, his hand could just slide right up.

"Take your sweatshirt off." Her voice was thin. Joe smiled and obeyed, hissing when her hands touched him before he was even through. Whatever she said, he touched her while she touched him, until she pulled on the thin cotton tie holding up his pants. That was enough to make him grab her. "No," she said, "let me." He counted backward from a hundred and let her.

There was nothing more exciting than doing this to him, Sara thought. Undressing him. Touching him. Loving him. Every time he gasped or groaned, every time his body responded to her touch, it was like an aphrodisiac, heightening her arousal. He wasn't exactly standing still for this, though. His hands were all over her. "Get on the bed," she ordered, and her voice sounded like she'd just swallowed a mouthful of sand.

He hesitated and then obeyed. She hesitated and climbed on top of him, straddling his hips. She realized she'd forgotten something and moved to the side so she could take the tap pants off.

"Wait!" Joe grated out when she started to throw her thigh over him again. "I'm not going to make the same mistake twice." He started to scoot off the bed.

Sara frowned. "What are you talking about?" She felt like an icy hand had just trailed up her spine.

"Protecting you."

Sara caught him and kept him from getting up. "I'm on the pill. I should have told you before. I'll bet you worried all week, wondering if I was going to have your baby or not."

Joe leaned back. It was strangely disappointing that she wasn't. But he couldn't very well stay disappointed when she was climbing on top of him, letting her body trail across him. She was playing with fire, and they were both going to go up in flames any minute now. She started to take the camisole off. "Leave it," he commanded. Her eyes got big but she obeyed. She was just hovering there, teasing him. And then he realized she was hesitating like she didn't know exactly what to do. He reached for her hips and drew her against him, helped her join him. How could she not know what to do? She'd been married. He guided her movements with his hands, showing her how to rock and twist.

And then they did explode into flames. Flames and flashes of light and booming explosions and bells and sirens and fire engines and skyrockets.

She was collapsed on top of him like a limp rag doll, and he hoped she never moved again, unless it was for an encore. Joe moved his hand so it rested on her head and ruffled her curls. "Anytime," he said in a slow voice still deepened with passion, "you want to be in control, honey, I'll be ready, willing and able."

Sara smiled against his shoulder. She couldn't resist. She flickered her tongue against his skin. "Anytime?"

He hugged her hard and then collapsed back against the mattress. "Almost anytime. Are you insatiable, too?"

"I don't know. I never did that before. I kind of liked it."

"I kind of liked it, too. I kind of like you." Joe hesitated and then asked, "Why didn't you do it before?"

Sara moved away, and he regretted the question even though she was still lying beside him, with her head on his shoulder, looking up at the ceiling. "I don't know. With Michael, at the beginning, he was really afraid of hurting me. We were both virgins. We just never got really wild in bed. It was always slower and real gentle. It was the only time he wasn't exuberant. He liked it that way."

"Am I too, uh, wild?"

"It's different with you." She sat up suddenly and stared down at him with huge eyes. "Am I too...aggressive?" She blushed and wrapped her arms around herself. "I've been acting like..."

Joe grabbed her and tumbled her back against him. "You've been acting like the woman of my dreams, honey. Don't you change a thing. Except you can take that silk thing off now so I can kiss you," he growled.

"Ooh," Sara gasped, "don't you sound forceful. Going to be in charge this time?"

"You better believe it," Joe said, laughing. He frowned suddenly and got up. "Wait here," he said and left her. Sara crawled under the sheet, wondering where he had gone and why.

He returned with a single red rose in a crystal vase that he set on the bedstand by the alarm clock. "Not one of my brother's roses," he informed her. "I bought just one. I'm afraid I don't have Tim's flair for the dramatic."

"I think you flare just fine," Sara observed with a wicked smile.

"Be serious now."

"How can I be serious with you sitting there like that?"

Joe threw a corner of the sheet over his lap. He handed her a scroll of paper bound with a gold ring. Sara's hand trembled as she took it.

"Joe," she whispered when she saw that it wasn't just a ring of golden paper, but a gold ring, with the most beautiful setting of sapphires, like a star, around a central diamond. "It's beautiful."

"I'll read it to you," Joe said and slipped the little roll of paper from her fingers. He looked into her eyes. "It's a gilt-edged guarantee. I can't promise you anything more than this." He bent his head and read the words from the paper, although he already knew them by heart. "I promise you all the time and all the space and all that I have that you ever need. All the understanding, all the forgiveness, and all the love I have in my heart." He looked up and saw that her eyes were dark blue, sparkling with tears. "For as long as our forever lasts."

"Oh, Joe, I love you so much," Sara cried out and threw her arms around his neck as tightly as she could.

"Will you be my wife someday?"

Sara pulled back and looked at his wonderful, strong, beautiful face and said, "I'm already your wife in all the ways that count. We can have a ceremony for everyone else, but I'm already your wife, Joe. Forever."

Joe touched her as if she was the most precious thing on the face of the earth. He slipped his ring on her finger and it fit perfectly. "Remember when I complimented your pearl ring? And you let me see it? It fit right up to this mole on my little finger. The guy in the jewelry store thought I was crazy, but he said we could have it adjusted."

"It's perfect. See, we're made for each other. Why else would you have that mole?" she asked and kissed it.

"That's not the only thing that fits perfectly," Joe commented saucily and rubbed up against Sara.

They made love again, and Joe got his chance to cherish Sara during the long, gentle act. Afterward they lay in each other's arms and talked.

"I still can't believe my mother called you," Joe said. "I yelled at Tim for interfering while Matt was sending you a hundred and forty-four roses, and I never even knew my mother was on your case."

"You should be glad she called. She's the one that made me look at what I was doing. I'd decided, subconsciously, I guess, that it was better to be in control and hurt than to live every day not knowing if something might happen to you. But she told me not to make any mistakes in the pain of losing my child that I'd regret later. You know, you once told me *you* felt responsible for Jeremiah's death, but she doesn't blame you. She says it was her fault for being careless and getting mugged, and your dad thinks it was his fault for not protecting her.''

Joe's body was suddenly rigid against hers. ''Mugged?''

Sara propped herself up on her elbow and looked at him. ''You don't know?''

''I have no idea what you're talking about.''

''She said she never talked about it, but I guess I didn't realize she meant *never.*'' Sara quickly told him the brief facts of Vera's story.

Joe tugged Sara back against him. ''And I always thought...''

''It was your fault? Sorry, you weren't in control...''

''Okay, I admit it. I don't control everything. I'm not always in charge.'' He deepened his voice. ''And sometimes it feels damn good.''

''Joe,'' Sara laughed. ''Not again?''

''Not yet, anyway.''

''I was going to tell you before we made love that if I get the job I'm going to take it. And you made me forget,'' Sara teased. She frowned when Joe stiffened and pulled away. ''Now what, Joe?''

''I can't move to Florida. My job is here. My family's here. I'll need at least a year to get a new job. Professors are supposed to write articles as well as teach. But it takes me a long time to get my articles to turn out the way I want them. Besides, I like teaching. So I don't always work on my articles zealously enough. I suppose I could try for a sabbatical or something while I looked for a new..."

Sara put her fingers across Joe's mouth. How had she ever doubted that Joe believed in her abilities? Or doubted the depth of his love? That he would sacrifice so much for her. Tears prickled behind her eyes again. "Not that job, Joe, the one with Vos Landscaping. My interview is on Monday morning."

"Oh."

"It might only be part-time, but at least it's something. My life still feels empty without Lala."

"Do you think you'll ever want more kids?"

"You'd live with it if I said no, wouldn't you?" Sara hugged Joe as hard as she could. "I don't deserve you, Joe."

"I promised."

"But you deserve a gilt-edged guarantee in return. I think we'll have two boys and a girl. Or two girls and a boy. Which do you think?"

"I think we should get started."

"I'm still on the pill."

"Practicing then."

"Joe," Sara chastised him, but she was already rubbing her smooth leg against the pleasant roughness of his muscular thigh. It was quite a bit later when she asked, "Do you have any plans for this afternoon?"

"Give me awhile. I think I can come up with something."

"Joe," Sara complained, drawing his name out into two syllables. "I meant, I have something I want to do. And not in bed, either."

"Kitchen table still interests you, huh?"

Sara resorted to tickling his ribs.

IT WAS THE MIDDLE of the afternoon before they finally made it down to the beach. Roly, despite being left outside for so long that morning, didn't seem to be holding a grudge as he danced around them. Or maybe he was, Sara decided, pushing him away when he got in her way yet again. Did licking a person's face count as revenge? "Control your dog, Fisher," she ordered. "He's as fresh as you are."

"The French poodle down the beach thinks he's a perfect gentleman."

"Sure, Joe," Sara said, but her laugh sounded funny, like it was stuck on the lump that was clogging her throat. She struggled with the red-and-yellow kite, trying to get it put together right, trying to untangle the knots in the long tail that were left from the day when she first met Joe, when she'd packed the kite up quickly, wanting to get Lala out of the cold.

"You know," Joe drawled softly, "when Lala couldn't get that kite to fly, she said, 'Hey, mister, you wanna help me fly my kite?' Like that was the greatest privilege in the world. I would think it was kind of great if you let me help you."

There was a split second of hesitation that seemed to last forever and pass in the blinking of an eye, and then Sara launched herself into his arms. Joe caught her and held her thin body close against him, absorbing her sobs into his body, her pain hurting him bone-deep. He rubbed the back of her parka and pressed a kiss against the smooth skin of her temple. What were they doing out here with this blasted kite? He rocked

Sara against him, trying to ease her pain. He could understand it all too well: he missed Lala, too, and he had barely known her. "It's okay, honey," he murmured. "It's going to be okay."

Sara pulled loose from his tight embrace and wiped her cheeks with the backs of her hands. "I still miss her. I wasn't supposed to miss her," she said in a raw voice. She stared at the dampness around Joe's eyes and knew he was special.

"Of course you still miss her," Joe soothed. "Us getting married isn't going to change that any." He kissed her tenderly. "Do you really want to fly this kite?" The last time he helped fly this kite he'd been feeling sorry for himself. Lala had brightened the day for him. And now Sara was brightening his whole life. He'd do anything in the world to ease her pain.

"I can't remember how," Sara confessed, sniffling back the remainder of her tears and almost giggling. "Lala told me a hundred times, at least, and I still can't remember right. She said I had a jinx."

"She wasn't overly impressed with my kite-flying abilities, either," Joe admitted ruefully. "And the wind's blowing in the wrong direction. This kite's not getting caught in any trees today, so I won't even be able to show off my climbing skills." He handed Sara a couple of tissues he had prudently tucked in his coat pocket and untangled the kite's tail in a moment.

It took them a couple of tries before they coordinated their movements and had the kite flying in the air, rising up and out over the edge of the lake on the unusual northeastern wind. The sky was a clear bright blue, sprinkling diamond dust over the banks of snow and choppy rows of ice. It was a wind that would bring a storm, the meteorologists said, and it was a wind that would serve Sara's purpose well. She fed out the string while Joe stood with his arm wrapped around her shoulder protectively.

The kite rose until it was just a tiny speck in the sky, and Joe squinted against the bright sunlight and tried to decide if he really could see it or if it was just his imagination. It took him a few moments after Sara caught his hands in hers to realize that she was no longer holding the kite's string. "It got away?" he asked in a whisper. What was he going to say to make her feel better? It was Lala's kite. What if Sara started feeing like a failure all over again?

He'd give her understanding, forgiveness and love. And it would be enough.

"No, I let it go on purpose," Sara explained. "I don't want it to come down again. I want it to soar and sail away. I know, it's a little silly, but I was thinking it would symbolize letting Lala go."

Joe stood holding Sara's hands, thinking she was strong, brave, knowing he loved her. She was staring into the sky, watching the tiny dot until it wasn't visible any longer.

Finally Sara turned away from the sky and slowly brought her eyes up to meet his. "Isn't it perfect?" she asked, and he smiled at the look of relief and happiness on her face. "Watching the kite disappear is a little like losing Lala. She's not stuck in a tree, she's soaring. Oh, I don't mean she's a little angel with white wings, I mean her memory. She's like the wind that can't be caught in a jar, she's not a memory to be kept in a box or a roomful of things. She's a memory that has to be lived, by celebrating life."

Joe searched the sky again for some speck he could imagine was the kite. He hadn't realized how clearly Sara had thought out what she was doing, how exactly perfect the symbolism was.

"Lala would be glad we're getting married. She'd be throwing rose petals and singing and dancing. Celebrating. It's what she did best," Sara told Joe. "And Lord knows, we have enough rose petals!"

"My brothers can get carried away, especially Timothy. We better elope or our wedding will put Princess Di to shame."

"My parents will never forgive me. Let's do it."

"I don't want to make them mad."

"I guess you'll be joining a monastery then, to keep them happy?"

"Uh, on the other hand..."

Joe's deep laughter joined with Sara's as they turned and walked up the beach toward his house...toward their house and the start of a whole new life together. Loving each other like Fishers, for as long as their forever lasted.

Harlequin Superromance®

CHILDREN OF THE HEART
by Sally Garrett

Available this month

Romance readers the world over have wept and rejoiced over Sally Garrett's heartwarming stories of love, caring and commitment. In her new novel, *Children of the Heart,* Sally once again weaves a story that will touch your most tender emotions.

You'll be moved to tears of joy

Nearly two hundred children have passed through Trenance McKay's foster home. But after her husband leaves her, Trenance knows she'll always have to struggle alone. No man could have enough room in his heart both for Trenance and for so many needy children. Max Tulley, news anchor for KSPO TV is willing to try, but how long can his love last?

"Sally Garrett does some of the best character studies in the genre and will not disappoint her fans."
Romantic Times

Look for *Children of the Heart* wherever Harlequin Romance novels are sold. SCH

PENNY JORDAN

Sins and infidelities...
Dreams and obsessions...
Shattering secrets
unfold in...

THE HIDDEN YEARS

SAGE — stunning, sensual and vibrant, she spent a lifetime distancing herself from a past too painful to confront... the mother who seemed to hold her at bay, the father who resented her and the heartache of unfulfilled love. To the world, Sage was independent and invulnerable— but it was a mask she cultivated to hide a desperation she herself couldn't quite understand... until an unforeseen turn of events drew her into the discovery of the hidden years, finally allowing Sage to open her heart to a passion denied for so long.

The Hidden Years—a compelling novel of truth and passion that will unlock the heart and soul of every woman.

AVAILABLE IN OCTOBER!
Watch for your opportunity to complete your Penny Jordan set.
POWER PLAY and SILVER will also be available in October.

The Hidden Years, #97121-4, Power Play, #97108-7 and Silver #97120-6 are available wherever paperbacks are sold, or send your name, address and zip or postal code, along with a check or money order for $5.99 for The Hidden Years, $5.95 for Silver and $4.95 U.S./$5.95 Cdn. for Power Play, plus 75¢ postage and handling ($1.00 in Canada) for each book ordered, payable to Harlequin Reader Service, to:

In the U.S.
3010 Walden Ave.
P.O. Box 1325
Buffalo, NY 14269-1325

In Canada
P.O. Box 609
Fort Erie, Ontario
L2A 5X3

Please specify book title(s) with your order.
Canadian residents add applicable federal and provincial taxes.

HIDDEN-RR